The Heart of Arorea

"I was more than pleasantly surprised with this action-packed, inspiring novel and Nicole's amazing storytelling talent! A humble blacksmith makes for an endearing hero as he embarks on a perilous journey (in Lord of the Rings fashion) ...Nicole Sager is a bright, new talent who I believe will go far in the world of Christian fiction. Great read!" ~Lisa Norato, Author of *Prize of My Heart*

"It is a wonderful Christian adventure...with Nicole's book they walk away challenged to improve their character, spiritually uplifted, and feeling not only entertained, but encouraged and inspired to live a better Christian life!"

~Mirren Martin, *Biblical Discipleship Ministries*

"Once I started reading I couldn't put it down...I really enjoyed it. I read it as an adventure novel but...I'm sure there was a lot of symbolism in it that I may have missed with the different characters and settings...somewhat along the lines of *Pilgrim's Progress* or *The Chronicles of Narnia*."

~Leo B., Reader in MD.

"This is an AMAZING...book that everyone of ALL ages NEEDS to read! It has a fast moving plot that never gets boring and is so exciting (with tons of unexpected turns and discoveries...) and TONS of amazing characters; some that you love, and some...not so much. 6 out of 5 stars!"

~Alice S., Reader in TX.

The Fate of Arcrea

Written & Illustrated by

Nicole Sager

Books written by Nicole Sager

The Arcrean Conquest

The Heart of Arcrea

The Fate of Arcrea

The Isle of Arcrea

Companions of Arcrea

Hebbros

Burdney

Cleftlocke

Classic Chats

A Tale of Two Siblings

Great Expectations

Valley of the Roden

The Retrievers

Illustrations: ©Nicole Sager
Cover Design: ©Rossano Designs

Printed in the United States of America

ISBN-10: **1480260274**
ISBN-13: **978-1480260276**

For Mama ~ My Prayer Warrior

"Let GOD be magnified."
From Psalm 70:4

ARCREA
{MIZGALIA}
{MIZGALIA}
BRIK BONE MOUNTAINS
Oak's Branch
Roughton
Frederick
Ranulf
Quinton
Tiltman &
Morgway
Balgo
Knavesmire
Rebel's Lair
Heartland
Saxby
Waterfall
Coswell
Kally
Osgood
Stephen
Dragon Coast
Clan
Qualc
Campbell
Brentwood &
Licklee
Geoffrey
Hugh
Dormay
Arcrean Sea

TABLE OF CONTENTS

LIST OF ILLUSTRATIONS

Acknowledgements

I want to give another big THANK YOU to my family—Dad, Mom, Christal, Mike, Caity, Caleb, & Caroline—for being such a wonderful support system! You all have been so kind and patient to let me ramble, rant, & rave about my books. I LOVE YOU!

And, again, most importantly!
A giant thank you to my Lord & Savior, Jesus Christ, without whom, none of this would have been possible!
When I am weak, He is strong!

It could be a severe coincidence...

Or one miraculous solution.

Prologue
* Conspiracy at Mockmor *

Night's shadows cloaked the royal city of Mockmor in the kingdom of Mizgalia. The vicious kingdom was a place of constant war and adversity between its native people and those of the neighboring realms, particularly with the kingdom of Arcrea—located to the south, on the opposite side of the vast region of Brikbone Mountains.

A single candle occupied a table in a private room at the heart of the castle Mockmor; the dancing flame lent a shifting appearance to the walls of stone. A wealthily clad man stood perusing a stack of well-worn parchments; his short black beard, laced with gray, had been oiled and shaped into a fine point that jutted from his chin. An unmistakable crown engulfed his head. His fingers, loaded with rare gems, suddenly shoved the parchments to the table as he lifted a cold gaze to the room's only other occupant and hissed,

"The kingdom of Arcrea is experiencing a dramatic change in the system of her leadership. Now will be the perfect time to destroy the Arcreans—test the skills of their boy-king…their first king. All that is lacking is an unarguable reason for our attack," he turned to face the other man, "But you have already seen to this, correct?"

Sir Kleyton, captain of Mizgalia's innumerable armies, gave a sharp nod, "The informant has been sent with three guides as promised, Sire."

A wry grin twisted the face of Mizgalia's evil king, "You always placed far too much confidence in that boy, Kleyton. Do you regret now that you agreed to prepare him for this particular fate?"

Sir Kleyton stiffened visibly, "I have trained him well, Sire."

King Cronin's brow lifted, indicating that this reply had not sufficiently answered his question.

Kleyton cleared his throat, "Sire, I understood the orders given me that day, and I have kept him in ignorance of the truth since I took the actions to—"

Cronin waved one hand and returned to the problems previously under discussion, "I have long awaited this day when Mizgalian blood, spilled on Arcrean soil, would create a reason for us to make war with these stiff-necked people! Now, at last, the ideal moment for their destruction has come, for they are preoccupied with a new king. If only the Brikbones did not create an obstacle for a swift advance."

Sir Kleyton lifted his chin and studied the opposite wall, "The Brikbones have always been a natural adversary in our campaigns against Arcrea…but there are other methods of attack, my king."

Chapter 1
* A Seaman's Fate *

A brisk January wind tugged at the sails of the *Seabird*, an Arcrean vessel recently set sail from the southeastern city of Dormay. The lowering gray clouds told of coming snow as the ship was whisked east beyond the peninsula of the area known as Geoffrey's region.

Though the kingdom's seven regions were no longer ruled by evil lords, but instead had been joined under King Druet's reign, the boundaries and titles of each had been kept in place for the purpose of forming local authorities, and to simplify the people's adjustment to the new form of government.

The *Seabird* continued its race east and then north, following the outer boundaries of Arcrea, but keeping a safe distance from her often-jagged coasts. The vessel's belly held a merchant's cargo, which the captain was anxious to deliver in the eastern city of Lowell before the skies released their own weighty burden.

Captain Marsh squinted at the gray tower of clouds and scowled deeply as he turned to bellow across the decks, “Keep her out to sea, lads; the storm won’t hold and she’ll splinter on the rocks of Stephen if we run her in now!”

Nathaniel of Dormay, in the region of Geoffrey, grinned as he and several other crewmembers scrambled up the rigging to adjust the ropes. Captain Marsh was never a pleasant man when his arrival at port was delayed. The sailor to Nathaniel’s right began to whistle a merry rendition of “Clouds o’er an Arcrean Sea” and Nathaniel chuckled and joined in bringing the tune to life.

During the months of the previous summer and autumn, Nathaniel had traveled through the land of Arcrea with Druet on a quest to discover the kingdom’s legendary and mysterious heart. The quest now complete and Druet crowned as Arcrea’s first king, Nathaniel had returned to his beloved Arcrean Sea in time to sign on with Captain Marsh for the *Seabird’s* nine-month voyage.

“Drop the sails, lads; we’ve got company!”

Even as the warning command was shouted from below, Nathaniel’s eyes darted upward to spot another vessel on the horizon. From this distance, it was impossible to distinguish her flag, but the ship itself was clearly foreign. Captain Marsh kept his sea-weathered gaze on the mysterious “company” as it continued to glide over the waves, slowly and silently drawing closer to the *Seabird’s* position.

“You think she may be trouble?”

Nathaniel’s eyes narrowed as he studied the strange vessel; his strained silence was answer enough to his comrade’s question.

Night fell quickly and with the help of the moon-thwarting clouds dropped a thick blanket of cold darkness over the earth. The foreign vessel had continued to draw nearer, but now disappeared from sight in the impenetrable blackness.

On watch in the rigging, Nathaniel's gray eyes strained to see something—anything. Suddenly, a deep thunderous noise sounded from across the water and a flickering light appeared, making a broad arc in the sky. Nathaniel's face registered his shock as he leaned down and cupped a hand to his mouth, "We're under attack!"

The ball of flame completed its arc of destruction and slammed into the *Seabird's* hull. A moment of panic seized the crew as they raced to recover from the hit. Captain Marsh stilled his men with a few bellows and they calmed to a pace of orderly chaos in response to his commands.

As Nathaniel worked his way down through the rigging, two more balls of flaming ammunition struck the Seabird in quick succession. The flames spread quickly and began to eat every inch of the vessel with uncontrollable speed. It soon became obvious that it would be impossible to save her.

The crew lowered the smaller boats into the water and prepared to make an attempt at reaching the shore safely. From his perch in the rigging, Nathaniel watched the boats being cut loose without him. Flames licked at the masts and climbed upward, trapping him high above the quarter-deck before he had a chance to reach its safety.

Suddenly, the *Seabird* gave a sharp lurch and Nathaniel yelled as he felt his grip wrenched from its hold on the ropes. His body was tossed through the air and for a moment the world around him felt surreal; the flaming vessel illuminated the night and snow began to fall in thick curtains as he plummeted to an uncertain landing.

The next moment, Nathaniel felt himself plunging into the icy Arcrean. Immediately, he propelled himself toward the surface, ignoring the sudden tightness in his chest when the numbing water closed in around him; his lungs felt as if squeezed by a grip of iron. Finally feeling the water break over his head, Nathaniel swallowed a gulp of freezing air and snowflakes as he tried to focus on treading water.

A board from the deck of the crumbling *Seabird* drifted nearby and Nathaniel forced his stiff limbs to propel him toward the floating object. Throwing his arms over the wooden plank he whispered the prayer "God, help me!" through chattering teeth. Despite the heat of the flames that engulfed the nearby *Seabird*, his body was numb in the freezing seawater. Nathaniel gripped the plank, unable to move even a finger. A miniature snowdrift was piling on his head and arms, and icicles were forming over the tips of his hair and eyelashes.

The knowledge that he was about to die suddenly struck him and he wished for a fleeting moment that he could have seen his father, mother, and two sisters again. He longed to see his brother-like friend, King Druet, and the others who had been his companions on the quest for Arcrea's heart. He had promised Lady Alice that he would return to see the royal palace upon its completion, as well as the plans she was drawing up for the queen's garden.

These fleeting thoughts passed through Nathaniel's numb mind along with a prayer for God's will to be done; and then the dark night wrapped closer around him, his eyes closed, and he felt the wooden plank slip silently from his grasp.

ꟓꟓ

Two weeks later.

The docks at Dormay were quiet. Snow still rested in thick drifts over the landscape and lent an atmosphere of peace and quiet to the quaint row of shops that lined the large harbor. Over the door of one of these shops hung a wooden sign indicating the proprietor within was the *Sailor's Tailor.* The man himself was seated before a fire in the front room, using the bright flame's light to better see the work performed by his agile hands.

The shop also served as the tailor's home. A door at the back of the room led to the kitchen, where a narrow staircase on the wall to the right climbed to the upper rooms occupied by himself and his small family.

The middle-aged tailor lifted his brown eyes from the torn doublet in his hands and then lowered them again with a twinkle, a small smile pulling at his lips. Across the fire, in the chair opposite his own, his younger daughter sat with a needle in her own hand and a determined glare on her face directed at the tunic held an inch before her pert nose.

"Brigit, you'll go blind if you hold everything so close."

The fifteen-year-old dropped the tunic to her lap and pushed dark brown curls out of her face; her soft gray eyes, flecked with blue, pleaded for understanding, "Father, I do believe with all of my young and frightfully exasperated heart that I have no skills where the art of tailoring is concerned! Shouldn't I fetch Anne and let her help you?"

"Anne is in the kitchen with your mother."

"I could help Mother!" Brigit bit her lip guiltily when her father glanced up again, "It's true I'm no better in the kitchen than I am with a needle…and Mother's had more of my help today than a soul ought to be forced to bear in a year, I know…"

"You're getting better."

"At which? Tailoring or…kitchening?"

He chuckled at her choice of words, "Both."

Brigit sighed, "Yesterday I sewed Captain Carro's sleeve shut and puckered the hem of Mistress Fanny's sash. Today I burned the bread, broke a spoon, and melted our only ladle by leaving one end in the fire!"

Her father smiled, "I suppose that does sum it up."

Brigit turned to gaze out the front window at the gray sea, "I wish Nathaniel hadn't had to leave so soon; he was gone for months and then left for the sea only days after he had returned from the Heartland and King Druet's quest."

The tailor followed her gaze and his thoughts mirrored those she had spoken. His eldest child—his only son—was a born seaman, and rarely able to remain at home for an extended period of time.

"He'll be back before you know it, Brigit."

It was silent for a moment as each returned to their work. Brigit absently murmured something about being "unable to stitch straight to save her young life."

The shop door suddenly opened, ushering in a gust of cold air along with two men in seamen's garb.

When the door was closed, the elder of the two held out his hand to the tailor in a seemingly reluctant gesture.

"Peter," the two hands clasped, "I…hope all is well."

The tailor stared back in shock, "Captain Marsh! We didn't expect the *Seabird* to return to Dormay until—"

Marsh lifted a hand for silence as he stared at the floor, "The *Seabird* has not returned, Peter," he glanced up and nodded respectfully when the tailor's wife, Martha, and elder daughter, Anne, appeared in the kitchen door opposite, "I'm afraid I've got bad news."

Martha instinctively clapped a hand over her mouth and began to shake her head, as if her denial could refute whatever was to come.

"We were attacked by a foreign vessel off the coast of Stephen two weeks ago, and forced to take to the boats. Praise God, we made it to shore in safety, but it was only there we discovered that not all had made it to the boats before…"

Martha gave a small cry and her knees buckled; Peter quickly helped her into his vacated chair. Anne's face was pale as she moved to offer her mother a trembling hand of reassurance, and Brigit was already in tears.

Peter's voice shook as he asked, "What is it you're trying to tell us, Marsh?"

The captain's jaw clenched with emotion, "I'm sorry, Peter. Your son Nathaniel was still aboard the *Seabird* when she went down."

Chapter 2
* The Mízgalían *

Trenton of Mockmor rode south at a brisk pace with the natural ease that evidenced years of practice. His well-developed frame spoke of years spent in his father's garrison. Years of rigorous training and never-ending routines enforced for the sole purpose of making or breaking a man—and ultimately to form the strength of his native kingdom's army: the great forces of Mizgalia. Trenton's eighteen years had been spent in adding to this strength.

Trenton's eyes, a singular light blue in color, shifted to the two horses on the snow-covered road ahead of him. His two Arcrean companions, both five to six years older than himself, were as different as night and day, and yet they seemed to be inseparable…cantankerous at times, but inseparable.

Bracy, a clansman from Ranulf, was a stocky figure with nearly-black hair pulled into a short club at the base of his neck. His dark eyes occasionally darted in Trenton's direction, but more often moved to check on the state of the second Arcrean. Talon of Quinton was a bit taller than Bracy; his hair was a pale shade of blond that could almost be called white. Two swords rested in matching sheaths crossed at his back; he had refused to remove them in spite of the fact that his shoulder had been punctured by a Mizgalian arrow during a recent run-in. Bracy was clearly displeased at his inability to convince Talon to ease the weight of the swords from his shoulders, nevertheless he had become grudgingly silent when his arguments fell on deaf ears.

The screech of a hawk drew Trenton's gaze to the pale wintry sky where the bird circled over the trio and then glided effortlessly away on the frozen air.

Trenton pulled his cloak tighter around his neck and nudged his horse's flanks, moving the animal closer behind Bracy's mount. If he would be successful in Arcrea, he had to ensure that his two guides remained convinced of his story: that he was a mistreated young slave running from an oppressive Mizgalian master in order to seek refuge with the heroic Druet, recently crowned as Arcrea's first king.

The light blue eyes searched for signs of the hawk while Trenton's thoughts reviewed his current position. In truth, the young Mizgalian had been trained as an informant for his father, Sir Kleyton—captain of the Mizgalian armies and close councilor to King Cronin. The knight had sent his only son across the Brikbones to infiltrate Druet's system in search of weaknesses, holes, and the secrets to his incredible success.

Trenton had managed to cross the border unseen with the help of three Mizgalian soldiers. His companions had attacked Talon and Bracy for sport in an Arcrean forest and only one of the three had survived the ordeal—the archer who had struck Talon's shoulder. Trenton had signaled for the lone man to withdraw and sent him back to Mockmor to report to Kleyton; he had then joined himself to Talon and Bracy under his fabricated identity as a runaway.

His new guides hadn't told him much about themselves besides their names and where they were from—eastern and western Arcrea—and the fact that they were traveling to see King Druet. Trenton had matched these particulars with previously known facts and quickly figured that Talon and Bracy were the two clansmen who had traveled with Druet on his quest for Arcrea's heart. The fact that they hadn't revealed this to him, along with their admission of where they were now headed, left Trenton certain that they still had intimate ties with their king. Their presence in northeastern Arcrea hinted to the young informant that they were probably on some mission or other for Druet.

Trenton couldn't believe his success in meeting up with these two men; they were sure to be great assets to his mission. The sooner he could get to Druet, the sooner he could find what he needed and return home to Mizgalia.

The hawk appeared again and Trenton whistled three peculiar notes. The majestic bird gave a shrill cry and disappeared again.

"What tune is that?"

Trenton lowered his gaze to Talon, "I'm not sure it's an actual tune at all," he shrugged, "only some notes I put together for moments of boredom."

Bracy grunted, "Somehow I fail to see that as a compliment to present company."

"I didn't mean to say that you're boring," Trenton glanced at an unconvinced Bracy and then back at Talon, who was still staring at him.

"Huh…the tune sounded familiar, but with only three notes I suppose one can hardly tell one song from another."

Bracy snorted, "You wouldn't know a pipe from a drum, Talon, let alone what song it was playing!"

"I've heard it somewhere before, Bracy!"

Trenton offered a slight laugh, practiced to sound natural, and deftly changed the subject of the conversation. He huffed inwardly; eager to steer away from the dangerous topic of the signals he used to communicate with his carrier-hawk, Link. Had he known it would cause such a stir, he would have left the bird at home and found some other way to send messages back to Mockmor!

"Did you say you're from Mockmor?"

Trenton eyed Talon, wondering if the clansman could read his thoughts, "I did."

"The royal city?"

Trenton gave a nod, running a hand through his warm-blond hair, "Terrible dark place, it is. King Cronin has his subjects pinned beneath his thumb…just like my master held me down before I escaped."

"Why didn't you escape before?"

Trenton was ready with an answer, "If I left before I turned eighteen, they could have tracked me down and taken me back across the border. When I turned eighteen I became my own man by law; I'm free if I can get away, and I did!"

The other two were silent until Talon winced and gripped his shoulder in a manner that had become familiar over the past few days of travel. Bracy insisted that the wound was healing, thanks to some "Ulric's Rose" tonic he had used. Nevertheless, Talon still experienced sharp pains on occasion, and Bracy was always ready to badger him with a fresh opinion about the placement of the two swords.

As Talon silenced Bracy's words with a glare of protest, Trenton sighed and let his horse fall a ways behind. The sooner they reached Druet, the better. He couldn't wait to be rid of this quarreling twosome.

ഇര

"The swords stay, Bracy," Talon rubbed his shoulder with the palm of his other hand.

"Fine," Bracy grumbled and glanced behind him; Trenton had fallen back a short distance…again, "There's something strange about that one."

"He's a Mizgalian," Talon offered, "That's strange enough."

"But don't you think it singular that we both think there's something familiar about him, and yet we also admit we've never seen him before?"

"For once I agree with you. There is something more to Trenton than meets the eye."

"Well, perhaps Falconer will be able to figure it out; he's usually a good judge of character. I say the sooner we reach the Heartland the better. I, for one, am eager to rid him of our 'boring' company."

Chapter 3
* Of News & Preparation *

King Druet sat atop his horse on a rise overlooking the site of his future home, Castle Eubank, in the western Heartland. Progress on its construction had slowed as winter settled to reshape the land with ice and snow and freezing temperatures. Nevertheless, the Arcrean craftsmen who had been hired to build Eubank continued with whatever tasks were possible considering the conditions.

Druet gave a satisfied sigh and turned to address his father, also mounted and staring down at the developing castle, "The master builder says it will be done within a year."

"A year," Gregory repeated, his breath showing white on the cold afternoon air, "Much is capable of happening in a year's time," the blacksmith looked at his son, "Why, only a year ago you'd never thought of leaving Oak's Branch to search for the heart of

Arcrea, and now here you are today, the heart discovered and Arcrea's first crown on your head!"

"A crown fashioned by the greatest blacksmith in Arcrea," Druet ran a finger along the golden band.

"Ha!" Gregory's laugh shook his muscular frame, "I'm not the blacksmith whose name is known by every man, woman, and child in this persevering kingdom! Only think—a year ago you were an unknown peasant, and now king! And that is only the beginning of changes that have taken place."

"It is awe-inspiring to see what God can do in so short a time. I am truly grateful for all the help I've received…I am so inexperienced for this task that now rests on my shoulders; to rule Arcrea wisely."

"But you know and acknowledge the Source of all wisdom," Gregory pointed a finger heavenward, "and that sets you far ahead of where you believe yourself to be, my son."

Soon afterward, the two men turned their horses and parted company, Gregory toward Eubank and the work that awaited him there, and Druet east to the large native village of Olden Weld, where he and his wife, Queen Aurenia, were living temporarily.

Druet dismounted before the solidly built cottage he called home and handed the reins to a waiting servant. He thanked the man with a smile and nod and watched as his horse was led away. Being waited on by servants was something that Druet was still unaccustomed to, but the men on his council had been honest when they said that Druet would not be able to do everything—he was going to need people who were available to help him and he would need to be accepting of this help. Not long after this decision had been reached, a group of willing peasants had been hired and trained as the first installment of the royal staff.

The door of the large cottage was opened and a young woman appeared in the opening. Her violet eyes brightened when she caught sight of him and she brushed at several strands of raven-black hair that had escaped from her braid. Druet returned his wife's smile and went to greet her.

"Hello, Renny!" He still enjoyed using the nickname that she had introduced herself by.

"Druet, you're freezing," she brushed at snowflakes on his shoulders.

"And you will be too if you don't move away from the open door," Druet crossed the threshold and closed the door as he glanced over the queen's head to her giant guardian, standing in silence on the far side of the front room, "Did the queen behave herself while I was gone today, Grikk?"

The man from Dragon Coast had the remarkable ability to keep his features drawn in an unaffected expression. Yet now, as his gaze fluttered momentarily to Renny's face and then back to Druet, the young king caught the faintest spark of amusement in the giant's eyes.

Druet looked down at Renny and tried to frown at her mischievous grin, "What did you do?"

"I only went to practice archery in the meadow."

"Renny…"

She motioned one hand toward the giant, "Grikk went with me and kept a close watch on whether or not I was tiring easily. Kellen was there too, and he said that I didn't look weary at all."

"Your brother wouldn't dare tell you otherwise, for fear of risking your wrath."

Renny laughed, "Kellen is almost as anxious as you are about my strength, and is always the first to reinforce your petitions for me to rest! I can assure you, Druet," she placed her hands over the barely-perceptible round of her abdomen, "I am always very careful of the baby's safety."

Druet nodded and ran a hand through his dark-brown hair with a look of resignation. The kingdom of Arcrea had celebrated the news of Renny's pregnancy with feasts and parades of well-wishers, and now all were looking forward to the birth of the throne's heir. Druet, too, eagerly awaited the day; not only would it mark the birth of the royal couple's first child, it would also mean that his energetic wife could once again move about without sending him into a state of anxiety for her health and safety. Druet had never known such terror as the day he had found her perched on a limb of her favorite tree. He prayed that God would give him grace to endure the next seven months.

"When we heard you coming, Alice offered to heat some spiced cider," Renny adjusted the shawl around her shoulders, "How did the site look today?"

Druet shifted his thoughts back to Eubank, "Better than last week," he pulled the cloak from his shoulders and Grikk reached to take it from him; Druet nodded his thanks, "The craftsmen are grateful for the work and eager to complete Eubank as quickly as possible—within the year."

Lady Alice entered the room then, followed by a servant girl, and the two served mugs of steaming cider. Alice was the niece of the former Lord Osgood. She had joined Druet's quest for Arcrea's heart and

Grikk

then agreed to remain as Renny's companion and close friend.

A knock sounded on the door and Grikk opened it. Druet's chief of informants, Falconer, who had served on the former Lord Frederick's staff, stepped inside and bowed before the king and queen.

"Good afternoon, Falconer."

"Sire," Falconer's face was drawn in a tense look.

Druet studied the man, "Any news from Talon and Bracy?"

Falconer shook his head, "I expected their mission in Quinton to take several weeks; they should return any day now."

The informant paused, obviously reluctant to reveal what he had come to say. Druet waited patiently. Finally, Falconer cleared his throat and spoke again.

"Sire, I bring news that, for several reasons, is most unpleasant. An Arcrean vessel was attacked near the coast of Stephen by a foreign vessel, believed to be Mizgalian."

Druet stiffened visibly. The armies of the seven former lords had retained their employment as soldiers in the Arcrean forces, though they were no longer paid the outrageous amounts that had been used by the noblemen to bribe them into service. These soldiers had continued to guard the northern border, where the Mizgalians were known to hide their armies in the vast range of Brikbone Mountains—but an attack at sea? This was unexpected.

"The crew? Did anyone survive?"

"Most...did...Sire," Falconer's words came haltingly and he looked at Druet with a pained expression that willed his king to understand so that he would not be forced to utter the words aloud, "Word has just been received from the captain of the *Seabird* that one man did not survive the attack."

"The *Seabird*?"

Druet's heart gave a fearful lurch. The only seaman he knew as a personal acquaintance was the man who had come to be like a brother during the length of his recent quest. Swallowing the lump in his throat, Druet worked his jaw back and forth as the news began to register in his mind, slowly cutting deeper to pierce his very soul. When, at last, he was able to speak, his voice grated in his throat like rocks.

"Nathaniel...?"

Lady Alice gasped. Druet knew that she too had come to be a close friend of Nathaniel's, and was eagerly looking forward to the seaman's return from a voyage at sea.

Falconer dipped his head, "I'm sorry, Sire."

A moment of shock gripped the room with silence, and then a sob escaped Alice and she began to cry. With deliberate effort, Druet turned to see Renny place a comforting arm around the other woman's shoulders even as tears filled her own eyes and she looked with a dazed expression to Druet.

Druet's mind screamed that it couldn't be true. Nathaniel couldn't be dead! Only two short months ago he had stood with them, talked with them, worked with them here in the Heartland. He had been the one to bring order to the chaos of Druet's journey through Arcrea. His ready smile and easy laughter had settled the nerves and tension of those around him.

More than once Druet had thought that Nathaniel would be the man to discover Arcrea's heart and become king.

Druet took a shaky breath. Not only did he have an extensive enemy to deal with on land and sea both, but also the shocking death that had come by their hands.

"Falconer, please inform Leland that I've returned from Eubank, and tell him to call the council together immediately."

ꟸ

King Cronin entered his private study to find Sir Kleyton waiting in attentive silence. Beside the knight stood a lanky, dark-bearded soldier who kept his gaze locked on the far wall. The two men saluted upon their king's entrance.

"Kleyton?"

"Sire," the knight motioned toward the soldier, "One of the men who accompanied Trenton over the Brikbones."

"Ah, at last," Cronin closed the door behind him, failing to notice that the soldier eyed the sealed exit with a fear-tightened jaw. The king stepped to the parchment-littered table below a central chandelier of dripping candles and sat in the elaborate chair. His eyes passed from one man to the other, glittering with dark pleasure over the soldier's return to Mockmor and the dastardly consequences it would bring.

"The deed is done, then?"

Kleyton glanced at the soldier.

The man finally lifted his gaze, but only to Cronin's chin, "Trenton is…in Arcrea, Sire."

The king's smile tensed uncertainly, "Dead?"

The soldier glanced fearfully at Kleyton and the knight turned to address the king, "Our four travelers came upon two Arcreans in the forests of Quinton and the three guides attacked them for sport," he tilted his head to indicate the man beside him, "Only Thomas survived; the other two soldiers were killed by the Arcreans."

Cronin's fingers balled into a fist, but otherwise he remained motionless, "I fail to understand what this ordeal has to do with my orders regarding Trenton."

"The attack on the Arcreans occurred before our men had the chance to carry out those orders, Sire."

King Cronin's eyes shifted and slammed into Thomas's terrified gaze, and his voice escaped through clenched teeth, "Were my words not clear? Did I not inform you and your comrades that this mission was the key to launching our campaign in Arcrea?"

"You did, my king."

Cronin slammed his fist on the table and rose with a suddenness that sent his chair toppling to the floor with a crash, "Then why did you not obey my orders?" he shouted as he came around the table to tower over Thomas, "I gave strict commands that you were to take Trenton across the Arcrean border and kill him there so that I might blame his death on those insufferable Arcreans."

"But Sire," Thomas cowered, "if you wish to blame them for the death of a Mizgalian, why not blame them for the deaths of my two companions who died in the forest?"

"Two reasons," Cronin lowered his voice to an ominous rasp, "First; your two friends died while antagonizing the Arcreans, which is not reason enough for me to flood their borders in war. Second, soldiers are a disposable lot. I lose soldiers in battle every day, on every front. However, Trenton is the son of my esteemed councilor, Sir Kleyton—his death would give me cause for revenge."

Thomas glanced at the knight with confusion in his wide eyes, "You would kill this man's son to make war?"

Kleyton's gaze flitted from Thomas to the king and back again, "I am willing to make a sacrifice for my sovereign's noble cause. Though the cost is great, the rewards will surely be greater."

The king turned to study the map of the Mizgalian/Arcrean borders, pinned to the wall behind his table, "Thomas…?"

"Yes, Sire?"

"Why did you not kill Trenton yourself, after your companions had fallen?"

Thomas's eyes widened as he scrambled for an answer, "My…my king, I…! You sent the three of us…that there might be more than one witness…of the death. I only thought—"

"You thought wrong! It would not matter if there were one witness or a thousand so long as he was dead! We're Mizgalians, you simpleton. Foreigners always believe our words are lies, and nine times out of ten this is true!"

Thomas was frantic, "Then why not lie to this Arcrean king, and insist that a Mizgalian lord has been killed within his borders? Then you need not kill Sir Kleyton's son!"

"Fool!" Cronin turned and glared at Thomas, "You think that I did not consider this myself? Trenton was chosen for this fate for more reasons than you will ever know," the evil king glanced at Kleyton and waved a dismissive hand at Thomas, "Dispose of the wretch."

Kleyton drew his sword to obey, but Thomas fell to his knees with a desperate plea.

"No! Please, my king! Give me another chance to please you! I will kill Trenton; only have mercy on me!"

Kleyton froze with his sword arm in the air and looked up that the king might signal his desire. Cronin watched Thomas for a moment and took pleasure in the man's helpless groveling; he lifted a hand and Kleyton lowered his blade.

"Very well, Thomas; I will grant you your request. As soon as we receive word of Trenton's whereabouts in Arcrea, you will be sent to carry out my orders." Cronin grabbed the front of Thomas's tunic and the soldier cried out when he was jerked within an inch of the monarch's face, "And this time, you will succeed."

Chapter 4
• Dangerous Creatures •

The three young men set up camp in a forest of southern Frederick. Bracy set about preparing three rabbits they had managed to catch earlier in the evening, while Talon applied a fresh dose of Ulric's Rose to his shoulder.

"A few days more should bring us to the Heartland and then Rodney can tend to it properly."

"It's healing well. You did a fine job with it, Bracy. Anyway, you couldn't really go wrong with the tonic already made for you."

"Rodney?" Trenton's bass voice drew the clansmen's attention across the cook-fire, "Is he the healer spoken of in the songs of Druet's quest?"

"He is that," Talon replied, "He's a good man."

Bracy turned the rabbits while staring at Trenton, "Do you sing?"

Talon shifted to eye Bracy with a bewildered look as Trenton's brow lifted in surprise, "I beg your pardon?"

"I wondered if you sing. Your voice is uncommonly rich and every time you speak, it nearly puts me to sleep."

Talon grinned as he reached for one of the rabbits and drew his knife, "Bracy, would you like for him to sing you a lullaby?"

Bracy scowled, "I was merely asking!"

Trenton gave a small laugh and accepted the hunk of meat offered to him, "I've never had time for singing, Bracy."

"Just random notes for moments of boredom."

Trenton detected a hint of suspicion in Bracy's eyes, but merely nodded, "Exactly."

The smell of cooked rabbit permeated the air long after the three had rolled into their cloaks to sleep. Talon jabbed Bracy in the ribs and hummed the first line of a lullaby before Bracy cut him off with a thump on the head. Talon laughed and belted another line, dodging Bracy's second swing.

Trenton listened to their lighthearted banter and wished for the first time that he too was free to enjoy a time of leisure. His father had never allowed him to maintain friendships for long, and so he had never reached the stage of brotherly familiarity that Talon and Bracy shared. Trenton had been forced to live a life at the furious pace kept by the Mockmor garrison and the no-nonsense Sir Kleyton. He had been trained to eat, sleep, and breathe in a state of constant preparation. For what? Attack. Betrayal. Weakness.

Friendships would only serve to make him lenient.

Suddenly, Trenton realized that instinct had pulled him to his feet and he was drawing his sword. Talon and Bracy were doing the same. The three stood in absolute silence for the space of several breaths and then the noise came again.

The distinct tongue-clicking of a catawyld beast.

Trenton felt a surge of energy course through his frame, "It's close."

"It smells the meat from our supper," Talon murmured.

Trenton nodded, "It won't be alone."

"Do we have time to get the horses ready and…?"

"No. They'd be sure to find the campsite deserted and track us before we were far enough away."

"And they're fast enough to catch us."

For a moment, Bracy looked panic-stricken, "Talon, your shoulder…"

"I'll be alright. Prayer and a good rush of adrenaline will keep my blades swinging."

Trenton's eyes scanned the trees, "Have you battled these creatures before?" Only when they didn't answer did he realize the intensity had caused his tongue to slip back into his native speech and he had spoken the words in Mizgalian.

Before another word could be uttered, a fierce shriek rent the cold air and a dog-sized creature with pointed features and a long cat-like tail pounced through the trees, landing several paces away. Its feet were webbed and capable of scaling any surface with astonishing speed. Its large ears looked able to detect the slightest noise. Two glittering eyes peered at the three young men and the catawyld clicked the back of its tongue in warning.

"I hate these things," Bracy growled as he set himself in a ready stance.

"I'll take the fist one," Trenton murmured softly.

The Mizgalian watched the beast closely. Catawylds were native to his homeland, driven over the Brikbones years ago in an attempt to overrun Arcrea. Many times Sir Kleyton had ordered Trenton into a training arena where the ground was thick with impossible sand; there he would single-handedly battle against two or three of these vicious beasts.

Trenton's fingers adjusted around the hilt of his sword. He remained motionless as he waited, feeling out each moment in preparation for the attack.

The hungry catawyld stalked closer and Trenton suddenly lunged forward. The surprised beast leapt over him and Trenton turned immediately to grab it by the tail. The animal's natural reaction was to turn on him, and when it did Trenton was ready. His sword made a quick cut and the beast was disabled; another thrust and it was dead.

Talon ran forward as another catawyld emerged from the darkness beyond Trenton.

"Bracy, build up the fire so we can see better!"

"Talon! Now?"

"Now!"

Talon's swords kept the second beast at bay while, behind him, Trenton rose from his vulnerable position by the first.

"Ready?" the blond clansman shouted.

"GO!" Trenton yelled the word and Talon lunged for the catawyld. The beast leapt over him and was met by Trenton's sword on the other side. Another catawyld pounced from the trees and jumped for Talon; the clansman jumped from his crouch and spun to open his crossed swords against the deadly creature while Trenton turned to face two more.

Bracy dropped an armload of kindling onto the fire and turned just in time to drive his sword at a catawyld as it jumped over Trenton. The Mizgalian immediately moved to finish the wounded beast while Talon imitated the earlier-used technique by grabbing the tail of the final catawyld and killing it when it turned on him.

Breathing heavily, Trenton jumped up and ran to bank Bracy's fire, "Now we leave! If there are any more, they'll be sidetracked by the fresh meat here."

Sheathing their swords as they ran, the three quickly mounted and were soon galloping southwest, following a well-worn road toward the Heartland. Talon and Bracy exchanged glances and then let out victorious whoops. Trenton shook his head at the two, but allowed himself the pleasure of a single laugh that was quickly carried away on the night air.

ꙮ

Word of Talon and Bracy's return reached Falconer long before the two men rode into Olden Weld. Queen Aurenia's father, Leland—the chief elder of the Heartland—also made his home in this village. He and the other native elders were currently serving as the king's council.

Falconer stood on the large flat stone that served as a front step into the meetinghouse. His sharp eyes were trained on the three approaching horses. Not only had he been alerted to the arrival of his couriers, but also that they were accompanied by a Mizgalian. Falconer let out a slow breath. Even from this distance he could see that the newcomer's presence was attracting many wary stares from the villagers.

Trenton

The stranger was young; younger than Talon and Bracy but older than Leland's son, Kellen. Blond hair neatly covered his head and tried to curl around his ears and at the base of his neck. He was dressed simply, like a Mizgalian peasant, but bore himself with a natural dignity that suggested another lifestyle. His powerful frame spoke of soldiering, and yet something about his noble features reminded Falconer of a dignitary.

The informant's brow suddenly furrowed.

The three young men dismounted and Falconer found himself staring into a light-blue gaze that rivaled the clear sky for cold brilliance. He continued to study the young man's face as Talon gave him the details of Trenton's story; he watched for any sign that might betray a secret hidden behind the calm mask, but quickly realized that Trenton was either accomplished at hiding his thoughts, or had none to hide. The blue eyes never wavered and Falconer quickly gained the impression that he, too, was being scrutinized.

"The king is meeting with his council now. You will have to wait to see him. Talon, Bracy, make your guest comfortable and then meet me in my quarters."

Some time later, when Talon and Bracy stepped into the small outbuilding behind the meetinghouse, Falconer waited as the door was closed and Talon stepped forward.

"We delivered the message to Sir Walter in record time. We were slowed on our return by the fight with the Mizgalians, and occasionally my shoulder forced us to camp early."

"Because you wouldn't take your swords off," Bracy interjected, "Your wound would have healed days ago if it wasn't being reopened by the weight of two heavy sheaths!"

"Bracy, I told you…"

Falconer cleared his throat and the two fell silent.

"Talon, have Rodney look at your shoulder. Thank you for your report. You may go now," when the younger men remained where they were, Falconer lifted his brow in question, "Was there something more?"

Bracy leaned closer and whispered as if an outsider might hear him, "What do you think of the foreigner?"

Falconer almost smiled at the suspicious tone, "I think we should be very careful—"

"But do you think he's honest?" Bracy interrupted.

Talon placed a balancing hand on the room's side table, "Bracy and I have tried to determine whether or not he can be trusted, but we can't decide one way or the other. Some things don't seem to fit together quite as they should…but we have no proof otherwise."

"And we both feel as if we've met him before, which isn't possible. We come from two different ends of Arcrea, and we would have remembered had we just met him during Druet's quest."

Falconer stared at them, his usually controlled features etched in shock.

"What is it, Falconer?"

The informant shook his head, "I'm not sure…only, when I first saw Trenton, I could have sworn that I too had seen him somewhere before!"

Chapter 5
* Trenton's Walk *

Bracy and Talon quickly learned of Nathaniel's death and were deeply affected by the news of their friend. Word of the beloved seaman's demise had been spreading beyond the borders of the Heartland and soon all of Arcrea mourned the brother-friend of their king.

Trenton stood by and observed the kingdom's sadness as if from a far country. He didn't know this seaman except through the sonnets and tales told of Druet's quest, but he supposed by the response to his death that Nathaniel must have been a good and honorable man.

Trenton's trained ears picked up traces of news from here and there. Among other things, he heard that a Lady Alice of Brentwood, Queen Aurenia's companion, had left Olden Weld several days before in answer to a summons received from the chatelaine of her castle on the southern coast of Osgood. Queen Aurenia would miss the lady dearly while she was away, but was glad that Alice had something to distract her from the news of the seaman's death. Apparently, the two had been particular friends.

Trenton was introduced to King Druet. Despite himself, the youth found himself impressed with Mizgalia's chief adversary. Druet was known to have been a blacksmith by trade, and yet he possessed a quality about him that would easily lead one to believe he had been born a prince. Druet's bright blue eyes shone with a ready humor, and yet his features, etched in a noble face, wore an expression of determination for the task that lay before him.

Trenton found himself marveling over this "boy-king." Druet was less than a decade older than the Mizgalian spy and far less trained for combat and military affairs, and yet he was facing the reshaping of an entire kingdom and the responsibility of a lifetime with the steadfastness of a seasoned warrior!

In accordance to his role in Arcrea, Trenton allowed an obvious measure of hero-worship to shade his eyes as he asked the young king about his amazing accomplishments in Arcrea.

Druet smiled in reply and humbly lowered his gaze, "I have not accomplished anything, Trenton, merely allowed God to work through me towards *His* accomplishments, no matter the cost."

Trenton was taken aback by this confession. As Druet's words tumbled through his mind, he began to silently fume. How could he report to his father and King Cronin that Druet's successes were believed to be supported and caused by an invisible God?

Trenton ambled along the village street, outwardly an innocent observer, but inwardly tossed in turmoil. He could see his father's eyes rolling in disgust as King Cronin's laugh mocked Trenton's feeble attempts to gain information—to perform the work of a grown man.

"You place far too much confidence in that boy," King Cronin had often said to Sir Kleyton, and Trenton had never understood why. He had lived as no other Mizgalian boy had been privileged; raised in the shadows of Castle Mockmor and annually examined in the presence of Cronin himself, Trenton had proved himself worthy of the king's praise time after time…only to receive a silent nod and the bitter words addressed to his father by the monarch's lips.

Now here he was in a foreign land, ready to take on this mission of utmost importance in his king's eyes, and all he could gather was that the Arcrean king was relying on the strength of the Unknown.

"Yes, father," Trenton muttered under his breath, "The long-sought secret to destroying the Acreans is to first tear down their invisible stronghold." The bitter words appeared before him as wispy tendrils of frozen white air. The morning promised another cold, clear day.

Trenton's thoughts were suddenly jarred back to the present when his path was cut off by a goat darting across the road. With a startled cry, Trenton swung his arms in an attempt to keep his balance, but it was too late; in another moment he was sprawled on his stomach in the street. Trenton sat up and brushed dirt and ice from his hair and tunic. Two figures appeared in breathless pursuit of the four-legged culprit, pausing to bend over the victim whose path the animal had crossed.

"You a'right, sir?"

At the sound of the strange accent, Trenton lifted wide eyes to see a girl's freckled face startlingly close to his own. The face was framed by a mass of curly auburn hair tied with a sorry ribbon, and the stubby nose was flanked by green eyes that were wider than his with panic.

"I asked, are you a'right?" she spoke louder now, obviously thinking he hadn't heard her the first time.

"I'm fine!"

The girl, in turn, looked surprised by his thickly accented voice.

Trenton drew back and brought his hand up to force her out of his way, but the girl mistook the motion as a plea for help and, grabbing the brandished hand, yanked him to his feet. Trenton bit back a roar of shock and tried to rub feeling back into his jarred arm. The girl, somewhere around sixteen years of age, watched him with a pitying shake of her head.

"Mean ol' goat, 'Umphrey is; knocks down ever'body in 'is path! Gran'mother says 'e sure can make a body mad an' she's right," the auburn head jerked to the left, indicating the grandmother, whose heavy breathing showed she was still recovering from chasing the goat. Trenton recognized the woman as Marie, an elderly native and a good friend to the royal household.

"I'm sorry," Marie huffed as she looked up at Trenton, "I can't seem to keep him in his pen. Are you hurt, sir?"

"No," Trenton shook his head and wiped his hands on his tunic, wondering why anyone would name their goat Humphrey.

"You sure?" the girl stood on tiptoe, bringing herself eyelevel with Trenton and peering at him with an odd look, "Looked pretty shaken t' me. You 'ad your 'ead in the clouds, you did; didn' even 'ear when I asked twice if you—"

"That's enough, Leyla," Marie hobbled forward to herd her granddaughter out of Trenton's way, "We must find Humphrey and take him home before he tramples the whole village to ruins."

"An' 'e will, too," Leyla blew a curl out of her face as the two set off down the road; turning to glance back, she grinned at Trenton, "Keep your eyes on th' road, Mizgal'yin!"

Trenton blew out a white cloud of frustration and turned to continue his walk.

He rolled his eyes.

Arcreans.

His father had warned him that these people were not ashamed to speak their minds. The northern Arcreans, like Talon and Bracy, were riotous warriors, and those from the south were carefree merchants who were accustomed to having their way.

Trenton's eyes observed his surroundings even while his mind was focused elsewhere.

King Druet was from the north. A warrior. Yet there was nothing about the man that suggested riotous behavior. He had conquered a kingdom, it was true; but he had done it gently.

Perhaps that was the secret to his success! He was gentle!

Trenton frowned at his own suggestion. His father would die of shame if Trenton sent back word that King Cronin's victory would come when he softened his heart. And Cronin himself would laugh

Trenton to scorn and then turn him out to serve as a lowly water boy or an aide to the kitchen staff. Anything that would bring him shame.

"Trenton!"

The Mizgalian turned at the sound of Falconer's voice. The king's agent strode toward him, his cloak billowing behind him. Trenton remained where he was and waited for the other man to approach him, studying his stoic features for any sign of what was to come.

Falconer came to a halt before the youth and returned his steady gaze, "Trenton, I am ordered to the village of Balgo—the dwelling place of the seven former lords of Arcrea. A close watch is kept over them at all times and I must gather a report for King Druet," he paused slightly over his next words and Trenton quickly perceived what they would be, "His majesty suggested that you accompany me and witness more of Arcrea."

Trenton remained silent, forcing Falconer to complete the offer, while a well-presented expression of anticipation hid his objective from the informant's perception.

"Would you care to accept the offer and ride with me, then?"

Trenton blinked. At last, here was his chance to leave the Heartland, "I would be honored to accompany you, sir. When should I be ready?"

"We leave at dawn."

"Very well. I'll be waiting outside the meetinghouse."

Falconer nodded and studied the Mizgalian for a long moment before turning back the way he had come. The shrill cry of a hawk suddenly lifted the seasoned spy's gaze to the sky, where the bird glided effortlessly over the village and disappeared from view beyond a border of trees to the south. Falconer's gaze darted back to Trenton, and he saw that the boy hadn't moved from the spot where they had spoken. The blue eyes shifted from the point where the hawk had disappeared, and he offered Falconer a small smile before turning to casually walk in the opposite direction.

Falconer's eyes narrowed the slightest bit as he watched the Mizgalian's back move farther down the street. Turning his head to the left, he gazed again at the border of trees to the south and murmured under his breath.

"Where have I seen you before, Trenton?"

Chapter 6
* Encounter at Balgo *

Northwest of the Heartland, in the region of Ranulf, the village of Balgo was tucked at the base of a steep rise in the rolling terrain; a lone mountain in a sea of foothills—some even called the lost Brikbone. A cluster of thirty or so sturdy cottages seemed to huddle together against the cold, forming a sort of ring around a central well.

"Those are the homes of the former nobility and their families," Falconer gazed down on Balgo from the top of the rise and spoke to Trenton, "The guards who are currently on watch occupy several of the cottages; others are the shops and homes of commoners who were willing to help conform the seven lords to their new lives in the peasantry."

"King Druet did not have them killed?"

Falconer glanced at the boy whose entire life had doubtless been molded by the idea that every opponent must be killed—every fight was to the death, "They are now members of Arcrea's heart and have therefore earned King Druet's protection."

Trenton stared at Falconer, clearly unable to fathom the informant's words, "But they don't deserve it."

"None of us do," Falconer pressed his heels to the flanks of his midnight-black mount and began the descent to Balgo, "The kingdom of Arcrea has long been a land of adversity, even amongst ourselves. In my opinion we did not deserve to have a man of Druet's quality and faith to take on the responsibilities of the crown. In any case, the former lords have been left to live and learn to serve one another."

Trenton heard the sound of rustling wings and glanced to see Link perched in a nearby tree. His gaze darted to see if Falconer had noticed, but the informant was carefully watching the trail before them. The hawk had been following them from the Heartland at a safe distance. If Falconer had seen it, he hadn't let Trenton know it.

During the two days of travel Falconer had spoken little, and seemed to take even less notice of Trenton's presence than he did of the biting cold. When the man did speak it was to point out any landmarks of importance, as King Druet had suggested. Trenton could sense that the man was accustomed to traveling alone.

Once, Trenton had looked up to see Falconer studying him and the agent had simply asked, "Have you lived in Mockmor all your life?"

Trenton's mind had raced to uncover what motive might lie behind the simple question, but had finally given a single nod and said, "All my life. First with my family, and then after they died, with the cruelest master who ever walked the earth."

Trenton's horse snorted, drawing the young man's attention back to the present. The cottages of Balgo released curling towers of smoke from their chimneys, reminding him that warmth would soon be available. They handed the reins to a young boy at the stables; Falconer placed a small coin in the lad's palm and then led the way toward a cottage on the village square.

A dark-haired young woman stood watching their progress from where she stood by the well. The bucket she had just drawn remained balanced on the well's wall as her eyes focused on Falconer with a look of half-bitterness and half-misery. When he paused and offered to carry the bucket home for her, the girl's thin fingers tightened around the handle and a splash of water escaped as she jerked away.

"I can do it myself."

They watched as she moved stiffly across the square and entered one of the cottages. Only then did Falconer speak.

"She is Elaina."

Trenton mentally reviewed the many songs and rhymes that had been ingrained into his memory, "She is Frederick's daughter."

Falconer glanced in his direction and then continued toward their destination, "You know much about King Druet's band of followers."

"I lived to hear each new sonnet that made its way across the border. I never heard about you, though."

"I did not travel with Druet until the end."

Trenton wondered if Falconer would have said more, but at that moment they reached the cottage serving as the guards' headquarters and Falconer gave the door a sharp rap.

Inside, the two travelers were fed and warmed at the fire. Trenton listened intently to every word spoken between the other men, but gave the appearance of one utterly absorbed by the hot mug in his hands and the bright flame on the hearth.

"Have the villagers given you any trouble of late?"

"None, sir. Osgood was recently ill with a fever, but that's passed now."

Another soldier leaned closer, "Some say the fever left him touched," he tapped his head to imply insanity, "But I can't say one way or the other…he's always been a bit odd to me."

Falconer glanced at the first man for more information.

"As you know, sir, Osgood has not taken well to the life of a peasant, and his wife died shortly after arriving in Balgo. What money Osgood makes in his new trade is usually squandered on wine, and he's often left begging his neighbors for a meal. He's not as large a man as he once was, for sure. Between the little bit of food he gets and the recent fever, he doesn't even look like the same man who ruled a portion of Arcrea just a short time ago."

"Is he insane?" Falconer sounded utterly unaffected.

The first soldier shook his head, "He mutters to himself and is sometimes known to sit outside and stare at nothing in particular, but he's done nothing that gives me cause for alarm."

Falconer cast a swift glance at Trenton and knew, despite the boy's ability to appear otherwise, that he had heard every word. It mattered little; this was not a private conversation. Still, the action was reason enough for Falconer to be a bit suspicious of the boy's intentions. After a glance through the window at the darkening sky, the informant declared that he would make the rounds through Balgo in the morning.

"Trenton, we'll bed down by the fire."

Trenton nodded silently and caught the looks of suspicion on the two soldiers' faces. Clearly, they were unhappy to be sharing a roof with this Mizgalian.

Trenton rose long before the sun and crept outside without rousing Falconer. Placing his right hand over the heart of his doublet, he felt for the scrap of parchment hidden there and took a step away from the cottage. Once beyond the cottages, he would signal Link, tuck the message into the small leather pouch attached to the bird, and then make his way back here before anyone knew he had gone. His father would be expecting an update of his location.

Trenton habitually made the shadows his friends as he moved through the streets of Balgo. He had nearly made it to the village's outskirts when he suddenly froze. Just ahead and to his left, the door of one cottage had been left open and a man was sitting on a stump outside the entrance. The firelight from within and the bright flame of a torch in an outdoor sconce showed the man's silhouette swaying back and forth. Trenton could hear the faint sound of his murmuring.

Trenton immediately thought of the soldiers' words the night before about the man called Osgood. If this was the same man, he was either drunk or indeed crazy. Figuring he would be in no danger of detection, Trenton stayed out of the light's reach and began to move forward once more. In the next instant, Trenton's foot kicked a crate left in the middle of the street and it slid noisily across the icy ground. He muttered a curse as Osgood bolted from his perch on the stump and stood staring into the darkness.

"Who goes there?" the man's speech was slightly slurred.

Trenton remained silent. Surely Osgood would return to his seat and…

"Come out of the shadows, whoever you are," Osgood grabbed the torch and stalked a step closer.

He'd been spotted.

Gritting his teeth in frustration, Trenton stepped forward, "Forgive me for causing your fright, good sir; I was just—"

Trenton froze when Osgood's torch cast a glow across his face and the former lord gave a frightful shriek that filled the still morning air and sent a shiver up Trenton's spine. The sound was far more unnerving than a catawyld's cry.

"No! It can't be!" Osgood covered his face with his free arm and stole glances at the paralyzed Trenton; his eyes were wide with obvious fear as he continued to shout at the youth, "Leave me and come no closer! Haunt me no longer, I beg of you!"

Trenton couldn't move. For the first time in his life, an eerie fear kept his feet planted where they were, refusing to carry him from the spot and this scene of terror.

Osgood's shouts had aroused many of the villagers, and people were quickly beginning to appear in the surrounding doorways. The torches they carried cast frightening shadows over Trenton and the crazy nobleman. Osgood's face was as white as the snow that covered the ground; terror gripped his features in an agonized expression.

"I knew it would come to this! Why must you…"

Suddenly, Osgood's face took on a look of wrath and he boldly marched closer. Before Trenton could force himself to move, Osgood gripped him by the arm and swung him around, pinning him to the cottage's outer wall with one hand. Trenton's mind screamed at him to resist—he was undeniably stronger than Osgood, it would be no hard task—but his body would not respond.

Osgood pressed his face closer until Trenton could smell the wine on his breath, "How did you escape?"

Trenton's eyes grew wider still. He had never been this close to a madman before, and he sincerely hoped this would be the last time. The murmurs of the gathering crowd told Trenton that the villagers were trying to coax Osgood to cease his attack without having to come too close to the man. Osgood's wild gaze remained fixed on Trenton's face in the gathering light of dawn.

"Did they let you go?" He growled.

Trenton finally found his tongue and forced it to stutter, "Who?"

"Your fate."

"I…don't know…what you're talking about."

"You do!" Osgood's grip suddenly slackened and his eyes were filled with fear once again, "You've come back to reward me for my deeds!"

As Osgood began to back away, Trenton quickly turned to make his escape, only to collide with Falconer. The informant opened his mouth to question the youth, but stopped when Osgood shouted his name.

"Falconer! You must save me, Falconer!"

Falconer's glance took in the large crowd of former lords and ladies sadly shaking their heads at the man shouting in their midst. Frederick and Elaina stood to one side watching Osgood with disdain. Falconer shifted his gaze and saw the look of terror on Trenton's face, a look that was mirrored by Osgood's expression.

"What is it, Osgood?"

"Take him away! He's come to haunt me!"

"That's absurd, Osgood. No one is here to haunt or harm you."

"He escaped from them!"

Falconer was nearing the limit of his patience. He had been alarmed to wake and find that Trenton's pallet was empty, only to be drawn outside by frightened shouts. Despite the guard's assertion otherwise, Osgood was obviously insane and would need special attention. Stepping forward, Falconer encouraged the older man to sit down on the stump. He pulled the cottage door shut to keep the cold from going in, and then asked,

"Who escaped, Osgood?"

Osgood lifted a shaky hand toward Trenton and spoke in a hoarse whisper that, regardless, reached every ear in the street, "Eric."

A deep hush suddenly fell over the crowd as everyone turned to look at Trenton. Returning their wide-eyed gazes, he could see that they were studying him as if for the first time. Falconer, too, seemed captivated by some sudden realization.

Suddenly, Falconer left his place by Osgood and with a determined stride made his way to Trenton. Without pausing he grabbed Trenton's arm and turned him back toward the square, simultaneously lifting the hood of Trenton's cloak to hide the boy's face from the curious people.

"What are you—"

"Silence," Falconer's voice was clipped and Trenton detected a hint of eagerness.

Trenton bit back the urge to resist the man's guiding hand, and was instead grateful that it was at least moving him away from the insane Osgood and the stares of the entire village.

With a sudden feeling of angst, Trenton realized he hadn't gotten the message to Link. He scowled within the shielding folds of his hood. Perfect. He had failed to get the expected message through, and instead had been the victim of a terrifying old man.

Trenton turned to glance back, but Falconer stopped him with a quick command to keep his eyes forward. Trenton took a deep breath through his nose. Something unknown to him had occurred back there in the dirt street of an Arcrean village…and he had the distinct feeling that he didn't want to know what it was.

Chapter 7
* Secrets From the Past *

Falconer pulled Trenton into the guards' cottage and pushed the door shut. Without releasing his grip on the boy's arm, he stepped over to the hearth and pulled Trenton's hood back. Pressing against one of Trenton's shoulders, he situated the young man so that the fire cast a full glow across the confused young face. The informant's sharp eyes studied the youth with a new intensity. The scrutiny lasted several minutes before Falconer finally took a sharp breath and released Trenton's arm. He turned and leaned against the mantelpiece.

"You have always lived in Mizgalia?"

"What?" Trenton had clearly expected an explanation, not an interrogation.

"Answer the question, Trenton."

"I've answered it before…many times!"

Falconer ignored the boy's annoyed tone, "And the answer you gave me is the truth?"

Trenton's brow furrowed in bewilderment, "Of course! Why do you doubt me? What's going on?"

Falconer stared at the youth's face for another long moment. He had plenty of reasons to doubt Trenton. He was a Mizgalian who had made his appearance in Arcrea shortly after the beginning of Druet's reign; he was extremely observant, even taking note of the slightest details; and he hadn't yet explained to Falconer about the hawk that had followed them from the Heartland. There was also the question of why Trenton had left the cottage so early, heading to the outer edges of Balgo alone.

All of these thoughts crossed Falconer's mind in an instant's time, hidden behind his customary mask of calm. The door opened and the two guards who had been present the night before entered the cottage; they cast a wary look at Trenton and waited for Falconer to speak.

The informant shoved away from the hearth and headed for the door, "Keep an eye on the boy while I'm gone."

Trenton took a step after him, "Falconer, I'm not—"

Falconer cut him off with a sharp look that was accompanied by the unarguable command, "Stay in the cottage, Trenton."

The door slammed shut with the informant's urgency and the three left inside stood staring after him with a thousand unanswered questions swirling in the space between them.

ꙮ

Osgood turned with a start when his door was closed with a soft thud. The morning was bright, but the windows had been covered, leaving the task of illumination to the fire on thc hearth. The flames now cast a yellow-orange glow on the figure by the door.

"Falconer?" Osgood sank into a chair at the table with a sigh of relief and reached for the lone mug that sat on the crude surface before him, "Did you send him away?"

Falconer approached the table's opposite edge as Osgood took a swallow of the mug's contents, "What's this about, Osgood?"

The former lord pulled the mug away from his face with a sloshing sound and placed it in a just-so manner on the table. He stared at the informant with wide eyes.

"Didn't you see him? I know he was a real being, for I felt him when I gained the nerve to approach him and…!"

"Who did you see?" Falconer waited, testing the clarity of Osgood's mind.

"Eric."

Osgood tipped his head back to take another drink but Falconer's arm shot out and slapped the mug away, tossing it directly into the hearth's flame with a hiss.

Osgood was on his feet, "That was my only mug!"

"I'll buy you another!" Falconer leaned across the table with a fierce glare and spoke in a barely suppressed shout, "This is not a matter to treat carelessly! You and I both know that Eric has been dead for nearly twenty years," he pointed toward the door, "That boy couldn't possibly be your elder brother!"

Osgood began to tremble; sinking back into his seat, he tapped his fingers on the table and muttered, "He's not dead."

"What?"

"Eric and his wife, Adelaide; they did not die at sea twenty years ago. They were kidnapped."

Falconer stared at the older man in shocked silence.

Osgood began to sway back and forth as the words spilled out, "This secret—I've carried it for twenty years. I've lived with the knowledge of my victory, and now it will turn against me in my final days."

Falconer dragged a crate over to the table and sat down, "Are the rumors true, then? Are you responsible for your brother's disappearance?"

Osgood's jaw clenched.

"Osgood, there is no longer any need to hide the past. You are no longer the ruler of a region trying to remain in power. Tell me what happened."

Osgood turned and stared at the flames that were melting his mug, "It's simple, really. Eric was to be lord of our father's region and I despised the fact. I convinced him to take a holiday with his wife before the ceremony had taken place and even arranged to care for their daughter, Alice. I would have had them take her too, but that would have appeared far too suspicious—the entire family disappearing at once."

He paused and Falconer waited a moment before urging him to go on.

"I had made secret arrangements with a Mizgalian vessel to attack Eric's ship far from the coast, and to take him and Adelaide. I told the captain that I did not care what happened to them as long as no one ever learned what I had done."

"Then you do not know for sure that Eric is still alive," Falconer was enraged by Osgood's tale, but kept his anger in check to ensure that the man continued to speak freely, "This captain may well have killed them immediately."

"Eric was strong. The Mizgalians would not kill him when they might make a fine slave of him, or keep him for negotiations," Osgood's eyes suddenly filled with the fear of that morning, "And now he has returned for revenge! He escaped them, and will surely…"

Osgood's words withdrew to murmurs that Falconer could not distinguish. Pressing his fingers together or tapping them on the table, he returned his gaze to the flames and took on the expression that obviously caused others to believe he was insane. Falconer studied the man closely, trying to determine whether or not his words were resulting from this supposed insanity or if they were indeed the truth at last coming to light. He asked several more questions and then left Osgood to his startling memories. As he traveled towards the square, Falconer's mind reviewed Osgood's words and then focused on one realization of his own.

Though he had never met the man face-to-face, Falconer had long before seen a painting of Osgood's elder brother. He, like Osgood, had been struck that morning by the amazing likeness between the painting and the strange Mizgalian boy in the street. This recognition had at last reminded Falconer of where he had seen Trenton before…only he hadn't seen Trenton—he had seen the painting of Eric.

Trenton was an exact copy of Eric's likeness.

Falconer thought of the day when Talon and Bracy had insisted that they, too, recognized something familiar about the Mizgalian. But they had never seen Eric or the painting—probably had only heard rumors of the man's existence. The only person beside Osgood who still held this story close to heart and mind was Lady Alice.

Falconer froze.

Alice.

Eric's daughter.

Trenton looked like Eric.

Talon and Bracy had never seen Eric, but they were acquainted with his daughter. Could it be that Trenton, who so closely resembled Eric, also bore a likeness to the man's daughter?

Yes…he could.

Falconer slowly started forward once more, his mind swirling with new thoughts. Talon and Bracy had recognized in Trenton the singularly-blue eyes and honey-colored hair that mirrored Lady Alice's features.

Falconer's sharp gaze moved to the cottage on the square. Without pausing to knock, he entered and closed the door behind him. Trenton sat scowling by the hearth, obviously angered that Falconer had treated him like a child and ordered him to remain in the small confines of this room without any explanation.

When the blue eyes shifted to return his stare, Falconer was left with no doubt. There was a definite and strong resemblance shared by the lost nobleman, his daughter, and this Mizgalian youth.

It could be a severe coincidence…

Or it may be that the likenesses could only be explained by one simple but miraculous solution.

Chapter 8
* The Tapestry *

Old Simon had served the noble family at Castle Brentwood for seventy-three years. Alice's late grandfather, the regional lord prior to Osgood, had known him as a young man. Now, at the age of ninety-two, Simon was dying. It was while lying in bed, slipping further from life with every breath, that Simon had begun to ask for Lady Alice, and it was in answer to his wife's summons that Alice had returned from the Heartland.

Simon and his wife, Flora, lived as tenants on Brentwood property. Their small cottage held a warm and friendly glow, despite the obvious proximity of death. Alice entered with a comforting smile for Flora and was then led across the small room to a low stool set by Simon's bed. Flora apologized that she had no other chair to offer, and then stepped to the cook fire to draw off a pot of hot cider.

Simon's small frame was nearly hidden by the mountain of blankets that Alice had sent ahead from

Brentwood. A massive pillow framed his head and his eyes searched her face as she turned to greet him.

"Hello, Simon. I was sorry to hear that you are unwell. Are you feeling any better today?"

"You've come," he boldly reached for her hand and Alice was astonished by the strength in his grasp; his fingers clutched hers as if his last few breaths depended on it.

"Of course I've come. I wouldn't think—"

"You must…hear."

Alice tilted her head to one side and honey-colored curls fell over her ear, "Hear what?"

Simon's eyes grew wide, stretching the weathered skin that framed them, "I carry…a secret. Sworn…to silence," his gaze darted momentarily to the door, as if whomever the secret belonged to might appear to prevent him from speaking.

Flora handed her a steaming mug, and Alice thanked her before returning her attention to Simon, "I don't understand."

Simon's breathing became labored and Flora bent over him, "Let it wait, my Simon. The lady will return to hear when you've rested."

"Of course," Alice nodded in agreement and started to rise but Simon's grip on her hand tightened.

"No! Please…I must. I will die…but first I must…tell you."

Alice glanced at Flora and then nodded to Simon, "I'm listening."

"The tapestry."

"The tapestry?"

He nodded, "In the great hall."

Alice remembered, "Over the large hearth? The one depicting a battle at sea?"

"Yes," his eyes closed but she knew that he was still listening.

"My uncle Osgood had it specially made for Brentwood, and ordered for it to be hung…" Alice stopped when Simon's eyes opened; he was nodding, suggesting that he already knew the tapestry's history, "What about the tapestry, Simon?"

He began to tremble beneath the mountain of blankets, and his voice quavered from more than a chill, "I feared death…as punishment if I spoke. So I said…nothing."

"Simon, I don't wish for you to be afraid. Remember, God has not given us the spirit of fear. I will not force you to tell me the secret if you feel that you should not break your word to remain silent."

He stared at her for a long moment and then seemed to decide on how much he would say. Closing his eyes, he spoke, "The tapestry—the ships—hold the truth."

"The truth about what?"

The small eyes opened again and seemed to stare at nothing, "Master Eric."

Alice's eyes grew wide, "My father? Do you speak of his disappearance with my mother at sea?"

She almost missed the slight nod of his head. Her heart pounded in her ears as she waited to see if he would speak again, but he remained silent and with his gaze locked on a distant memory.

"Simon?"

He stretched a quivering hand toward the far window, facing the castle, "The tapestry."

Alice rose and quickly took her leave. Her mind was a frenetic whirlwind. Could it be that her father and mother's disappearance at sea had been planned as she had long wondered? Had the truth been hanging over her mantel for nineteen—almost twenty years?

After a hurried ride back to the castle, Lady Alice marched through the doors of the great hall, absently handing her cloak to her personal attendant, Bess. Her sights were set on the large tapestry over the mantel, her vision suddenly capable of handling only one object at a time. She called for several servants to remove the piece and carry it up to the spare room where Druet had been laid after the carnatur's attack months before.

Alice stood back by the window while the tapestry was spread across the bed and torches were set in the surrounding wall-sconces. She quietly ordered the servants to leave the room and to shut the door behind them. When their obedient steps had descended the staircase and silence had fallen like Simon's thick blankets over the room, she turned to open the window, eager to relieve the room's stifling atmosphere with a wintry breeze. Taking a deep breath through the window, Alice finally turned and began to move slowly toward the tapestry. She watched as her shadow crept across the floor, climbed up the side of the bed, and fell across the two ships warring on the restless waves. She squeezed her eyes shut, afraid of what this search may reveal.

She knew her parents were gone. This truth had stuck like a thorn in her heart for two decades. Did she want to uncover more of the awful truth now? Clenching her fists at her sides, Alice swallowed the bitter tears that wanted to come and opened her eyes.

One of the ships was Arcrean.

She had noted the ship's familiar flag—that of her family's region—many times before, when the tapestry had glared down at her from over the hearth, a constant reminder of her pain. She knew now that her discomfort had been Osgood's purpose in ordering the piece.

Leaning closer, Alice studied the wind-whipped flag on the second vessel and then gasped in sudden realization when the colors began to take shape in her mind.

Mizgalian.

Alice bit her lip. Simon had said the tapestry held the truth about her parents' disappearance and that he had been threatened into terrified silence about what he knew. Anyone who knew of Eric and Adelaide's tragic tale also knew that Osgood had been a prime suspect of causing the catastrophe, but no proof had been found to establish these suspicions.

Alice stared at the Mizgalian vessel and wondered if her uncle had hired the foreigners to attack her father's ship. Had her parents died at sea, as she had always believed, or had Arcrea's enemy carried them away into exile? Were they still alive?

Alice blinked.

And leaned closer.

At the bow of the Arcrean vessel, barely visible to the human eye, were the letters that made up the name of her father's ship.

Instinctively, her gaze drifted to the left, landing on the second vessel. Here the letters were even harder to distinguish. Alice shifted so that her shadow would not cover the spot as she slowly spelled it out.

F…

A knock came at the door and a hesitant voice called, "My lady…"

"I wish to be alone, Bess."

F…A…

The woman called again, "My lady, it's Simon."

…*T*…

Alice straightened, "What is it, Bess?"

"He…he's dead."

Alice stared at the tapestry in silence. The ship's name now stood out like a glowing emblem, and beside it she imagined the face of an old man who had carried this dreadful secret for nineteen years.

Slowly, Alice doubled over and sank to her knees beside the bed. Her arms stretched across the two ships and the tears finally managed to overwhelm her carefully-kept wall of defense. She didn't know how long she cried, but sobs and shudders still shook her frame long after her tears had been spent.

Alice cried for Simon.

She cried for Flora's loss.

She cried over Nathaniel's death.

She cried over her past, shaped as it was by painful lies.

But most of all Alice cried for her father and mother, the two people who had been closest to her heart, lost to an uncertain and terrible *Fate*.

Chapter 9
* In the Rigging *

"Get up, slave! The sun is about to rise and will wish to greet you this fine morning," the massive Mizgalian laughed coarsely and delivered a kick to one young man's side, "Get up!"

Nathaniel stifled a groan as he rolled over and pushed himself to his hands and knees. The chains that bound his wrists and ankles clanked noisily against the plank floor beneath him. Rising to his feet, Nathaniel joined the line of slaves inching their way up the rickety stairs toward the patch of sky that was visible through the hatch above.

In spite of his surroundings, Nathaniel's lips formed a slight smile when he heard the familiar voice behind him.

"Sleep well?"

"Does anyone sleep well aboard the *Fate*, Thumb?"

A chuckle escaped the fifty-year-old man before he was silenced by a harsh snap from the guard.

The ship lurched when he reached the top of the stairs, but Nathaniel's body habitually balanced against the tossing motion. Shifting his gaze to the blue dome of sky overhead, he breathed deeply of the salt air, trying to force from his senses the awful scents of the hold where he had spent another restless night.

The overseer stood to the right of the stairs with a tablet in his hand. His cold gaze glanced at the number that had been branded just below Nathaniel's right shoulder and then shifted back to the tablet. His voice was thick and gravely, casually releasing the Mizgalian language that Nathaniel had begun to recognize after spending weeks in their midst.

"Captain Black has ordered you to the rigging today."

Nathaniel felt like crying for joy. For one month now he had been ordered to clean the decks, prepare ammunition, wash the captain's clothes, and even cook the crew's meals. He had been assigned every task on board *except* manning the rigging. The dangerous place where every slave knew they could find a taste of freedom.

The overseer barked that Thumb, too, would be in the rigging, and the two slaves moved to where another guard would unlock their chains for the day. The Mizgalian soldier let the irons fall from their wrists with a wry grin.

"Be careful you don't slip and fall into the water," he moved on to the other slaves preparing to climb the ropes and continued with his threats, "the archers will not waste an opportunity to…catch you…should you fall."

He laughed and shoved Thumb out of his way. Nathaniel caught the older man and helped to steady him before they turned and lifted themselves from deck to sky.

Nathaniel climbed upward until he felt that he could reach out and touch the clouds. The cold wind tugged at his hair and clothes, sending exhilaration through to his fingertips. After a month of imprisonment, he felt that he had been set free for the day.

After the sinking of the *Seabird*, Nathaniel had been spotted by those on board the enemy vessel and hauled from the icy waters to live as a slave. Tossing with fever for three days, he had been brought back to health and befriended by the man called Thumb.

By the strength of God alone, this middle-aged man had remained strong throughout the long years of his servitude. It was true that after every three years on board, he was sent back to his home in Mizgalia for twelve months, but when this allotted time had passed, the cycle was begun again and he was returned to the ship.

The *Fate*.

The dark Mizgalian vessel lurked within Arcrean waters, attacking ships that strayed too far from shore. Once, Captain Black had even taken a Mizgalian vessel in order to restock his dwindling supplies below deck. The man had no principals. Rumor said that his real name was unknown to the public, and that everyone called him Black to describe the condition of his heart.

Thumb climbed to a perch beside Nathaniel and laughed into the wind. The young seaman had been amazed the first day he had seen Thumb scrambling through the rigging like a youth.

"God is good, Nathaniel!"

"He is indeed."

"Six more months of this misery and then I'll see my wife and daughter again."

Nathaniel shifted, "Ho, there, you've never spoken of them before. How old is your daughter?"

Thumb's jaw clenched in a brief showing of emotion, "Nearly seven. I've missed much of her life, being aboard the *Fate*."

"What is her name?"

"Caroline."

Nathaniel watched the deck below, waiting for a signal from the captain. He glanced at the man beside him. The years had washed Thumb's hair to a dull yellow that was beginning to gray. His creased face showed the effects of strenuous labor and hardship, but his eyes remained a clear blue that sparkled with fortitude and spoke of God's grace.

Thumb glanced over, "I have been blessed to know you, Nathaniel, though I wish it had been under better circumstances," his eyes shifted to study the tossing sea, "If I had raised a son, I would wish for him to be like you."

Nathaniel studied the man's distant expression. They had become close friends, and yet knew so little about each other. Friendships on board the *Fate* were based on the present—no one spoke of their past.

The captain gave his signal and the slaves set to work unfurling the sails. Thumb began to whistle a lively tune and Nathaniel suddenly jerked his head around to stare at him.

"Ho there, mate!"

"What is it?"

"That song…it's Arcrean."

A knowing twinkle appeared in Thumb's eye and he smiled, "So it is."

"Clouds o'er an Arcrean Sea."

Thumb nodded, "You know it?"

Nathaniel grinned, "It's my favorite, but…how do you know it? A Mizgalian?"

Thumb tied off a rope and answered without lifting his gaze, "Perhaps I'm not Mizgalian."

Nathaniel could only stare, "Are you Arcrean, mate?"

A slight nod.

"But why—"

"SAILS!" the overseer bellowed from below.

Nathaniel finished with the rope beneath him and moved on to the next. He wondered fleetingly if Thumb had been waiting for a day when they were both in the rigging to tell Nathaniel more about himself—away from the overseer, the guards, the Mizgalian crew, and those bloodthirsty slaves who looked for reasons to take offense with other men.

Nathaniel glanced to ensure a safe distance from the other rigging-slaves, "Why do you live in Mizgalia, Thumb?"

"I have no choice. Since the day I set foot on their shores, they will not let me return to my native land. They constantly watch my family. They force me to work, on land and sea, in exchange for my life."

"But why?"

Thumb paused long enough to give Nathaniel an intense stare, "That is best left untold."

They were silent for a time as they worked their way through another sail. Finally, Thumb broke the stillness.

"What about you, then? I've opened my mouth today and told you something about myself…"

"Ho, there! It was a month in coming, you'll recall," Nathaniel offered a grin.

"Better late than never, son. So spit it out!"

"What do you want to hear, mate?"

"Anything to divert an old man's thoughts from his own sad story. Have you a family of your own at home?"

"My parents and two sisters live by the sea in the region of Geoffrey. No doubt they'll hear that I'm dead. I also have many friends, the closest being Druet, Arcrea's first king."

"I've heard of him. They say he is a good man."

"He is that. A godly man."

"And you're a friend of his?"

"I joined his quest for the heart and came to see him as the brother I never had."

There was a short pause as Thumb focused on a relentless knot, "You've no wife and children, then?"

Nathaniel moved toward the final rope and grunted over the task of untying it, "No, Thumb, I'm not married. There is a young woman who was waiting for me in the Heartland, but she too will hear that I've died and may marry some—"

"The Heartland? You were to marry a native?"

Nathaniel shook his head and a thatch of sun-washed brown hair fell over his eye, "Not a native. She lives there now, but before joining Druet's quest a year ago she lived in the region of…"

"*All hands at the ready!*"

The slaves looked to see Captain Black studying the eastern horizon through a spyglass. Nathaniel craned his neck to peer in the same direction and then felt his heart sink at the sight of an Arcrean vessel. Thumb's next words voiced the same agony.

"After all my years of slavery, it still cuts me to the core when I'm forced to aid in the destruction of my native people."

"*Let go the main sail!*"

Nathaniel knew that the bellow had been directed at him, for he had yet to release the final rope. The other slaves were waiting on him to release the rigging together, allowing the sail to unfurl and drive the *Fate* east to battle. Every fiber of his being resisted the cord's release, but to disobey the captain's order meant certain and immediate death. Nathaniel turned to exchange glances with Thumb and in that moment both men were filled with the firm resolve that they would somehow escape the terrible *Fate*. The young seaman gave a single nod of commitment and then cringed as his fingers opened to release the sail.

Chapter 10
• Ambushed •

Trenton shot another glance over his shoulder and then finished scrawling a message across the piece of torn parchment. The Olden Weld meetinghouse remained empty as he folded the scrap to half-an-inch's width and then rolled it into a tight cylinder. Mentally, he reviewed the words he had written:

Seven lords at Balgo. Heavily guarded.
Lord Osgood crazy—swears I am "Eric."
Druet's weakness—wife, Aurenia. With child.

Trenton wasn't absolutely certain that the queen was Druet's weakness, but he could no longer afford to delay sending word. His father and King Cronin would be expecting some word from him. Trenton frowned over the entry about Osgood; he had included the bit as small talk to amuse Sir Kleyton, nevertheless the memory of that night in Balgo still sent chills up his spine.

Putting the writing materials away, he tucked the message into his belt and then slipped through the door and out onto the quiet village street. It was dusk and most of the natives were home for their evening meal.

As he walked, Trenton's mind reviewed the recent trip to Balgo. Falconer had refused to explain Osgood's strange behavior, and had remained silent all the way back to the Heartland. The informant had obtained a private meeting with King Druet and then disappeared. No one but the king knew where he had gone.

Veering off of the main road, Trenton walked to a broad meadow just south of the village; there he was hidden from the natives' sight by a border of trees that ran along a steep embankment behind the cottages. Darting to a mound of rocks in the center of the meadow, Trenton whistled three notes and then waited for Link.

The hawk appeared a moment later and circled Trenton's rock before floating to a perch in the trees at the meadow's edge. Trenton frowned. The bird wouldn't hide itself from sight unless…

"What you doin' out 'ere, Mizgal'yin?"

With a start, Trenton jumped and whirled away from the rock pile, simultaneously drawing his sword. He stared in disbelief. Old Marie's granddaughter, Leyla, had appeared from the far side of the rocks and now leaned against one side with a barely suppressed smile on her face.

"My, aren't we jumpy t'day?"

Trenton scowled and sheathed his sword with a quick snap, "Don't sneak up on me like that!"

Her green eyes flashed with shock and a ready temper, "Sneak up on *you*? I was the one sittin' over there, min'in my own business, when you came 'round an' started whistlin'," she crossed her arms and huffed an auburn curl from her eyes, "You sure are an odd one."

Trenton clamped his mouth shut. If the observation were his, he certainly wouldn't have dubbed *himself* as the odd one in this scenario. He studied the tree line and quickly spotted Link, waiting for a signal. Trenton stood for a moment in indecision; he had to convince Leyla to leave so that he might finally finish this transaction.

The girl hoisted herself to a niche in the rocks, clearly intending to remain where she was. Leaning her head back against a boulder, she closed her eyes, "This is my fav'rite place t' be," she opened one eye and frowned down at him, "'cept when hoity-toity Mizgal'yins intrude."

Trenton kept his back to her, "Shouldn't you be at home eating?"

"Shouldn' you?"

"I ate early."

"So did I," the tone of her voice told him that she was grinning.

Trenton ran his tongue along his front teeth and turned to face her, "Where are you from? Your accent is foreign to the Heartland."

She gave half a laugh, "Not as for'n as yours!"

Trenton shifted impatiently, "You already know where I come from."

Leyla sat up and balanced herself on the rock ledge, "I come from the region of Hugh. Orph'ned a year ago. Gran'mother 'eard 'bout my parents' death an' sent for me t' live with 'er."

"Her and Humphrey," Trenton muttered, allowing his gaze to casually drift toward the trees.

"You miss your 'ome in Mizgal'ya?"

"No," Trenton lied. Truth be told, he'd rather be in the familiar arena with two deadly catawylds than standing here with this Arcrean. Peering at her from the corner of his eye, Trenton resumed the conversation, "Do you? Miss your home in Hugh?"

Leyla stared at him for a moment, as if she could sense that his question was not sincere.

"I miss some of it. I miss the mount'ns. I don' miss the drag'ns, though, or the clan at Drag'n Coast—pillagin' knaves! It's rumored they detest King Dru't with a fierce passion, they do."

Trenton's interest was sparked by this report, "Why do they hate him?"

"'E rescued Queen Renny from 'em, 'e did. They were goin' t' sacrifice 'er."

They were silent for a moment as Leyla watched the last rays of sunlight fade to a dull purple. Trenton's mind eagerly grasped at the beginning threads of an idea.

"Well," Leyla suddenly jumped to the ground, "I best be goin' 'ome now."

She paused to retie the ribbon in her hair and then started off toward the border of trees that sheltered the village. When she had gone several paces she looked back over her shoulder and sent Trenton a mischievous grin before calling, "You can call your bird now."

Trenton failed to hide the look of shock that sprang to his face. Leyla's musical laugh drifted back across the meadow as she disappeared from sight.

Trenton shifted his gaze to Link and whistled for the bird to approach. Taking the message from his belt, he bent to find a piece of clay on the ground and quickly set about adding a final note to the scrap of parchment.

Link landed on the rocks and peered at Trenton with sharp eyes. Trenton held one leather-clad arm out and the hawk lifted slightly to reposition himself there. Trenton opened the small pouch that was held flush against Link's chest by a light strap that looped around the bird's neck and back. Slipping his message into the pouch, Trenton closed it back up and then gave the signal for Link to return home. Sending the bird into the air with a quick lift of his arm, Trenton watched until Link had disappeared from sight.

As he turned back toward Olden Weld, Trenton glanced ahead to the shadowy tree line and remembered Leyla's words about the Dragon Coast clan. He thought of her freckled nose lifting in clear disdain for the rebels of her native region and smiled in spite of himself. Her pluck did her credit. Trenton's smile suddenly disappeared when he thought how his mission for information would bring war to Arcrea and to the Heartland.

Trenton's steps brought him to the village's main road and he paused. If war came to the Heartland, old Marie and her spirited young granddaughter may die. Trenton shook his head fiercely and urged himself forward; this was exactly why his father had never allowed him to cultivate friendships! The fate of these people did not concern him. It was the victory of his homeland that mattered most.

Leyla was an Arcrean. He was a Mizgalian. They had been born enemies and would remain so. He had a mission to complete for his king, for his father, for his kingdom; and no green-eyed Arcrean lass with an ornery streak a mile wide was going to stop him.

ᘓᘐ

Several days later, Link drank from a cool stream in the Brikbone Mountains. Suddenly, the hawk tilted his head to one side in tense preparation and then lifted in startled flight when a rider appeared at the edge of the clearing.

Falconer watched as Trenton's hawk made a lazy circle over his head before shifting to sweep north. The informant's eyes lowered to gaze on the vista below and he was overwhelmed with the sense that he was now abandoning all measure of safety. Clucking to his horse, Falconer began the northern descent toward his dangerous destination.

Mockmor, Mizgalia.

Chapter 11
* In Search of Truth *

A loud pounding sounded on Osgood's door.

"Enter!"

The door opened and two soldiers stepped inside and to either side of the entryway, making way for the young woman behind them. Osgood failed to rise from his place at the table, but looked at her with wide eyes, "Alice?"

Alice froze on the threshold and stared at her uncle in shock. His once-gluttonous frame had shrunk to half its former size, and his strangely intense stare left her almost certain that the rumors of his insanity were true. His small cottage showed signs of his old desires for perfection—everything had a place and was where it should be—but the layer of grime and dirt that covered the room left his just-so-neatness lacking.

Tears sprang to Alice's eyes as her gaze took in the small loaf of rye bread and the even smaller portion of cheese on the table before Osgood. The platter was set directly in front of him and a bent mug was situated at the familiar angle from his food. She wanted to pity him, but knew that his love of wine had brought him to this level of poverty; any attempt at an honest day's work would place a fine meal on his table.

He motioned toward a crate in the corner, "Set yourself a seat," he glanced down and seemed to remember his manners, "Care for a bite?"

Alice bit her lip and shook her head; her curls quivered with the slight movement. One of the soldiers stepped forward and placed the crate by the table, taking a moment to dust the top off. Alice nodded her thanks and sat down across from Osgood.

A thick silence filled the room as the two stared at one another. Finally, Alice turned and asked the soldiers to wait outside, "I'll call you if I need you."

The two men bowed and stepped out into the fading sunlight, pulling the door closed behind them.

Alice swiveled back around to face her uncle. The left side of Osgood's face bulged with a slice of bread and cheese, and his eyes studied the table's surface as his jaw worked to chew the meager portion.

"Is it true that you sent a Mizgalian vessel called the *Fate* to attack my father and mother at sea?"

Osgood's jaw froze mid-chew and his eyes darted upward to meet hers.

"Did he tell you?"

Alice's brow furrowed. Was he speaking of Simon?

"Who, Uncle?"

"Did Eric tell you?"

"My father?" Alice was confused, "How could he tell me anything when I haven't seen him in nineteen years?"

Osgood's chair scraped the floor as he pushed it back and rose to his feet. Leaning over the table, he towered over his niece, "He didn't come to see you?"

Its true, Alice thought, *He's gone mad.*

"Uncle, please tell me—what was the cause of my parents' disappearance? I saw the tapestry…"

Alice rose from the crate and stared with uncertainty as her uncle moved to stand in the corner of the room. His eyes darted fearfully about and he rubbed his hands together in agitation.

"Uncle, what's wrong?"

"He'll come back for me!"

"Who?"

"Eric!"

Alice frowned, "Uncle, my father has not been seen for nineteen—almost twenty years! Everyone said…"

"I did see him!"

Alice's heart was beginning to beat a quick echo of her fear. Her eyes shifted to the door and she was about to call the soldiers, when Osgood spoke again in a hoarse whisper.

"I saw him! I know it was him—it was Eric! He spoke to me. I felt him! He was here…in Balgo!"

"When?" Alice couldn't believe she had just asked such a foolish question.

"Days ago! Weeks ago! I don't know. He came to haunt me!"

Alice peered into Osgood's frightened face, "What happened?"

"He appeared out of nowhere, in the middle of the night, and attacked me! Falconer took him away."

Alice felt herself lurch forward, "Falconer?"

Osgood suddenly sank to his knees and fell forward, collapsing into an unconscious heap.

"Uncle!"

Alice's cry brought the soldiers through the door. The young woman watched as from another world as they lifted Osgood to the bed and one felt his pulse. The soldier then looked to his comrade with a grave expression.

"Fetch a healer."

Chapter 12
Catastrophe at the Sailor's Tailor

While Osgood lay ill on his bed, and the *Fate* continued its work of destruction on the high seas, King Druet traveled with a contingent of soldiers to the city of Dormay in Geoffrey, where the Arcrean Navy was being formed and trained under the instruction and oversight of a certain Captain Hull. The short squatty captain sported a rather bulbous nose and thinning white hair that stood on end whenever he doffed his hat. His barrel-chested voice barked commands with a volume produced by many years of practice, but his eyes showed a delight in his work that made him agreeable.

Captain Hull greeted Druet and his entourage when they rode into Dormay one February afternoon. The king was led along the docks and through the shipyards, where a fleet of new ships was nearing completion, and Captain Hull explained in a voice scraped raw by sea-salt how Druet's orders were being followed to the slightest detail.

"I've divided the men up into prospective crews and set them to training under the watchful eyes of Arcrea's most trusted captains. I make rounds to each crew every other day to see how the process is coming along. The shipbuilders give me daily reports regarding the status of each vessel, and several have already been out on trial to taste the waves."

"Well done, Hull. You have exceeded my expectations. Thank you for your thoroughness," Druet's eyes swept over the fleet, "Did you see Peter the tailor about the navy's garb?"

"I did, Sire, and he was honored by the request. Subsequently, there were also a number of weavers hired to prepare the materials for the job."

Druet nodded, "I'd like to visit Peter today and pay my respects for Nathaniel…" Druet paused and clenched his jaw; though the seaman's death had occurred a month and a half ago, the pain of losing his closest friend still managed to pierce sharply every time he thought of it.

He turned and glanced at the two young men nearby, "I'll send the majority of my men to set up camp west of Dormay. Talon and Bracy will ride with me to Peter's, as well as a small company of guards," the young king cast a lopsided grin at the captain, "I'm still growing accustomed to the fact that I can't go anywhere without at least ten armed men to protect me. Don't you think ten is a little more than necessary?"

Unsure what his response should be, Captain Hull plucked his hat off in respect; tendrils of white hair stood out in all directions as he snapped a sharp salute, "God bless you, Sire, and grant you a long reign…ten men to watch your back or no!"

Some time later, Druet dismounted before the Sailor's Tailor. As friends of Nathaniel's, Talon and Bracy accompanied him inside while the other soldiers guarded the shop from outside. Nathaniel's father hastily cleared his worktable and pulled chairs up for the three visitors, while his younger daughter Brigit sat with a tunic held frozen in mid-stitch and stared at the sovereign guest in open-mouthed awe. Peter's wife, Martha, and older daughter, Anne, appeared in a doorway at the back of the room. They each dropped in a curtsy at Druet's polite greeting and then disappeared again when Peter suggested they prepare the evening meal for their guests.

Peter glanced toward the chair by the fire, "Brigit…Brigit! You can rest your eyes a while and see if your mother needs help."

Brigit's head gave a slight nod as she dropped the tunic into the basket by her chair. When she had passed into the kitchen through the opened doorway, Peter turned with a shake of his head to face Druet.

"You cannot know how honored I am to meet you, Sire. My son, Nathaniel—may he rest in peace—spoke very highly of you when he was with us last. He called you his brother and said that he would have considered your quest a success even had the heart remained hidden from knowledge. It was a blessing to our hearts to know that he had been blessed by your friendship."

Druet smiled, "We were the ones blessed by your son's friendship, Peter. Talon, Bracy, and I agree that our band would have fallen apart had it not been for Nathaniel's steady hand at keeping peace."

Druet glanced at his companions and found them peering through the kitchen door with looks of concern. In the next instant the small shop erupted in a state of pandemonium.

Anne's voice shrieked "Oh no, Brigit!" and the men cringed when a loud crash followed. They jumped to their feet and rushed through the kitchen door to see a black cauldron turned on its side with a pool of stew crawling out of it across the floor. One chair had caught fire, and Anne was turning in circles, trying to extinguish the hem of her dress. Brigit was screaming wrathfully at a flaming piece of…something, and trying to flick it into the hearth with an iron poker. Martha came running through the back door with a still-empty bucket in her hands.

Soldiers burst through the front door and looked around in confusion. Peter shouted for Martha to go for water and she quickly turned back outside and ran for the well on the nearby square. Talon darted across the kitchen and, grabbing Anne's arm, rushed her out the back door to douse the hem with snow. Bracy rushed to the flaming chair and lifted it by an untouched arm to follow Talon and Anne outside. Peter pulled Brigit away from the hearth just as she managed to trip herself, while Druet grabbed a knife off the table, speared the burning…something, and tossed it into the fire.

The sounds of Talon and Bracy extinguishing the chair floated in from outside and then everything fell silent. The boys and Anne reentered the smoke-fogged kitchen and everyone stood staring at one another in shock over the suddenness of all that had happened.

When Martha panted through the door with a full bucket of water, she glanced from one face to the other, "Is everyone alright?"

"No!" Brigit wailed, bringing a hand to her forehead, "Of all the frightfully exasperating experiences that I have endured during the brief duration of my young life this has been the worst!"

Bracy nearly laughed at her but swallowed the impulse when Talon punched him in the shoulder.

Peter looked from one daughter to the other and finally asked, "What happened? What started the fires?"

Anne bit her lower lip and glanced at Brigit, "Well…when Mother went for more water, I asked Bri…"

"She's innocent!" Brigit burst into tears and sank dramatically to her knees before her father, "It was me! It was all my own fault and Anne had nothing to do with it!"

Druet glanced at Peter and knew that the older man was accustomed to this sort of behavior in his daughter. The tailor rubbed a smile from his mouth and placed a hand on Brigit's shoulder.

"My dear child, I didn't say there would be a death penalty to the guilty party, I only want to know what caused the trouble."

From behind the curtain of dark curls that hid her face, Brigit's hand emerged and motioned toward the smoldering…something that Druet had tossed into the hearth, "I was browning the bread."

Chapter 13
* Discoveries *

The city of Mockmor emanated a sense of darkness that Falconer was unable to shake as he walked the crowded streets as just another citizen. Drifts of snow-turned-sludge lined the streets and hemmed in every building like a dirty frame. The royal palace rose from the city's center in a daunting show of power, the Mizgalian standard fluttering from every pinnacle and tower, daring all who passed by to still the authority that it represented.

All day the Arcrean informant searched for clues to the information he was after.

No one had heard of a slave called Trenton.

Not that Falconer believed the boy's story about running from a cruel master; he had simply decided to start with what he had been given.

Finally, toward evening, Falconer spoke—using his rusty knowledge of the Mizgalian language—with an old woman who had once served in the royal palace. She told him that the only Trenton she had ever known was the son of Sir Kleyton, King Cronin's close councilor and chief captain of the Mizgalian armies.

"He was a fair-haired boy, with the bluest eyes I ever saw in a lad," the woman selected a bunch of parsley from a roadside stand and shook her head over the memories, "He was always watched very closely, as I recall, and never had any friends. Sir Kleyton molded him into a hard warrior."

Falconer casually turned to gaze up at the formidable palace walls, "He lives at the palace still?"

"I wouldn't know," the old woman paid for her parsley and turned away, "Sir Kleyton still lives over the garrison barracks, far as I know, but I've heard naught of Trenton for several months now."

Falconer watched her hobble down the street. When a company of soldiers appeared, patrolling the city, he turned to walk in the opposite direction. Several blocks later, he suddenly altered his course and disappeared into an alley. Melting into the shadows, he headed swiftly for the castle that dominated the city's core.

ꕥ

Queen Aurenia stepped briskly along the main road through Olden Weld. Grikk followed several paces behind like an enormous shadow, listening to young Renny's low-spoken ramblings but refraining from any reply.

"There's something suspicious about this, Grikk. If Trenton were an honest man, he would have had no cause to vanish from the Heartland in the middle of the night. He could have mentioned his desire to leave instead of disappearing like a puff of smoke when no one was looking! And I think it highly suspect that my bow vanished when he did," she turned with a sudden thought, "Unless you took it to keep me from practicing in my condition…"

Grikk's face remained a picture in stone.

Renny pushed open the door of her cottage and paused at the sight of a young woman sitting in the front room, "Alice! I didn't expect you back so soon!"

Alice rose and helped Renny out of her cloak while Grikk shut the door and took up his usual position in a corner where he could see out the window to the street.

"Renny, I need to speak with Falconer, do you know where he is?"

"No," Renny turned to study her friend's face, "Falconer left on a mission some time ago and Druet is the only one who knows where he went. Druet left to check the progress of the Arcrean Navy in Dormay a week ago, or I would ask him how soon Falconer will be returning. Alice, is something wrong?"

Alice pressed a palm to her forehead and sat back down, hugging Renny's cloak, "My uncle is ill, and I think he has gone mad."

"Hmm. Why does that not surprise me?" Renny lowered herself to sit next to Alice and caught the other woman's look, "I'm sorry! Druet is always reminding me to think before I speak."

"It's alright," Alice shook her head, "I understood what you meant. Somehow I feel that my uncle's behavior shouldn't be a surprise to me, either," she paused and set Renny's cloak aside, smoothing the fabric with one hand, "He said that my father appeared to him in Balgo some time ago, and that Falconer took him away. But if Falconer isn't—"

"Falconer was in Balgo some weeks ago. When he came back, he met with Druet privately and then set out on a secret assignment. He seemed to be in a hurry."

Alice allowed these facts to register in her mind. She wasn't sure what to think.

Renny laid her head against the chair back and patted her rounded abdomen with a chuckle, "I feel huge."

Alice laughed and stood to retrieve a long object from the side table, "My dear queen, don't forget you have six more months of growing to do."

"Thank you, Alice."

Alice sat beside Renny again, holding a rolled canvas, "I brought this back from Brentwood to show you," she untied the strings and unrolled it in her lap, "It's an old painting of my fath—"

Renny suddenly gasped and sat forward, staring intently at the painting in Alice's hands, "Why, that's Trenton!"

Alice looked up in confusion, "Who is Trenton?"

Chapter 14
* Penetrating a Fortress *

Falconer silently scaled the outer walls of castle Mockmor with the practiced ease of a cat. Timing his arrival at the top to occur when the sentry had progressed to the other end of the walk, Falconer moved like a shadow over an embrasure and through the door of the corner tower.

Inside the rounded turret room, Falconer allowed a quick glance of surveillance through the window over the courtyard. He turned to check the progress of the sentry, now heading back towards the tower, while the picture he had glimpsed of the courtyard registered in his mind. A fire warmed a crowd of gossiping servants in the middle of the yard. The doors of the keep were closed to the night air and guarded by two heavily armed soldiers. The sentry on the southern walk was turned away from his position, looking down into the city; the guards to the north and east would not see his next move from their distant positions, as the sun had set and draped the informant's arrival in the cover of darkness.

Falconer hoisted himself to perch in the shallow windowsill. Tuning his ear to the approaching sentry's steps, he waited until the guard's next stride would bring him to the turret's door. In a flash, Falconer reached to grip the edge of the tower's roof and pulled himself up and out of sight, making his disappearance just when the stone doorframe would block the sentry's view of both inside and out.

Seeming to float effortlessly onto the roof, Falconer settled himself in his new vantage point and surveyed the castle. His dark eyes followed the outer wall to the south and quickly located a point where its central tower was connected to the keep by a guardhouse that ran between. Grunting his approval of the plans forming in his own mind, Falconer quickly glanced to check the positions of the sentries. Claiming a moment when both the western and southern sentries had their back to his tower, Falconer slipped over the roof's edge and dropped nimbly onto the southern walk. The Arcrean informant moved forward noiselessly, following behind the sentry, until the man reached the point where he would turn and retrace his steps along the wall.

Falconer was halfway to the central tower and connecting guardhouse.

As the sentry turned, Falconer leapt into an outer embrasure, using the flanking stone merlons to hide him from sight. Lowering himself on the outside of the wall, Falconer used the uneven face of the stones to grip his way to the next embrasure while the sentry passed by on the walk overhead. When the guard had passed his position, Falconer silently scrambled up over the next embrasure and raced along the remaining distance to the wall's center tower.

Once inside, Falconer took another surveillance glance at the courtyard and then paused to catch his breath. His fingers were numb and bleeding from the frigid temperatures and climbing over the rough stones. He carried leather gloves in the pouch at his waist, but wearing these would reduce his ability to maintain a firm grip, and increase the danger of slipping on the icy surfaces. He would wait to put them on.

The sound of footsteps ascending the tower stairs from the guardhouse below gave Falconer his cue to leave the turret. Perching once more in a shallow window, he waited for the sentry's stride to time his exit and then dropped lightly to the roof of the guardhouse inside the yard. Melting into the shadows where the roof met the tower wall, he listened as the sentry met the man coming up the stairs.

"Any trouble in the south, Brone?"

"None, sir," Brone spoke with a clipped tone of respect.

"Sir Kleyton has ordered three additional men to each sentry-walk…"

Even as the officer spoke the words, Falconer could hear footfalls echoing in the tower stairwell. A company of soldiers emerged from the guardhouse below him and started across the courtyard towards the north and west towers. Another group crossed the garrison yard behind the guardhouse and headed for the eastern wall.

Falconer ran his tongue over his front teeth. Getting out of Mockmor would prove a greater challenge than getting in.

The officer stood in the tower window above the spy and continued, "Old Candice—you know, she once served in the castle kitchens—reported to our patrol that she was approached in the streets by an Arcrean seeking information about Sir Kleyton's son."

"An Arcrean?" Brone sounded doubtful, "Was she certain?"

"Fairly. She claims his accent left her without doubt."

The muscles in Falconer's jaw clenched tightly. He had known speaking in the streets would alert those around him to an Arcrean in their midst, but he hadn't thought the old woman would report him to the castle guard.

The officer sent the three additional sentries from the tower and took his leave from Brone, who waited until his superior had left to bark his own orders at his new companions.

Falconer shifted his focus to the building at the other end of the roof. The lower portion of the keep rose into a sentry-walk just above the roof of the guardhouse. The walk was several paces in width and created a border around the base of the keep's upper stories. A door into the keep was situated directly across the point where he would climb. Two guards were usually sufficient to keep watch from this post. Thanks to Candice, tonight there were five.

Falconer watched their pacing for fifteen minutes, memorizing the pattern they made along the balcony. Simultaneously, he listened to the slow steps of the sentries on the outer wall above him. At last he calculated the coming moment, the brief lapsing of seconds when all nine of the sentries—on balcony and south wall—would either be out of sight or walking with their back to him. Falconer's heart pounded with the thrill of adrenaline as his arms and legs tensed in preparation for the next instant.

Finally, with an instinctive shove, the Arcrean informant suddenly lifted from the shadows and darted the length of the guardhouse roof. Dropping into the shadows there, he took several deep breaths as he watched the south-wall sentries and counted out the pattern of the balcony guards, who were now outside his range of vision.

Praying that the sentries would remain blind to him, Falconer jumped up a second time and expertly scaled the keep wall in seconds. According to his calculations, the two sentries closest to his position would have their backs to him in three…two…one… Falconer lifted himself onto the ledge of an embrasure and slipped between the flanking decorative merlons. His calculations proved correct. Soundlessly, he slipped across the walk and ducked through the door just as the two sentries turned back around.

Falconer glanced right and left and then started down the long corridor, lined on one side with candlelit alcoves that gave off an eerie glow. Falconer thought back to his private audience with King Druet. The informant had revealed his suspicions regarding Trenton to the young king and asked to be allowed to travel to Mizgalia in order to ascertain the truth one way or another.

Druet had given permission, but only after Falconer had sworn to hold to a code of peace. As long as he was the foreigner, trespassing in Mockmor to gain information, he was to refrain from combat if at all possible. Entering a struggle should only be resorted to if he was the one under attack. There was no reason to start a war and bring the enemy spilling over the Brikbones. The border wars, mostly contained within the southern slopes of the mountains, provided more than enough opposition for Arcrea to be handling just now.

Falconer grinned. Druet was not after a fight, only truth; he was so unlike the other men whom the spy had formerly served.

Falconer mentally reviewed the castle floor plans he had discovered years ago and made his way upstairs. Another alcove-lit corridor stretched before him.

Halfway down the hall was King Cronin's study.

Hearing voices approaching from another sector of the keep, Falconer moved from the stairway and entered the study, closing the oak door behind him. A fire had been lit on the hearth. The king was expected.

The voices were coming closer.

Quickly, Falconer crossed to the massive fireplace and felt along the pillar-like trimming, searching for a lever, a knob, a knothole…anything! Finally, his finger caught a lip in the wooden frame. Falconer pulled this and the wide piece of trimming swung out like a door, revealing a narrow recess hollowed out of the stones behind it. Slipping inside, Falconer stood encircled by stones that radiated heat from the fire on the other side.

He pulled the trim door shut and listened. Several quick heartbeats later, the study door opened and Falconer distinguished the voices of three men. King Cronin, Sir Kleyton, and a man they called Thomas.

ꕤ

King Cronin waited only until the study door had been closed. He turned to face Kleyton and Thomas with an impatient lifting of his brows.

"What news? Trenton's bird has returned, yes? Does he send word of his whereabouts?"

"Yes, Sire," Kleyton held out a scrap of weathered parchment, and Cronin took the piece to read the contents by the light of the fire.

" 'Seven lords at Balgo. Heavily guarded. Lord Osgood crazy—swears I am "Eric." Druet's weakness—wife, Aurenia. With child. Going to Dragon Coast.' "

The king's gaze snapped back to Kleyton, "Who is going to Dragon Coast? The queen or Trenton?"

"Sire, I highly doubt that Druet would send his queen to a vicious dragon-infested coast, known for its inhabiting clan of ritualistic savages."

Cronin grunted, "The boy needs to learn how to categorize his information properly," he gave a sickening smile, "but then, he won't be in need of the knowledge for much longer, will he Thomas?"

The soldier's head shook readily, "No, Sire."

King Cronin set the parchment on his table, "Take one other soldier with you and leave for Dragon Coast immediately."

Thomas made a nervous bow and started for the door.

"And Thomas…"

"Yes, Sire?"

"Should I need to send you further word, my men will know how to find you," the king's lips spread into a thin smile when Thomas' pale face showed he understood Cronin's meaning, "And if you should fail a second time, they will find you then, too. You cannot hide from me, Thomas. I suggest you use this opportunity to your advantage."

Thomas swallowed and bowed and then quickly left the room.

Kleyton ensured that the door had shut, and then, turning to face his sovereign, he spoke the words that neither wanted to consider, "He has seen Osgood."

"And Osgood has seen him!" Cronin grabbed Trenton's message and threw it forcefully at the knight, "If that boy learns of his true identity before Thomas reaches him, then all of our plans—the eighteen years spent in molding his mind as a Mizgalian—will prove to be a waste!"

"Thomas will succeed, Sire. I have assigned Delaney to accompany him into Arcrea, and I have no doubts regarding their capabilities as a team."

King Cronin leaned heavily against his table. Slowly, a deep laugh built within his chest, just managing to surface, "I cannot imagine a more pleasant way to create war in Arcrea," he pushed away from the table and placed one hand against the mantel, staring into the flames, "Blaming them for the death of a Mizgalian nobleman who is, in truth, an *Arcrean* nobleman."

Cronin turned with an evil grin as Kleyton approached with the scrap of parchment and tossed it into the flames. The knight watched the message curl into itself and finally disintegrate, and then he looked to the king with a slight nod,

"And neither the Arcreans nor Trenton will ever know the difference."

Some time later, when Kleyton had left the room, Cronin summoned one of the soldiers posted outside the study door, "Bring my private courier with all haste."

The soldier bowed and several minutes passed before a knock was heard.

"Enter."

The door opened and the courier bowed before Cronin. The king signed his name at the bottom of a document and pressed his seal into a fresh puddle of wax. He held the document out to the courier.

"Sir Kleyton has great confidence in the two men he has sent to find Trenton. I do not. Take these orders and alert the trader that I am in need of his assistance with several matters. Tell him that Trenton's fate must be sealed. Do you understand?"

"Yes, my king."

"Good. Go now, and tell no one of these orders."

Chapter 15
• A Concealed Fate •

Still absorbing the information he had overheard in Cronin's study several hours before, Falconer opened the window of Kleyton's private quarters from the outside and slipped cautiously into the room. As planned, Falconer found himself in Sir Kleyton's study. Pale moonlight spilled inside, illuminating the interior. A small table, piled with historical records and accounts of ancient battles, stood in the center of the room. A locked chest, trimmed with gold and studded with silver, stood by the right-hand wall. Through a door to the left came the rhythmic sound of Sir Kleyton's breathing.

Falconer moved to crouch before the chest and ran his index finger over the keyhole in the lock. Silently, he rose and crossed into the knight's sleeping quarters. A smaller chest on the bedside table caught Falconer's eye as the probable hiding place for Kleyton's ring of keys. A closer look confirmed his suspicion that it too was locked; the single key dangled from a thin chain around the sleeping knight's neck.

Falconer stood for a moment by the bed and rested his chin on one fist. He glanced back at the larger chest in the adjoining room.

In a few swift strides the informant crossed back into the study and softly closed the door behind him. He pulled the chest away from the wall, sparing a single glance for the mouse that scampered out of his way. Two hinges at the back of the chest rotated on iron pins. Falconer drew his dagger and wedged the blade behind the head of one pin. Using the blade as a lever, he slowly worked the pin out of the hinge, grimacing when the iron gave with a shudder. Falconer set the pin aside and shifted to remove the second; when this was done, he stepped to the door and peered into the bedchamber.

Kleyton was still asleep.

Falconer pulled on his leather gloves, crouched behind the chest, and lifted the lid at the back, where the two hinges now separated freely without the pins to hold them in place. Inside, parchments and scrolls were stacked neatly and in order of documentation. Falconer grinned at the precision and thought how his mother would have shed tears of joy had his own belongings been kept this tidy. With one hand propping the lid open, the gloved fingers on his other hand crawled through the records until he found the year he was looking for.

Eighteen years back.

Falconer caught sight of a stack of parchments wrapped in a leather cover and bound with twine. Drawing the stack out, he gently closed the lid of the chest and pulled the twine loose from the parchments. Pulling back the front piece of leather, he glanced over the document at the top of the stack and grinned.

Just what he'd been looking for.

I, Cronin, king of Mizgalia and the known world (Falconer exhaled half a laugh)*, do exercise my great power this day in approving Sir Kleyton of Mockmor to be granted full right and parentage of one, Trenton of Brentwood, formerly of Arcrean descent and of the household of one, Eric of Brentwood. Trenton is hereby declared reserved for future service, to be rendered on behalf of his king and kingdom, Mizgalia. Death to the adversary!*

The page was sealed in blood-red wax.

Falconer carefully folded the document and slipped it into his pouch. His jaw remained clenched as he leafed through the other parchments. The neatly written script on one bore record to Osgood's tale of a Mizgalian vessel—one, the *Fate*—hired to attack Lord Osgood's elder brother, Eric, on the high seas. Another document tracked Trenton's progress in the Mockmor garrison and arena. Falconer scanned the page, impressed, and shook his head; the boy had been raised as a faultless Mizgalian to die a pathetic Arcrean.

A map near the bottom of the stack caught Falconer's eye and he quickly realized that it pinpointed the location of Eric and Adelaide's imprisonment. His studied gaze took in every detail of the grid while his mind raced to plan his next move.

Did he have enough time to rescue the long-lost nobleman before Thomas reached Trenton at Dragon

Coast? Regardless of his confused methods as a Mizgalian, Trenton still deserved his help as an Arcrean. Then also, King Druet would need to be warned about Cronin's plans for war.

The sudden screech of a hawk out in the royal mews pulled Falconer's gaze to the window. A thought struck him and he quickly began to replace the twine around the parchments.

He needed to find Trenton's bird.

ꟾ

The screech of a hawk pulled Sir Kleyton from the depths of sleep. The knight opened his eyes and glanced toward the window with a yawn.

He sat up.

The door between his bedchamber and study had been open when he retired for the evening.

Now it was closed.

Pulling back the bedcovers, Kleyton swung his feet to the floor. A faint sound, as of metal clicking and sliding against metal, came from the next room. Kleyton reached for his sword belt. Clutching the sheath in his left hand, he gripped the sword's pommel with his right and moved silently to the study door.

Taking a deep breath to calm his pounding heart, Kleyton shoved the door open with his shoulder, drew his sword with a fierce cry…and froze. His eyes darted across the dark study, searching for the intruder. He quickly strode to open the window and frowned when shafts of pale moonlight illuminated the quiet room.

If someone had indeed been in his study only moments before, then they had completely vanished in seconds.

Chapter 16
* An Untested Arena *

The stench of death permeated his surroundings and clung to his clothes. Trenton's gloved hand kept a firm grip on the pommel of his sword as his horse inched forward through the forested mountains of western Hugh. His blue eyes maintained a constant vigil for danger. Gradually, the sound of waves crashing against the cliffs alerted him to his proximity to the coast. The sheer walls of rock rose nine hundred feet or more above the tossing sea, housing hundreds of dragons in caves and crevices that could not be reached and conquered from land. As he sat and studied the surrounding trees, Trenton's ears detected the distant shrieking of one of these legendary monsters.

Trenton dismounted in a fairly cleared area and studied his map. He was several miles south of the Dragon Coast clan's encampment. If everything went according to plan, he would be ready to move in that direction within a week's time.

Trenton tied his horse in the shelter of a rock outcropping. He set up camp and hunted for fresh meat; the bow that he had stolen from Queen Aurenia downed him a young deer. He skinned the animal and set the pelt aside for later use, then selected a portion of meat for his evening meal. The rest he wrapped within the folds of a stolen cloak and buried at the base of a tree.

When he had eaten, Trenton cut slits in the deer's hide and looped a length of rope through them. After hanging the hide from a tree, he stepped back to survey his work. In the gathering shadows it looked alive—a living deer standing at the edge of his clearing. Trenton chuckled to himself as he finished his preparations and then wrapped in his own cloak to claim a few hours' sleep.

The rush of wings woke Trenton some time later. It was dark. The cook fire had died to only a few stubborn embers, which was just what he wanted—fire would have kept the dragons away.

Pillars of pale moonlight cast a soft light over the clearing. The rush came again, like the sound of a strong wind, and Trenton lifted his eyes to see the silhouette of a dragon floating by on leathery wings. When it disappeared over the trees, Trenton tossed his cloak aside and moved to stand behind the cover of a tree, where he could watch the clearing from the shadows. With sword drawn, the young Mizgalian waited in tense silence.

Finally, the dragon reappeared and floated momentarily above the clearing. Then, in a flash, it dropped to the earth and stood peering at the hanging deer hide. Trenton's heart thumped in his chest. Though it looked to be a fairly small dragon, the monstrous beast still stood nine feet tall without including the length of its tail.

Trenton remained motionless as he waited for the dragon to step closer to the deer. It inched forward. Trenton's grip tightened around the pommel of his sword. The dragon took another step and was no more than two feet from setting off Trenton's trap. Suddenly, the dragon's nostrils flared with the recognition of another scent and the beast whirled to its right, toward Trenton's hiding place. Just then a slight breeze played with the deerskin, causing it to sway back and forth in lifelike motion, and the dragon turned back to the hide with a fierce hiss.

In another instant the trap was set off.

A taut branch whipped back and tightened a rope around the beast's left foreleg, and at the same time, Trenton darted from his cover to advance from the right. The dragon shrieked at the rope and reared back to sever the tight cord, but Trenton's sword fell to its target before it had the chance. The dragon's right wing was severed before Trenton's blade. The dragon stretched its neck to the sky with an angry bellow as Trenton prepared to circle around to its left.

The beast turned to glare at Trenton and a puff of white powder blew from its nostrils to coat the ground at his feet. The animal lunged for its human prey and Trenton tripped in his attempt to jump clear of the open jaws. The dragon lowered its head and twisted its neck to come at Trenton from behind, but the young man rolled beneath the monster's belly and then jumped up to strike his second target. The left wing was severed from the torso and the dragon roared as it backed away to nurse its wounds.

Trenton quickly circled to the spot where he had

buried the wrapped venison. To the cadence of the wingless dragon's fierce breathing, he attacked the mound of freshly thrown dirt and brought out a hunk of meat. Across the clearing, the animal lifted on its hind legs and then dropped again on all fours with a bellow directed at Trenton. Trenton stood with the meat in his hand and kicked the dirt back over the rest while keeping a wary eye on his catch.

Gradually, the dragon became silent as it watched Trenton slowly approach with the meat in his left hand. Its black eyes glared at its human captor with glittering bitterness, and once again a white powder blew from its nostrils with a snort. The rope around its foreleg kept it from coming any closer, but it kept its neck arched back over its body, ready to strike. Suddenly, as if to prove its own capabilities, the dragon lurched to its left and snatched the deer hide in its jaws. With a few jerks of its head, the dragon pulverized the hide and then dropped it to hang in a pitiful state from the ropes.

Trenton reached the cook fire and carefully set about bringing it back to life. When the embers began to catch and a small flame appeared he stood to watch the dragon. The beast snorted like a frightened horse and backed as far away from the fire as the rope would allow. Lifting its head toward the sky it willed its body to lift in flight, only to remember with a fresh complaint of pain that it no longer had wings. Tilting its head to stare at Trenton from an angle, it hissed a threat and then crouched in defeat at the clearing's edge.

Trenton released a breath he hadn't realized he was holding. Taking one step closer, he tossed the hunk of meat to land close to the dragon's head, and then set about the task of removing the creature's severed wings from the clearing.

Over the next few hours, Trenton used the influence of venison to creep ever closer to his catch. On one venture he tied a thick length of rope around the trunk of a nearby tree; another time he managed to lasso the rope's other end around the dragon's neck.

The next morning, while the dragon slept curled in a ball to keep out the sunlight, Trenton fashioned a strong cord into a muzzle that would permit the beast to open its mouth just wide enough to eat. After several attempts, Trenton finally managed to hold the dragon's neck down long enough to slip the muzzle over its jaws. Trenton then stepped back and observed the animal with his arms crossed and a triumphant grin in place on his face.

"You look like a long-necked lizard without your wings."

Trenton brought a large portion of meat and held it out on a flat palm; the dragon watched the familiar routine warily and finally reached to pluck the coveted venison from its captor. Trenton smiled at the progress he was making and bent to look the beast in the eye.

"You're making things a lot easier than I'd expected. I'm nearly ready to head north to the clan's encampment," he backed up a step when the dragon huffed its annoyance at Trenton's nearness, "and you're going to buy my passage inside."

That evening, Trenton made his way to where the forest abruptly ended and the mountainside dropped away in a cliff wall to the sea. The sun was just setting in a brilliant show of orange and pink. As

Trenton watched, the miles of cliffs to the north and south became alive with dragons ready to begin their nightly hunts of death. He smiled when he thought that tonight there would be one less dragon in the air. An eagle floated on the breeze overhead and Trenton thought of Link; by now the hawk would have reached Mockmor with Trenton's message and his father would be aware of his location.

Trenton backed into the trees as the first dragon dropped from a cave in the cliff's face and swept low over the waves before starting a leathery-winged climb for the Hugh countryside. Trenton turned and started back toward the clearing. He would send another message to Mockmor. He would tell his father about his victory over the dragon, and then maybe, just maybe, he would earn King Cronin's approval.

Chapter 17
* Of Faith & Shepherds *

Druet smiled his approval as he studied Arcrea's newly fashioned royal insignia. The small silver plate was set with a simple cross of beaten gold, and a sparkling ruby was nestled in place where the cross's lines intersected.

Bracy peered over the young king's shoulder, "That's a fancy bit of work."

Druet glanced at his friend and then laced a thin chain through a hole in the top of the plate, "I had this one made as a necklace for Renny. A larger copy will be set in the royal armor, and the pattern will be embroidered in the garb of each man and woman on the royal staff."

Bracy darted an uncomfortable glance between necklace and king, "Does that include me?"

Druet grinned, "Of course it does, Bracy. Why?"

Bracy looked away, but not before Druet caught his look of disapproval, "It's a cross."

"It is the symbol of—"

"Your faith…I know! But it's not my faith. I shouldn't have to wear that!"

Druet studied the plate in his hand, "The ruby represents the people—Arcrea's heart—set in the midst of the cross to show that we are knit together as a kingdom only by the grace of God, extended to us by Christ's work on the cross," slipping the necklace into a leather pouch for safekeeping, Druet turned to face the other man with a serious expression, "Yes—it is my faith, Bracy, and no—it is not yours…yet," Bracy threw him a dark look, "But the fact that you have rejected Jesus Christ is no one's fault but your own. If you can not wear this symbol as a sign of your own faith, then wear it as a reminder of the source of your king's strength, and the strength behind the uniting of this kingdom."

They were silent for several minutes as they left the silversmith's shop and started down the street, preceded and followed by Druet's royal guard of ten men.

Finally, Druet broke the silence, "I will not force you to wear it. I would not wish you to turn further from the gospel over such an issue."

Bracy directed his gaze to the sea, "I'll wear it," he murmured, "for your sake."

Druet saw the need for a change of topic, "Where did you say Talon is?"

Bracy smirked, "He went to run errands for Nathaniel's father."

"Ah," Druet studied the crowds along both sides of the street as he walked, "Peter is grateful for the daily help. Ever since Nathaniel's death his work has seemed a burden to perform; now he has accepted the responsibility of clothing the entire Arcrean Navy, and he no longer has time to complete the manual household chores that his wife and daughters are unable to do."

"Especially Brigit," Bracy shook his head, "I wouldn't trust her to sweep the floor."

Druet laughed, "My Renny would love her. If my work here is delayed much longer, I plan to send for Grikk and Alice to bring the queen to Dormay," Druet glanced at Bracy as a sudden thought struck him, "Why is it that Talon is always the one to help at the tailor's? Just last week you were complaining to me that you have nothing to do here."

Bracy grunted, "Talon wants to go and so I let him," he glanced in Druet's direction and then rolled his eyes, "He's become rather fond of Anne."

Druet's steps faltered for a moment and he stared at Bracy, "Talon?"

Bracy nodded and a slight smile of humor pulled at his lips, "Besides, he likes to talk about Jesus as much as you do, and I'd rather not subject myself to an afternoon of sermons while I'm trying to chop wood."

Druet started forward again as a laugh boiled up from his chest, "Bracy, why do I have the feeling that it's only a matter of time before you realize that while you've thought you were running away from God, you were actually running *to* Him…and that He's been holding your hand and leading you the whole way there?"

ꕥ

There were two soldiers guarding the cottage where Eric and Adelaide had been held hostage for nineteen years. Falconer sat on a thick limb with his back to the tree's trunk. Though the winter winds had stripped the branches of their leaves, the afternoon shadows still hid him from the guards' view. Falconer shifted to study the horizon to the southwest and mentally calculated how far Thomas and Delaney would have traveled by now on their trek to Dragon Coast and Trenton's assassination. He turned his gaze back to Eric's cottage—first things first.

The stone cottage was a simple affair with a thatched roof, hardly large enough to house a family of mice let alone a grown man and his wife. It was situated in the foothills west of Mockmor, at the head of an unassuming little village inhabited mainly by shepherds. The fact that there were only two guards to watch the cottage indicated that nineteen years had eased any fears that the Mizgalians may have had over an Arcrean rescue. It also suggested that Eric had not worried them with an attempted escape.

As the afternoon began to wane, Falconer relinquished his perch in the tree and backtracked over the hill and to the base of the village. His horse, along with two others, had been tied north of the cottage, on the opposite side of the hill.

He entered the village and began in broken Mizgalian to inquire after a place to stay, making sure to emphasis the words with a thick Arcrean accent. He noted with pleasure that the shepherds eyed him warily and exchanged knowing glances when they thought he was turned away.

One of the cottages had an upper loft room that the owner said he'd be pleased to let for a price. Falconer paid the man for a night's lodging and climbed the ladder to his room. He shut the trapdoor firmly and immediately crossed to the back corner of the cottage. Below him he could hear the hum of suspicious conversation. Reaching up to the low ceiling, Falconer quickly pulled away the layers of thatch until he had cleared away a space large enough to crawl through. Gripping the outer edges of the cottage walls, the informant found footholds in the stones and silently climbed up and out through the opening he had made in the roof.

By now the sun had set and the village was cast in shadows of a deep purple hue. Perched on the corner of the cottage, Falconer watched as several men left by the front door and headed up the path to the prison-cottage and the two soldiers. He grinned to himself and quickly worked his way to the ground, and then, keeping behind the row of cottages, he too started toward the head of the village.

Like a silent shadow, Falconer moved up the hillside until he reached the corner of the last cottage. From there he watched as the shepherds spoke to the two guards in low tones and pointed back towards the place where they had left an Arcrean in the loft. The two soldiers peered down the darkened path and Falconer prayed that they would both leave their quiet post to investigate. A moment later, the guards glanced back at Eric's cottage and then one nodded to the other. Falconer breathed a prayer of thanks when they both set off with the shepherds.

The Arcrean spy immediately left his place at the corner of the wall and crossed to Eric's cottage as the group of Mizgalians moved in the opposite direction. Standing in the shadows that shrouded the threshold Falconer watched as farther down the path the shepherds ducked inside their destination. Behind them, the two soldiers paused to glance back at their post, failing to see the man who watched them from the prison's doorway, and then followed the shepherds inside.

Falconer turned and, drawing his dagger, used the hilt to deliver a solid blow to the lock that kept a bar in place over the door. The lock fell away with a clatter and Falconer sheathed his dagger with one hand while shoving the bar up and away with the other. In another instant, Falconer pushed the door open and stepped into the cottage's only room. His sharp eyes scanned the room in a single sweep and he paused in a moment of uncertainty at what he saw.

Or rather, what he *didn't* see.

A woman who Falconer guessed to be Adelaide sat in a chair by the hearth, staring at the intruder with wide eyes. Sitting in her lap was a young girl, about seven years of age, who so looked to be a miniature version of Alice that Falconer knew she must be another daughter.

A shout from the cottage down the path told Falconer that the soldiers had found his loft room empty. Moving further inside, he pulled Adelaide from her chair and spoke in the Arcrean tongue.

"You must come with me," he glanced at the child and continued in a hurried tone, "If you would keep your life, then you must remain silent and do as I say."

Falconer gripped the startled woman's arm and herded her and the child out of the cottage. His steps led them over the hill to the waiting horses even as his mind scrambled to explain what his glance of the cottage had just revealed.

Eric was not there.

Chapter 18
* A Thumb's Tale *

Nathaniel woke with a start and jerked back when his chains resisted the forward motion that his body had impulsively made. Once again, his dreams had been filled with the terrified screams of Arcreans under attack by his own hands. Always, the rope slipped through his fingers and swung like a whip to crack the side of an innocent vessel carrying Druet, Renny, Alice, and his other friends from back home. Then, as the *Fate* sailed closer for another blow, Nathaniel would see his father, mother, Anne, and Brigit, chained helplessly to the deck of the suffering ship.

"You see them in your dreams, don't you?" Thumb's voice came from close to his right ear. Nathaniel shifted as far as the chains would let him and stared into the darkness that shrouded the older man as Thumb spoke again, "Your family…attacked by the *Fate*?"

Nathaniel nodded, "Every night."

Thumb nodded and leaned back against the bowed wall of the hold, "It was the same for me…only I had reason to dream it, for it really happened."

Nathaniel continued to stare at Thumb in silence.

Thumb turned with an intense look directed at the younger seaman, "I want to tell you my story, because I know that you will do what you can to help my family if I fail to make it off the *Fate*."

"Ho there, mate, you'll make it," Nathaniel's whisper was fierce and he glanced to see that none of the other slaves were awake, "We will escape the *Fate* at the first opportunity we find—when we're closer to land."

Thumb nodded, "All the same—" he froze when a nearby body rolled over with a groan; when it was silent once more he continued, "I was to become lord of a southern Arcrean region, but my brother coveted the title and arranged to have my vessel attacked by Captain Black. My wife was aboard with me, and I…" Thumb broke off and waited as a tear escaped his eye, "We were taken to Mizgalia. We hoped to be returned for ransom…" he cleared his throat, "A year later when they came for me—my first voyage aboard the *Fate* as a slave—they also took my infant son. I never heard what they did to him. My wife was devastated—left alone in a strange land, everything familiar ripped from her grasp—but by God's grace she remained strong."

Nathaniel's jaw had dropped in shock long before this point in Thumb's narrative. The younger man tried to employ his voice as the other man continued.

"I had a daughter in Arcrea—"

"Ho, there! Alice?"

"Yes, Alice. I thank God she was not with us when we were attacked, but I regret that I never heard of her—" Thumb turned with sudden realization to stare at Nathaniel through the shadows, "You know of my daughter?"

"Lady Alice of Brentwood?"

"The same!"

Nathaniel couldn't believe what he was hearing, "Ho, there, you're…mate, you're the brother? Osgood's brother—the one who disappeared at sea nineteen years ago?"

Thumb could just make out the shock on his friend's face. He leaned closer to remind them both to keep their voices down, "My given name is Eric and yes, Osgood is my younger brother. Do you know the story?"

"I heard of it when I was a child, mate. People believed that Osgood was behind your disappearance, but no proof could be found and so Osgood reigned as lord until Druet claimed the throne several months ago. The seven former lords now live in a village of Ranulf, closely guarded by Druet's soldiers."

"But what of Alice? You have heard of her, yes?"

In the dark hold Eric couldn't see Nathaniel's face flush, "I have. She lived with Osgood in Quale for a time and then returned to Brentwood. She was always afraid of the sea, but overcame her fears last year when she joined Druet's band in search of the heart. Osgood had sent for her arrest when she gave us shelter."

"That fiend brother of mine!" Eric muttered, "You knew Alice as a friend, then? Oh, I have longed for this moment! What is she like now?"

Nathaniel nodded and cleared his throat, "Ho, there… She's very lovely, very kind…gentle. Lives now as the queen's companion…in the Heartland."

Eric heard the message implied by Nathaniel's slow speech and it was his turn to be shocked. Suddenly, a chuckle shook his frame and he pulled at the chains on his wrist to rest a hand on the younger man's shoulder.

"Your particular friend? My Alice is the woman waiting for you in the Heartland?"

Nathaniel gave another nod, "I hope."

Eric's low chuckle continued to rumble in his chest and Nathaniel joined the mirth with a smile of his own.

"Praise the Lord," Eric murmured, "I knew from the first time I set eyes on you there was something special about you, son," he leaned his head back and stared up into the empty darkness, "Ah, this has been a night for surprises."

A moment of silence passed as each man became lost in his own thoughts.

"Well, Nathaniel…we'd best get rested if we're to escape the *Fate*, fetch my wife and younger daughter, and then make it to the Heartland for your wedding!"

"That hasn't been settled for certain, Thumb."

The older man turned his head and studied Nathaniel's shadowy frame with a discerning expression, "Oh…I think it has."

Chapter 19
• Access to a Clan •

Several days passed and Trenton had finally taught the wingless dragon to ignore the fresh meat presented in the form of his horse. He removed the rope around the dragon's foreleg, allowing it a bit more roaming space on the length at its neck.

Every day the muzzled dragon curled into a tight ball to block out the sun and to sleep. At night it paced in circles around the tree and watched as other dragons flew overhead in search of food. At first, Trenton wondered why it did not cry out at these times or shriek for the other dragons' help, but he soon came to believe that the wingless creature was looking out for its own safety; if the other dragons knew of a disabled beast, even one of their own, then it was sure to be their next prey.

One week after the dragon's capture, Trenton broke camp in the late afternoon and prepared to move out. When his horse was ready, he tossed the dragon a portion of meat and then mounted. Urging his horse toward the tree where the dragon's leash was tied, Trenton used his dagger to sever the cord and quickly tied it to his saddle.

"Eat up, Wings," he looked down on the scaly captive, "I want to reach the clan's encampment before dark."

The dragon spared him a glance and snorted. Trenton took note that, once again, the action produced a fine white powder that coated the ground at its feet. Some of the particles were caught by the chilling breeze and tossed against the trunk of a tree.

Finally, Trenton convinced Wings to follow him from the clearing at a slow pace. Twice, the dragon planted its feet beside the horse and rose to its full height to tower over Trenton. With the muzzle still in place and Trenton's hand ready at his sword, it could do nothing but shriek in the boy's face. When this happened, Trenton barely managed to keep his horse from shying away as he cringed at the smell of rotting meat that had been blown up his nose.

"Ugh," he sputtered and glared up at the dragon, "This had better be worth it."

When Wings had been calmed and they were once again heading north, Trenton pushed his thoughts ahead to the encampment. Rumors swirled like a thick fog around the happenings at Dragon Coast. The clan was said to plunder the farmlands and cities as far away as eastern Hugh, and the story of Queen Aurenia's near sacrifice at their hands was known throughout the entire kingdom. Myths regarding the clan's rituals and beliefs were as plenteous as catawylds in the Mizgalian forests. Apart from Druet's experience, accounts of an outsider's escape from their midst were unheard of.

Which was why Trenton needed Wings to gain him an audience with the clan's chief.

If these wild Arcreans were as superstitious as everyone claimed, then his control over a conquered dragon should work wonders in their initial estimation of him. And if they were as averse to King Druet as Leyla had insisted, they would prove more likely to help a Mizgalian plan revolt.

The farther they traveled to the north, the more the air thickened with the pungent smell of decay. Wings followed behind Trenton, tasting the atmosphere with a forked tongue and hissing at the shadows to either side of the path.

"Keep quiet, will you?" Trenton licked his lips in apprehension as the sounds of a village reached his ears and the glowing of bonfires illuminated the mountainside beyond the next rise.

When he reached the top of the hill, Trenton reined in his horse and looked down. The path descended into a vast encampment that was teeming with savages intent on performing a strange ritual. Amidst wild dancing and discordant singing, the clan proceeded to usher a number of sheep to the edge of the cliff to the west. Once there, they pushed the sheep over the edge and cheered when hungry dragons swooped to catch the sacrifices.

Trenton shuddered at the thought that he was about to alert this clan of his presence. No amount of training in his father's arena had prepared him for the realization that he may follow the sheep over the cliff before given the chance to utter a word.

Beside the horse, Wings glared at the scene of utter chaos, crouching low when the bonfires flared over a fresh supply of kindling. When the dragon uttered a helpless moan, Trenton glanced to see the beast eyeing the few dragons that circled overhead, wishing to drop into the camp, but fearing the bright flames that had been lit to keep them away.

"Let's go."

Trenton spoke the words aloud, as if urging the animals forward, but knew that he had really been commanding himself from the hilltop. Wings resisted the pull of the rope all the way down the slope, until, between the first two huts, he finally stood and let out an angry shriek.

Which produced the very effect that Trenton had hoped for.

The clan froze with fear and searched the darkening sky to see if one of the hovering dragons had decided to make a dive. One woman spotted Trenton at the edge of the camp and pointed his way while screaming a rush of frightened words in a language foreign even to Arcrea. The men of the clan made a furious dash towards Trenton, but Wings lurched forward and stretched his neck with another shriek to keep them from coming any closer to his defenseless position.

The astonished clan assumed Wings' behavior to be in fierce defense of Trenton, and suddenly they began to move with one accord—away from Wings, and forming a living wall behind a tall man who Trenton knew was their chief. The chief stared at Trenton with a look of confusion in his dark eyes, which were framed with painted signs similar to those covering his arms and chest. The tall leader spoke a few words and a small man, half the chief's height, inched closer to Trenton and spoke in clipped

Arcrean while keeping a wary eye on Wings.

"Our honored chief says, are you, sir, the noble keeper of the dragons?"

"No."

The interpreter's brow shot upward and he turned to speak with the chief. Trenton watched the curious faces, hoping that his answers short would keep them guessing and bide him some time.

The little man faced Trenton again, "Our honored chief says, have you come to bring the terror of the dragons upon us?"

"No."

Wings paced back and forth at the end of the rope.

"Our honored chief says, do you bring the blessing of the sun upon us?"

"No."

"Our honored chief says, have you brought us praise from the dragons for our sacrifices?"

"No."

"Our honored chief says, do you come as an ally of our foe—Arcrea's king, Druet of Oak's Branch?"

The crowd seemed to stiffen at the mention of Druet's name. Trenton's mind swirled with images of Arcrea's king and queen, of Talon and Bracy, of Falconer and Leyla, but he quickly pushed them aside with a shake of his head. Was he a friend to the Arcreans?

"No."

A smile pulled at Trenton's lips when he saw the look of perplexity on the interpreter's face. Suddenly, the memory of King Cronin's face swam before his eyes and he heard the monarch saying to his father, "You place far too much confidence in that boy."

Clenching his jaw with decision, Trenton dismounted, keeping a tight hold on Wings' lead rope, and launched into his proposal before the interpreter had finished speaking with the chief.

"I am Trenton of Mockmor in Mizgalia, and I come seeking your aid in the destruction of Druet's reign."

The interpreter stared at him in open-mouthed surprise until the chief slapped the back of his head; with a start, he turned to relay Trenton's message.

The young man watched as the chief stiffened warily at the word "*Mizyala*" and then looked up sharply when Trenton's ultimate goal was revealed. The tall man studied the Mizgalian for a long moment and finally lowered his head in a single, slow nod. He spoke to the little man beside him.

"Our honored chief says, he will hear your plans."

Trenton nodded in return and then led horse and dragon forward. Some time later, as he outlined his own ideas and discussed others in the warmth of the chief's hut, he couldn't help but smile. Surely, his work at Dragon Coast, along with the tale of Wings, would prove that he was worthy of his father's confidence, and King Cronin's as well.

The following day Trenton oversaw the designs for a number of large cages and helped to locate timber that would prove strong enough for their purpose. When the cages were complete, he set off at the head of a selected band to hunt for deer. That evening the clan prepared itself for a night of battle.

After a lifetime of fearing the vicious creatures, it was time to capture some dragons.

Chapter 20
* The Mizgalian's Bird *

Falconer led Adelaide and her young daughter, Caroline, southeast through the Brikbones and across the border into the Arcrean region of Frederick. He learned from the former noblewoman that Eric was currently serving as a slave on board the *Fate*—the vessel that had attacked them long before, and to which Eric had been sentenced to serve three years at a time, with only one year to spend with his family between voyages. Adelaide hated to think what Cronin might do to her husband when he discovered that she and her daughter had escaped, but Falconer quickly assured her that everything possible would be done to attempt his rescue as well.

Falconer's eyes constantly studied the horizon, searching for signs of Thomas and Delaney. As Adelaide shared her story of imprisonment, he came close to telling her that he knew her "little Eric"—the estranged son of whom she spoke—but the informant ultimately remained silent, as he was uncertain whether he could reach the boy in time to save his life.

Young Caroline rode with her mother—the third horse having been sold—and spent many hours observing the passing landscape and singing "Clouds o'er an Arcrean Sea," a song that she explained had been sung to her as a lullaby.

Coming upon a camp of Arcrean soldiers, Falconer made arrangements for a company to escort the two ladies to the Heartland, explaining that urgent business called him to ride in a different direction. With the setting sun illuminating the landscape like a flaming orb, Falconer's horse was soon pounding a steady trail southwest towards Dragon Coast.

ഗ്ദ

Leyla sat perched on the outcropping in the meadow south of Olden Weld. Most of her afternoon had been exhausted with chasing Humphrey across the village, and her grandmother had expressed a desire to rest before preparations for the evening meal began. Burrowing deeper into her cloak, Leyla watched the clouds overhead and began to hum a song that her father had loved to sing—one about storm clouds bearing down upon a vessel on the Arcrean Sea.

A sudden commotion caused Leyla to turn just as a hawk landed beside her head. A startled scream tried to escape her throat, but failed miserably as she moved quickly away and jumped to the ground. Another look at the bird made her pause and stare.

"'Ere now…you're the Mizgal'yin's bird," Leyla took a step closer and peered at a small sack held

Leyla

flush against the bird's stomach, "What's that?"

Slowly and carefully, Leyla moved close enough to gently stroke the hawk. Opening the sack, she pulled out a folded piece of parchment and spread it out to read the message scrawled across the inside.

Forward to Druet. Am riding to Dragon Coast—Trenton in danger. Rumors of war at Mockmor. Falconer.

Leyla's eyes widened, "Dragon Coast? I told 'im those people don' like King…" she froze with sudden realization, "Why that no good scoun'rel took my words and ran off t' cause trouble by 'em, 'e did!"

The young girl wrapped her cloak in thick folds over her left arm and managed to coax the hawk to perch there. Heading homeward across the meadow, she tried to think of who she should take Falconer's message to. Queen Aurenia had left two days before to join her husband in Dormay, accompanied by Alice, Grikk, and a company of royal guards. Leland would be meeting with the royal council now, but she supposed that news of war would prove an urgent enough interruption.

Leyla glanced at the hawk on her arm, "You're 'eavy, you know that?" it quirked its head to stare at her with one eye and she frowned, "If Falc'ner's been in Mockmor, and 'e just sent you back from there, then that means the Mizgal'yin sent you there with a message to begin with," Leyla huffed a lock of auburn hair from her face and muttered, "Traitor."

Leyla received a multitude of odd looks as she moved through the streets of Olden Weld with a hawk perched on her arm. When she approached the meetinghouse, she found that she would not have to interrupt Leland after all, as word of the bird had preceded her and the Heartland's chief was already waiting for her on the front stoop.

A lengthy discussion ensued among the members of the council. How had Trenton, who had declared himself to be a lowly runaway slave, come to possess a nobleman's carrier-hawk? Why had he gone to Dragon Coast in secret, if not to cause trouble? Why had Falconer been sent to Mizgalia? What rumors had been heard at Mockmor? Was war imminent? And what had caused Falconer to take such an interest in this troublesome Mizgalian youth—who must be a spy in the service of their long-standing foe?

Leyla sat on the floor by the wall, listening with frustration to the evidence piled against Trenton's innocence, and wishing that she had held her tongue regarding the clan at Dragon Coast. She had been forced to sit through the meeting when it was discovered that the hawk would not leave her. It stood on the floor beside her or lifted to perch on her knee, but refused to part from the girl's company. One of the council members occasionally came to inspect the small pouch or the bird's wings, and then returned to his seat.

Leyla's eyes began to drift closed and she started humming her father's song again. When the hawk perched on her knee again, Leyla opened her eyes to see it peering at her with an intensity that lifted her brows.

"You like the song my father sang t' me?"

She started to whistle the tune softly and the hawk opened its beak to let out a piercing screech. Leyla cringed at the shrill cry and the councilmen paused to glance at the bird.

Kellen, Leland's son and brother to the queen, stepped closer, "What happened?"

"I was whistlin'."

Kellen stared at the bird, "Whistling what?"

"My father's song. 'Clouds o'er an Arcrean Sea'."

"Hold on," Kellen wrapped his arm and carefully lifted the hawk, taking a single step back from where Leyla sat, "Do it again."

Leyla obediently began to whistle the tune but got no farther than the first three notes before the hawk suddenly flapped its wings and dropped to perch on her knee again. It stared at her expectantly and gave another shrill cry.

Leland stepped away from the table, "It's a signal! Trenton must have used those notes to call the bird to him. Well done, Kellen. Leyla. If the hawk will let you, try the same pattern at a greater distance from each other."

They did so. With the same results.

Kellen turned to his father, "Why would a Mizgalian signal his bird with a favorite Arcrean song?"

Leland shook his head, "Perhaps he was not aware…"

Another councilman stood, "Or perhaps there is more to this situation than *we* are aware of. I say we send word to King Druet as Falconer says and trust God to take care of what we do not understand."

The rest of the council agreed and a royal courier was sent for. A copy of Falconer's message was made for the council and the original was passed into the rider's hand to be delivered with all haste to King Druet at Dormay.

Chapter 21
* Drop of Death *

Two weeks passed and a sufficient number of dragons had been captured. Trenton thought of the inhabited cages now lining the decks of the Dragon Coast fleet and smiled at his own ingenuity. The clan's ships would cart the dangerous cargo south and then east, and the dragons would be released to attack the southern coast of Arcrea, where the people were less accustomed to battle.

Their first target: Dormay.

Trenton turned when a fresh round of excited cheers arose from the encampment beyond the next rise. The ships would set sail within the hour. The clan had spent the entire day in wild celebration over the forthcoming ruin of Druet's reign. Trenton had spent the day alone, planning his return to Mockmor that would take place once the dragons had been launched into southern Arcrea. His father would doubtless now find him a position in an elite rank of the Mizgalian troops.

The snap of a twig caused Trenton to turn and study the trees behind him.

Nothing.

"Who's there?"

Silence.

Trenton laid a hand to his sword and sidestepped behind an outcropping. Had an animal caused the noise, he would have heard it darting away at the sound of his voice. If another human were close by, they would have answered…unless they didn't want him aware of their presence.

On the other side of the rise, the clan had begun a strange chant.

An eerie feeling wrapped itself around Trenton's heart and filled his lungs with every breath. Every sense was alive and tense.

"Where are you?" he whispered as his gaze flitted across the forested mountainside above him.

Suddenly, Trenton cried out when a hand covered his mouth from behind and the attacker's other arm shoved him against the outcropping. Immediately, Trenton pushed away from the rocks with all his strength, throwing his opponent off balance, but only for a moment. Another brute, wrapped in a black cloak and wearing a dark mask, appeared over the top of the outcropping and Trenton reached for his sword. When his hand failed to find the weapon, Trenton looked down and growled when he realized the first man had robbed him of his sword belt.

The masked man jumped from the outcropping and tackled Trenton, rolling the boy to his stomach and pinning him to the ground with one knee. Trenton thrashed about and tried to loosen the man's grip, but froze when he felt a dagger at his back. The first attacker quickly came to his partner's assistance and delivered a nauseating kick to Trenton's ribs.

One of the men tore a length of cloth from the hem of Trenton's tunic and used it to blindfold him. The dagger was lifted away, another kick delivered, and Trenton felt himself pulled from the ground. His arms were held in a painful position over his back as the attackers led him away from the outcropping. He tried to ask where they were taking him but was instantly rewarded with a slap to his face.

The clan's drums echoed the pounding of his heart as Trenton struggled to gain a sense of what direction they were headed in. He grit his teeth, angry over his inability to detect the attackers' presence sooner or even contribute a single blow in the sudden contest.

The drums suddenly became silent and Trenton's attackers froze.

"What…?"

"SH!" The attacker behind him hissed in his ear.

Just then, a dragon shrieked directly above them and a chill raced up Trenton's spine as he suddenly realized the brutes' intent.

"No!" Trenton shouted his refusal to die in such a manner and tried to twist out of the attacker's grasp. The iron grip only tightened, however, and Trenton felt with a rising panic that he was being driven closer to the cliff's edge.

Somewhere off to his left, the clan's discordant singing began again. Trenton shouted for someone to help, but knew that his cries would not succeed in penetrating the unearthly chants.

His feet slipped on loose earth and Trenton knew that they had reached a peninsula where the dragons' claws had ripped the rocks after decades of using the spot as a perch. His resistance took on a new urgency, which only increased his attackers' speed in pushing him forward.

They came to a stop once more, and the two attackers each gripped one of his arms.

"Let go of me," Trenton tried to jerk free.

One of the brutes let out a cruel laugh and Trenton was startled by the fleeting thought that he recognized the timbre of the man's voice. In the next instant he felt himself shoved forward and the plummet of death began.

The sudden drop caused Trenton's stomach to rise into his chest. If his scream succeeded in escaping, he didn't hear it. He thought of the sheep that had been sacrificed by the clan two weeks before and would have pitied them had he had the time.

The blindfold came off, whipped away by the wind, and Trenton shrieked when he saw how quickly the sea was coming up to swallow him. His shriek was echoed by something behind him and an instant before he would have plunged into the water Trenton felt a terrible grip take hold of his arms; his body was jerked upward. The sudden change in direction jarred his neck and shoulders and he cried out in pain as he looked up to witness the inevitable.

The claws that were wrapped around his shoulders tightened when the dragon lowered its head to peer down at the human catch. Trenton tried to peel his arms from the beast's grasp, but soon stopped when he saw that the fall would prove worse than the flight.

As the dragon circled to head for its cave, Trenton caught sight of the clansmen beginning their trek down the single path in the cliffs. His plans, his ships, his dragons, his victory, were about to set sail without him!

"No!"

Trenton's shout brought the dragon's head down for another look and the monster shrieked in his face.

"What are you looking at?" Trenton's rage had turned his face red. He tried his swing his legs upward to kick the beast, but was unsuccessful.

The dragon snorted and Trenton yelled in surprise when the same powder that Wings had produced blew from the beast's nostrils and covered his face in a chalky film.

Trenton gagged and spit when the substance touched his tongue, "Ugh! What is this stuff?"

The dragon groaned and suddenly dove for the sea.

Trenton tried to yell, but his tongue had suddenly gone numb. He watched as they fell closer to the waves but was unable to react in any way. His entire being felt sluggish—his body had begun to shut down as if he were falling asleep.

The dragon lurched upward again and was startled when a second beast suddenly appeared and grabbed for the human prey. Trenton heard his scaly captor's shriek and felt his arms accidentally released. He knew he was falling again, but for some reason that didn't worry him. The dragon continued to shriek and dove to retrieve its prize once more.

Trenton felt the sweeping blow of a leathery wing as it collided with his helpless frame.

He saw the flash of talons.

Sensed that he had been struck.

The waves rose to greet him with an icy welcome

and Trenton knew that he had plunged beneath the surface. The thunderous sound of water filled his ears until he heard nothing, and then, from some distant place that refused to register in his mind, came the strangely familiar sound of a woman's voice in song.

But she was only humming the first three notes.

Chapter 22
* Pieces of a Puzzle *

Druet's eyes studied the crowded inn, though his mind hardly took stock of his surroundings; the soldiers on guard at their various posts, Grikk standing near the door with his massive arms folded across his chest, and Talon and Bracy conversing with their fellow courier—the man who had just delivered the message that Druet now held in his hand. Falconer's written words had brought a thousand different thoughts into focus.

Beside him, Renny slipped her hand into his, "Are you alright?"

He nodded. At least he thought he did.

"Druet…?"

He started and turned to look down at her.

"Druet, what's wrong?"

He handed her the slip of parchment and watched as she read the short missive.

She stared at it as she spoke, "Falconer went to Mockmor?"

Druet maintained the quiet tone that she had used to ensure that no one else heard their conversation, "He went to learn the truth about Trenton. Apparently, he unearthed much more."

Renny looked up then, "What about Trenton?"

Druet told her about Falconer's visit to Balgo and the story that Osgood had revealed, "It appears that Trenton bears a remarkable resemblance to Alice's father…"

"He does!"

Druet quirked an eyebrow at Renny's sudden excitement, "What do you mean?"

"Alice returned to Olden Weld with an old painting of Eric. The likeness is an exact copy of Trenton…it could pass as the Mizgalian's portrait!"

"Did she bring it here to Dormay?"

Renny shook her head.

Druet leaned against the high back of the corner bench, "If Falconer learned of the danger involving Trenton while he was at Mockmor, it seems probable that the Mizgalians are behind the trouble. And if Falconer is taking such care to rescue Trenton then his suspicions must have been proven true. Trenton must be Alice's brother—and Eric's son."

"And a thief," Renny murmured.

Druet chuckled, "Renny, you don't know for certain that it was Trenton who stole your bow."

Renny gave him a sidelong glance that suggested she thought otherwise.

Druet pointed at the message still in Renny's hand, "It's no surprise that the Mizgalians will want to use my inexperience to their advantage by initiating war. My concern is that they will advance by sea. The armies in the north are accustomed to battling the

Mizgalians; they are experienced in pushing the enemy troops back across the Brikbone Mountains. The people here in the south are not ready to defend themselves against a fierce attack. Their ships have always been used for trade, and the royal navy has not yet had time to put their lessons to use on the water."

Druet ran a hand through his hair and fingered the golden circlet that framed his head, "Oh God, what should I do?"

Renny bowed her head and silently added her own prayers to his.

Talon approached the table and cleared his throat, "Sire. Captain Hull to see you."

Druet looked up to see the squatty captain standing at the inn's threshold, "Tell him to come sit with us, Talon."

Captain Hull doffed his hat and bowed when he had drawn closer, and then seated himself across from the king and queen, "I thought that you would like to know, my king, the last three ships were completed today—the entire fleet is now seaworthy!"

Druet smiled; here was the answer to his prayer, "Thank you, Hull. Send word to the crews that tomorrow they will put to sea for their continued training."

Captain Hull's eyes were lit with anticipation, "Aye, Sire!"

As the captain left the inn, Renny tapped Falconer's message on the table, "Should we tell Alice that she has a brother here in Arcrea?"

Druet sighed and shook his head, "I think it would be wise to wait until we're certain about Trenton, and that Falconer brings him back alive."

Renny searched his face for a moment and then

nodded, "I'll pray for him."

"Good," Druet rose from his place at the table and offered Renny his hand, "If Trenton is indeed Eric's son and doesn't know it yet, then he has a difficult decision ahead of him. He will need our prayers."

ഌ

Nathaniel dropped another handful of sliced onion into the cauldron and glanced up as Eric added an eel. It was the first time the two had shared work on the *Fate* since the day they'd both been in the rigging. Their conversations in the hold at night had formed a greater bond between them, as had their shared plans for escape. Nathaniel was honored that Eric had trusted him with the story of his past, though he continued to use the name Thumb when they were around the other slaves.

On this particular day they were in charge of preparing food for the Mizgalian crew.

Overhead, the captain's shouts had revealed to them that a ship had been spotted on the horizon. Some time later it had been discovered that the ship was Mizgalian. They had supposed that Captain Black would disregard the other vessel's flag and attack for his own pleasure, as he had done in the past; however, Nathaniel and Eric heard no such orders.

A sudden commotion brought Nathaniel's head up, "We're coming alongside the other vessel."

Eric tilted his head to listen.

A few moment later the two slaves froze when the sound of heavy footfalls descended the stairs to the galley and the door opened to admit three armed

Mizgalian soldiers, followed by Captain Black and a knight whose armor was marked by Cronin's royal insignia. The soldiers removed the sharp utensils from the slaves' hands and then stood at attention to one side of the room.

A moment of silence followed and the cauldron's contents began to bubble.

The knight's eyes never left Eric's face.

"You are the man called Thumb."

Eric nodded, "I am."

The knight's face took on a hard look, "To whom did you reveal the secret of your true identity?"

Eric's brow lifted a fraction and he motioned toward Nathaniel, "Only this man."

In a flash, the knight drew his sword and stepped toward Nathaniel, but was blocked when Eric moved in front of the younger slave.

Captain Black took hold of the knight's arm, "Sir Kleyton! I said I would allow you an interview with the man you sought. I did not say you might come aboard and kill my slaves!"

Kleyton glared at Eric, "Captain Black was to be the only man aware of your past!"

Eric spoke quietly, but firmly, "It was my past to live, it is my secret to tell."

The knight growled in Eric's face, "Who else did you tell?"

"No one, sir."

Kleyton shoved Eric against the table and held the edge of his sword to the slave's collarbone, "If no one else knew, then how can you explain the aided escape of your wife and daughter?"

A look of genuine surprise shaped Eric's face and his voice came as a hoarse whisper, "They were rescued?"

"They *escaped*," Kleyton hissed, "Thanks to your failure to obey orders."

Eric set his jaw, "I told no one save this slave. Thanks to *your* close surveillance of my family, I have had no opportunity to tell anyone else."

Sir Kleyton considered the captive for a long moment and finally snapped his sword back into its sheath, "I begged my king for permission to kill you this day, but he said that he anticipates your return from the *Fate* so that he might have the pleasure himself," Kleyton turned for the door and paused with his hand on the latch, "Bear this in mind: you will not be returning from the *Fate* until your wife and daughter are brought back to Mizgalia," he gave a sinister smile, "We wouldn't want you to come ashore without dear Adelaide there to greet you."

Eric stepped away from the table with a stricken look, "Sir, my three years on board have nearly expired!"

Kleyton turned to face the Arcrean with a condemning finger, "A small sacrifice to pay for the good of Mizgalia! You would be on your knees begging for your life, if not for King Cronin's edict to spare you a little while. Some of us have not been so fortunate," the knight's head lifted in a patronizing manner, "I have been forced to sacrifice my own son for the cause."

"Do not speak to me of sacrificing sons," Eric drew himself up and returned Kleyton's look with a glare, "for your king is guilty of abducting mine from the cradle."

Kleyton's head lowered in a menacing glower and his jaw clenched with unleashed wrath, "Mark my words, you will never set foot on solid ground again," the knight made a quick motion for his guards to follow and then stormed out the door and up the stairs with a furious bellow, "I will see that you remain on the *Fate* until the day of your death!"

Chapter 23
• Míjí •

The vision slowly became clearer. The woman's voice echoed in his mind as she continued to sing the oddly familiar tune. The rest of the words began to piece themselves together—lilting lyrics of a storm and the Arcrean Sea—and Trenton could just make out the form of the woman's head as she bent over him to say good night. Though Trenton had been very young when she had died, and his father, with a soldier's ability to silence the past, had never spoken of her, Trenton knew instinctively that this was his mother.

Gradually, the vision melted away and Trenton reluctantly opened his eyes. He was lying on his back in a dimly lit hut. The single lamp that hung from the ceiling was swaying back and forth to a rhythm, and Trenton was suddenly aware of a gentle slapping against the wall by his head. Water. He was on a boat.

Trenton blinked. His eyelids felt grainy, as though they had been scratched raw by saltwater. His throat felt equally scratched and was drier than the Mizgalian desert.

The door in the far wall suddenly opened and a man entered the small space. Trenton stared. The only word he could think of to describe the newcomer was Round. The man's round toes poked through sandals on round feet below rounded legs that supported a round body with round arms and a round head. Round ears perked at the sound of boiling stew, and a round nose led the man across the room to a cauldron; one round hand lifted the pot's lid and the other a long spoon to stir the contents. When he was done, the stranger turned to study Trenton with squinty eyes—the only feature he possessed that was not round.

"Ah, you are awake, my friend!" The man spoke in the Arcrean tongue as he bustled across the cabin and leaned close to Trenton's face, peering intently into the younger man's eyes, "I think you are going to make it!"

Trenton tried to respond but could only offer a dry croak.

The stranger immediately crossed the room again and dipped a clay cup into a pail of fresh water. Returning, he lifted Trenton's head and held the cup to the youth's mouth.

"Better?"

Trenton nodded, laying back against the rounded pillow and enjoying the feel of the cold water on his throat.

"Do you feel able to eat some stew, my friend?"

"Yes," Trenton rasped, "I'm starving."

The round man crossed to the cauldron and dipped a ladle of stew into a wooden bowl.

Trenton watched him.

"Where am I?"

The man glanced at him with a smile, "You are on my boat! It is a small vessel, with only this cabin on deck and a small hold below, but I am not too proud to call it home," he turned and bustled back to the bedside, "My name is Miji. You might say that I am a hermit. I live alone here, in a water-level cave below the cliffs of Dragon Coast."

Miji paused a moment and set the bowl on a tiny bedside table, "Let me help you into a sitting position. I say it is much easier to eat when you are not lying flat on your back!"

"No, I can do it…" Trenton started to sit up and then froze when his left hand refused to cooperate.

Miji's round face gathered into a look of concern, "It is numb, my friend. I had to…I have kept it…" he bowed his head, "I am sorry."

A disconcerted feeling came over Trenton as he observed the somber Miji. Using his right hand, he quickly reached across, lifted back the wool coverlet, and stared. His left hand was hidden within an excessive amount of bloodstained linen. Trenton moved to unwrap the length of cloth, but Miji gently laid a hand to the boy's arm.

"You must not remove the bandage just yet; I reapplied the salve only an hour ago and it will need to—"

"What happened?" Trenton's wide eyes searched Miji's face for any answer but the one he feared.

Miji pulled a low wooden stool from under the tiny table and set it by the bed. Lowering himself onto the stool, he clasped his hands and stared at Trenton's wrapped hand.

"I remember falling—being pushed from the cliff," Trenton pressed, "I remember the dragon taking me up and then spitting something in my face…"

Miji looked up, "Ah! That would be the Death Chalk."

"Death Chalk?"

Miji's head bobbed in a nod, "That is one name for it. Some call it Death Chalk, and others call it Dragon Dust or Deadly Powder. The ancients called it the Substance of Fate. When a dragon hunts it will often administer the Death Chalk on spirited prey. The chalk is effective to the very core of a being, enabling the dragon to gain better control over its victim."

"Miji?"

"Yes?"

"What happened to my hand?"

Miji sighed, "A second dragon challenged the first, and you were dropped. The first dragon tried to grab you again, but failed. In the frenzy that followed, I saw you struck by the beast and thought that you were dead. I have a contained fire kept on my deck for when I venture out, and this forced the dragons back to their cliff as I drew closer to where you had fallen. I fished you out of the water and hoped…"

Trenton closed his eyes and tried not to shout with impatience, but failed, "Miji!"

Miji started and lifted his eyes to stare at Trenton.

Trenton rebuked himself for yelling at his rescuer, and forced his tone to a quieter level, "What happened to my hand?"

"The dragon's final strike took your thumb."

Trenton felt as if a giant fist had a constricting grip on his chest. His heart wouldn't beat. His lungs failed to take a breath. A sharp sensation behind his nose warned of oncoming tears and he squeezed his eyes shut, refusing to let them make an appearance.

His entire life had been spent in training—the arena, the catawylds, the examinations, had all been endured so that he might earn an honored place in his father's army. Now, in a single moment, with the frantic assault of a wild beast, he had lost everything. Though he was right-handed, the loss of his left thumb would still prevent him from being promoted through the Mizgalian ranks. King Cronin would smirk and say to Trenton's father that he had always been right—Kleyton had been too confident of his son's abilities.

"Take heart, my friend! You are still alive, and that is far better than keeping your thumb in death."

Trenton kept his eyes closed and ignored Miji's attempts to cheer him. When the round man asked if Trenton was still hungry, the youth turned his head to face the wall in silence. Several minutes passed and Trenton heard his rescuer pour the bowl's contents back into the cauldron. The door opened and then closed, and Trenton knew that he was alone again. He shifted to stare up at the low ceiling and allowed two bitter tears to escape from the corners of his eyes.

The thought crossed his mind that he still did not know who his attackers had been, but it no longer mattered. Whoever they had been, they had succeeded in reducing his life to mere shambles. If his father didn't turn him out into the streets, as was lawful in Mockmor, he would be forced to live under the constant judgment and criticism of others.

Trenton closed his eyes and wished that the dream of his mother would return and forever remove him from this misery.

Chapter 24
* Mystery at Dragon Coast *

Falconer lay flat on a rise overlooking the Dragon Coast encampment. It was relatively quiet just now, if what he had heard of the place was true. There were people milling about the camp, performing the mundane tasks of life, but it looked to the informant as if the place was empty. True, there were many women and children and a good number of men that he could see, nevertheless, there were not enough people here to reckon for half of the huts that Falconer had counted.

And another thing—Trenton was nowhere to be seen.

Falconer's brow furrowed. The detached clan of Hugh was known for its rebellion toward King Druet. Trenton's choice of destination proved that he was striving to aid in the Mizgalian cause as he had, superficially, been raised to do.

So then, where had he and the majority of the Dragon Coast males gone?

Falconer moved away from the top of the rise and continued down to the base of the hill. Pausing near an outcropping of rock, he studied the base of the cliffs below. There were no ships or even signs of a cove where ships might be kept. If the rumors of a Dragon Coast fleet were true, then the clansmen had set sail.

Falconer turned from the edge of the cliff and his gaze immediately fell to see Trenton's sword lying in the dirt at the base of the outcropping. The informant crouched to study the signs of a tussle that had taken place. He retrieved the weapon and quickly scanned the area for any signs of Thomas and Delaney.

He had come too late.

Falconer gripped the pommel in frustration and turned north, wanting to put some distance between himself and the clan before nightfall. He had left his horse stabled on the other side of the mountains, so he would have to circle back around on foot.

Suddenly, Falconer paused and turned to look back at the rock formation.

Something wasn't right.

The informant searched his mind for a clue as to what might be out of place. A thought struck him and he returned to circle around the rock. The signs of the struggle combined with the discovery of Trenton's abandoned sword left Falconer with no doubt that Eric's son had been attacked.

But the attackers had not been Thomas and Delaney.

Falconer turned to study the landscape and figured that his best choice would be to continue north; perhaps he would still be in time to meet the

Mizgalian assassins.

Leaving the rocks, Falconer strapped Trenton's sword opposite his own and started off into the trees. In his mind, he reviewed the conversation that had taken place at Mockmor. It was obvious to Falconer that if Cronin would use Trenton's death as an excuse to create war, then Trenton would need to be found dead to prove the Mizgalian's point.

Trenton's attackers had not left him by the rock pile.

It was true the coast was infested with dragons, but Falconer's study of the site had shown no signs of a dragon landing to carry off a human. No, the dragons had not come to Trenton—Trenton had been taken to the dragons. The three sets of footprints that Falconer had seen had led away from the outcropping and directly towards the cliffs. From there, only two sets had marked a path up the hill toward the encampment.

Falconer shook his head and his jaw clenched with fury.

Trenton had been offered as a sacrifice.

And the only people so inhumane they would perform such a gruesome ritual were those of the Dragon Coast clan.

ഇൽ

Several miles to the north, Falconer found Thomas and Delaney camped in a clearing that was sheltered on the west side by rock formations. Even though darkness had fallen, Falconer could see that Thomas was a tall and lanky man, while Delaney, though just as tall, looked to be a wall of solid muscle.

As Falconer crept closer to the clearing, he saw that the two Mizgalians were deep in discussion. Silently making his way to the top of the rock pile, some six feet above their heads, he was finally able to hear and interpret most of what they were saying.

"...never been so shaken in my life," Thomas hissed.

"Why does it bother you? We would have killed Trenton if the clan hadn't done it first."

"Delaney! He was pushed, blindfolded, over the edge of a cliff—a nine hundred foot drop, mind you—and those people celebrated! Forget that his death was imminent! I would much rather have seen him die by my sword that at the mercy of dragons and chanting rebels."

Delaney grunted and murmured something Falconer couldn't hear before raising his voice to say, "We came all this way just to watch someone else get our victim. What a waste of a journey."

"That's the truth," Thomas agreed, "I only wish we could find some other rotten soul to fill King Cronin's demands and save us from inventing an explanation."

"That will not be necessary, my friends."

The third voice brought the Mizgalians to their feet. Drawing their swords, they turned to peer into the trees to the south of their clearing.

"Who's there?" Delaney called, "Show yourself!"

The voice called back in the Mizgalian tongue, "Am I correct to assume that you are the two men sent by Cronin for the assassination of one, Trenton of Mockmor?"

The two in the clearing exchanged a look of shock. Their mission had been carried out with all secrecy! Who was this stranger and how had he heard of Cronin's orders?

Their silence was answer enough for the voice.

"I see that I am correct. Hear me. I too have been sent on a mission that concerns you and the one who you seek."

"Trenton is dead."

"One would think."

"What do you mean? Why do you not show yourself?"

"Lower your swords and I will lead you to Trenton."

"Impossible! We watched from a distance and saw Trenton killed."

"Did you? Did you see him die?"

The Mizgalians exchanged another glance and Delaney gave the slightest nod. The two slowly sheathed their swords and a moment later a man appeared and motioned with one arm for them to follow him.

From his position on the rock pile, Falconer watched them go. He waited until they had gone a short distance and then dropped to the ground to follow as well.

Having studied the third man when he had first appeared, and then watching as they moved through the trees ahead of him, Falconer quickly came to the conclusion that there was only one word that could accurately describe the stranger.

Round.

Chapter 25
* Of Rescue & Defeat *

Trenton felt himself buffeted on all sides by the dragon's thick leathery wings. In a flash, the large claws lashed out and Trenton woke from his dream with a start that sent him tumbling from the bed. When his left hand struck the floor, he let out a howl that brought Miji hustling in from the deck.

"My friend, what are you doing down there on the floor?"

Trenton groaned.

Miji bent over his paunch to help the youth into a sitting position, "I have run out of salve for your hand. If you want my stitches to hold and the skin to heal up, then we must get you to a healer."

Despite the pain that flamed in his hand, Trenton's head shot up and he glared at the other man, "My people are forbidden to visit the healers. They are troublemakers and workers of dark magic."

"Ha!" Miji laughed, "That is nonsense! Have you

not heard of King Druet's healer, Rodney, and of the good he has done in Arcrea?"

Trenton used his right arm to force his way to his feet, "Miji, I forbid you to take me to a healer."

Miji sat on the edge of the bed and shrugged his round shoulders, "Very well, but do not complain to me when you lose the rest of your hand."

Trenton sent the man a dark scowl and cradled his left arm with the right; "I suppose I should thank you for pulling me out of the water and caring for me these past two days."

Miji chuckled, "I suppose you should!"

The round man sat waiting with his hands folded in his lap.

Trenton rolled his eyes, "Thank you."

Miji leaned forward in a bow, "You are most welcome!"

Trenton turned around and nearly ran into the lamp swinging form the low ceiling. Sidestepping to avoid a collision, he leaned against the door, "I have to get out of here, Miji."

"Good! We will go to the healer."

"No! I said no healers! I need you to get me back to Mizgalia. Once I get home, my father will provide the medical help I need." *I hope.*

Miji sighed deeply and lifted a petitioning gaze upward, "This is the thanks I receive for my help!" he lowered his eyes to look at Trenton, "Very well, I will take you to Mizgalia. It will be safest for us to travel by land to northern Hugh, and from there you will sail across to your homeland."

Trenton nodded and shoved away from the door, "Let's go."

"You are not fatigued?"

Trenton let out an exasperated sigh, "Miji, I want to go home. Today. Now!"

Miji nodded his way from the bed and lit a second lantern, "Then I will not keep us!"

Outside on the deck, Trenton found that Miji's boat was indeed moored in a cave at the base of the Dragon Coast cliffs. One hundred feet to his left, Trenton could see the cave's entrance, beyond which the moonlight reflected off of the relatively calm sea. To his right, the boat had been tied at a pier, carved from the cove's wall. Beyond the pier, Miji's lantern illuminated the base of a staircase that Trenton could see climbed upward through a dark tunnel.

"This staircase will take us up onto the land, about two miles north of the Dragon Coast encampment."

Miji hefted himself onto the pier and started up. Trenton glanced out to the moonlit waters once more and then followed.

The climb left Trenton exhausted. The attack at Dragon Coast and the following bout with the dragon must have left him far weaker than he had thought.

At the top of the stairs, Miji lifted a heavy bar from a door in the rocks. He pulled the panel open and motioned for Trenton to move ahead while he set the bar aside. Trenton stepped through the door and found himself on a forested mountainside. The door to Miji's tunnel had been wedged directly into one of the rock outcroppings that were so numerous in the Hugh Mountains.

Trenton breathed deeply of the salted air and managed half a smile.

He was going home.

But home to what?

Suddenly, a dark form separated itself from the shadows to his left. Another appeared to the right. Both figures held drawn swords.

The attackers!

"Miji," Trenton turned just as the door slammed in his face, "Miji, open the door! The attackers have…" the realization of the man's betrayal hit him hard, and he pounded his right fist against the panel, "You dirty traitor! Miserable dog!"

One of the attackers gave a throaty chuckle and Trenton turned his back to the door. Instinctively, he reached for his sword, though he knew it no longer hung at his side. The two figures continued to advance and Trenton braced himself.

"What do you want from me?"

The answer was given in Mizgalian, "Your life."

The attacker to the left lifted his sword to strike and Trenton sank helplessly to cower against the door as the weapon started its return swing. At the last possible second, another dark figure dropped from the rocks over the door, knocking the attacker to the ground and sending his sword flying out of reach through the trees. Trenton saw the flash of a dagger and heard the grunts of a brief struggle, and then the third man—his rescuer—rose to meet the second attacker. The first attacker remained motionless where he had fallen.

The two swords clashed and scraped. When the blades locked at the cross-guard, Trenton's defender growled as he resisted the other man's strength, until finally he shoved the attacker backwards with a fierce cry. A moment later all was silent except for the victor's heavy breathing.

Holding his left arm against his stomach,

Trenton used his right arm to lift himself to his feet, "I don't know how to thank you, sir."

The stranger remained silent, his shoulders rising and falling with the labor of taking a deep breath. Trenton stood still for a moment and watched in tentative silence as the defender held his sword ready and rolled the second man onto his back. Moonlight fell across the man's face and Trenton lurched forward with a gasp.

Delaney!

"I knew that man!" He turned to the first attacker and rolled him over with his foot.

Thomas.

Trenton shook his head in disbelief. Thomas had escorted him safely into Arcrea a short time ago. Why had he been out to take Trenton's life? There must have been a misunderstanding…

The stranger sheathed his sword and finally found his voice, "Why didn't you stay in the Heartland?"

Trenton froze in shock, "Falconer?"

The Arcrean informant pushed his hood back, "Are you mad, venturing to Dragon Coast on your own?"

Trenton could only stare. He didn't know how he should answer. When he had last seen Falconer, Trenton had been living under the guise of a runaway slave. Then Falconer had disappeared from the Heartland and Trenton had done the same. He had not revealed the truth to Falconer, but the fact that the informant was in Dragon Coast looking for him was a clear sign that he knew more than he should.

Falconer seemed to understand Trenton's pause; he lifted a hand to swipe at the space between them,

"And don't...don't tell me that you came to see the sights! I'll have no more of your Mizgalian games, Trenton. It is time for truth!"

Trenton's eyes narrowed, "How did you find me?"

Falconer shook his head, "Does it matter? At least I managed to rescue your foolish hide from assassins."

"They were my friends," in his agitation, Trenton's tongue reverted to the Mizgalian language, leaving Falconer to interpret for himself, "There must have been a mistake!"

"No, Trenton," Falconer refused to adopt the boy's foreign tongue for this conversation, choosing instead to address the issue in Arcrean; his voice was low, carrying the weight of conviction, "Thomas and Delaney were sent to kill you on Arcrean soil."

Trenton's adept brain caught the subtle clue and he continued to challenge in Mizgalian, "How do you know their names?" when Falconer remained silent, the youth offered, "You went to Mockmor, didn't you? You went to spy on my people and discover who I really am—to see if I was telling you the truth!"

"Which you weren't."

"And you found out that I had come to Dragon Coast by intercepting the private message I sent to my father and my king!"

"Wrong! I did not intercept, I overheard. Had I intercepted the message, Cronin and Kleyton would not have known where to send the two brutes."

Trenton leaned forward in shock at this Arcrean's presumption, "My father would not send men to kill me!"

The bantering back and forth between two

languages was getting on Falconer's nerves, and his calm finally broke with a shout, "He is not your father!"

Trenton's jaw dropped, "What are you talking about?"

"You are not Kleyton's son. You are not even of Mizgalian blood!"

The two suddenly fell silent, breathing hard and staring at each other in the pale moonlight. Trenton's face slowly formed a frown and he shook his head in disgust.

"You're mad," turning north, he started off through the trees.

Falconer called after him, "I speak the truth, Trenton. I can prove it!"

Trenton froze. He hugged his useless left arm as if for security and refused to face the other man. It wasn't possible. How could Falconer have proof of such insanity?

Falconer approached at a slow pace that matched his deliberate tone.

"Yes, I did go to Mockmor to discover who you really are. However, I did so only because I realized that you are not even who *you* think you are."

Falconer stood in front of Trenton and reached into his doublet. When he pulled out a folded piece of parchment, he paused before holding it out to Trenton.

"I had not planned to tell you so suddenly, but I feel now that it is necessary."

When Trenton did not move to take the parchment, Falconer's gaze shifted to the bloodstained wrap on his left hand.

"You were wounded by the dragon?"

Trenton looked up, astonished at the man's knowledge of what he had been through the past few days. Falconer returned his stare and unfolded the parchment. Tilting the page to catch the moonlight, he held it for Trenton to read.

The first thing to catch Trenton's eye was the royal insignia, molded by blood-red wax, at the bottom of the page. From there, his eyes lifted to scan the short but precise document.

"I, Cronin…approving Sir Kleyton…parentage of one, Trenton of Brentwood, formerly of Arcrean descent…Eric of Brentwood. Trenton…reserved for future service…Death to the adversary!"

Trenton took a slow breath. His shoulders drooped and he took a single step back, away from the angrily-scrawled words. First, assassins and dragons had dashed all his hopes for a prosperous future; now, a meddling Arcrean was trying to shred what was left of his very existence. It couldn't be true. Trenton drew himself up and tried to appear as though he didn't notice Falconer's sympathetic expression.

"Eric of Brentwood?" he spoke in Mizgalian to annoy the other man, "Is this your idea of jesting? This is a result of Osgood's crazy ramblings, isn't it? You think I am this 'Eric'."

Falconer slowly folded the parchment and purposely spoke in Arcrean, "In truth, your given name is Eric—you are your father's namesake. In his drunken delirium, Osgood—your uncle—thought that you were his brother."

Trenton's jaw began to tremble, "How do I know that you yourself are not the author of this document? How can I know this isn't false?"

Falconer leaned closer, "Did you not recognize the seal, boy? Rest assured, I would not degrade myself to bear a copy of Cronin's signet for my own purposes. I would swear my life to the probability that every document marked by this seal has brought meaningless death to at least one man, woman, or child, and I will not—"

"Meaningless dea… What do you call that?" Trenton pointed back to where Thomas and Delaney had fallen.

Falconer's jaw clenched and he pointed in the same direction with a clipped response, "That, Trenton, was the apprehension of two Mizgalian assassins bent on killing an Arcrean—the son of a former Arcrean nobleman."

Trenton felt his defenses crumbling and knew that he would soon run out of excuses. Taking another step away from Falconer, he glanced at the parchment and offered a challenge.

"*Bruviktzi.*" Prove it.

Even as he said the words, Trenton knew that Falconer would somehow find a way to produce evidence of his story, but he had to buy himself time to think through the whirlwind that had just uprooted his mind from everything familiar.

Falconer remained silent for a long moment. When he spoke, he pressed the folded parchment into Trenton's right hand and looked the younger man in the eye.

"I give this to you because it is the key that will unlock the door between your past and your future. You are the only one who can fully open this door or keep it shut, as you so choose. Only promise me that you will not destroy the document in haste, before you have given the matter considerable thought."

Trenton looked away and nodded, "I promise."

Falconer studied the youth, "Trenton, regardless of what Cronin and Kleyton have told you for the past eighteen years, you have every right to walk through this door and embrace the truth."

Trenton kept his gaze locked on a distant tree until Falconer began to walk away.

"Come, we'll find a place to build a small fire and rest a while. I want to see the damage done to your hand."

As if to prove his defeat, Trenton's tongue finally relented and claimed the Arcrean language, "I lost the thumb."

Falconer turned to stare at him for a moment, "Truly?" When Trenton answered with a nod, Falconer walked back and quickly began to remove the linen, "How has it been treated?"

"I haven't seen it. Miji says he stitched it and applied a salve."

Falconer grunted, "If he treated your hand anything like he treated you, I highly doubt he did anything at all."

With the final fold of cloth, Falconer blocked Trenton's view of the injured limb. The informant's expression became grim and he glanced up.

Trenton winced, "He didn't stitch the wound?"

"No."

"Or apply a salve?"

Falconer shook his head, "We'll camp here. I have a tonic derived from a flower that grows in the Heartland."

"Rodney's tonic? Ulric's Rose?"

"Yes."

"I should have known."

In an overwhelmed daze, Trenton allowed Falconer to lead him to a fallen tree, and then accepted the informant's help in being lowered to sit with his back to the log. Falconer built a small fire and set his dagger to sterilize in the flames. For a bandage, he tore a strip from the hem of his cloak and found a stream where he washed the length of cloth. When the dagger was purified and the bandage had dried by the fire, Falconer knelt beside Trenton.

"I'll wrap it securely once I've removed the infection and applied the tonic. The wound may not require stitching after I've cauterized it. Are you ready?"

Trenton wiped the nervous sweat from his forehead and nodded, "Is that my sword you're wearing?"

Falconer grinned, "It is."

"And were you planning to return it to me?"

"Do you still consider yourself my enemy?"

Trenton's eyes darted from Falconer's red-hot dagger to his own hand, still hidden beneath the last folds of linen; "I'll answer that when you're done."

Falconer's brow lifted in amusement as he reached to remove the wrap from Trenton's hand. When his fingers touched the linen, however, he paused and glanced at the youth, "It would be a mercy to both of us if you lost consciousness about now."

"I haven't seen my hand yet…I want to see it."

Falconer tilted his head with the acknowledgement, "That just might do it."

"Then let's get it over with," Trenton gritted his teeth and waited for Falconer to remove the linen.

The sight of his thumbless hand, swollen with infection and discolored by neglect, did not render him unconscious as Falconer had hoped; but in another moment, the dagger was drawn from the flames and Trenton's body began to tremble with resistance. Falconer poised the red-hot dagger with its flat edge hovering just above the swollen area, and Trenton lifted his gaze to see that the informant was watching him…waiting. Trenton returned the other man's stare with widening eyes until the strain of expectation overwhelmed him. A blanket of heavy darkness rose to engulf his vision and Trenton knew that he was unconscious.

Chapter 26
* Acceptance *

When Trenton woke some time later, Falconer had him swallow several drops of Ulric's Rose, and an hour after that they started a slow trek toward the other side of the mountains, where Falconer's horse was being stabled. As they walked at Trenton's pace, Falconer told the story of Osgood's treachery nineteen years before. Trenton had no choice but to listen.

He learned that his mother's name was Adelaide.

He learned that he had a little sister—seven years old—whose name was Caroline.

Queen Aurenia's companion, the Lady Alice, was his elder sister.

His father, Eric, was currently serving in bondage on board the *Fate*, a Mizgalian vessel with a history of piratical deeds. Trenton was surprised that he had never heard of the ship.

With each step another fact was delivered and another question answered until finally Trenton walked with his head lowered and his left arm cradled tightly against his chest, as if he walked against a stiff wind or in pain. However, there was no wind on the thickly-forested slope, and the pain that crushed him was not physical…but it was just as crippling.

Every detail that Falconer gave him served to draw back, just a little, the curtain that had, unbeknownst to Trenton, shrouded his past. Within the Arcrean spy's narrative Trenton discovered a native world to which he was completely foreign; a family that missed him, but to whom he was a total stranger. There was an entire life that he had never lived; one that, on the contrary, he had been raised to destroy.

As Falconer finished repeating what he had heard and seen at Mockmor, Trenton finally collapsed. Dropping to his knees beneath the weight of an unknown identity, the young man roared at the ground before him, slowly doubling over until his forehead touched the earth and his bellowing was somewhat muffled by dirt, leaves, and moss.

Falconer kept a respectful distance and averted his eyes to study the route ahead. He would wait to tell Trenton that his mother and younger sister should be in the Heartland by the time they reached the natives' central encampment.

Trenton clutched at the fallen leaves beneath him and pounded his fist into the earth. He grimaced when the ache in his heart threatened to undo him. It was too much. To discover that one was everything he had thought he wasn't, and that he wasn't everything he'd thought he was, was excruciating.

He had thought he was a Mizgalian, when he was really an Arcrean—his own sworn enemy. He had thought he was strong, but now realized it had been an illusion—he had been trapped beneath Cronin's thumb all along.

He had thought that he had a father's love.

He had thought that he was on an important mission.

He had thought that he could gain the king's approval.

Death to the adversary! The words of Cronin's decree flashed across his memory and Trenton knew that this "adversary" was none other than himself.

"Trenton?" Falconer's voice sounded from above him, to his left.

"What?"

"Where are the men of Dragon Coast?"

Trenton slowly lifted his head. How could the man ask such a question at a time like this? He stared at Falconer for a long moment and finally realized that the informant's question held a twofold purpose. First, he knew Trenton's visit to the rebellious coast of Hugh would have been for nothing but trouble, and no matter what Trenton was going through now, Falconer's first priority was to look after the protection of Arcrea. Second, the informant would be able to judge by Trenton's answer whether the youth would continue to protect the secrets of Mizgalia or claim his duty as an Arcrean.

"They set sail for Dormay…" Trenton swallowed, trying to ignore the feeling that his words were betraying his life-purpose as a Mizgalian, "with a load of captured dragons on each ship's deck to attack the southern coast."

Falconer masked his shock well, but Trenton's quick eye caught the slight signs.

"We must return to the Heartland with all haste. I must warn the king."

In his shock, Trenton did not think to tell the man that Druet was in Dormay.

Falconer held out a hand to help Trenton to his feet, but the younger man shook his head, "Leave me, Falconer. I'll only create more work for you when you could be riding ahead; my hand will hinder me from being of any help. Besides that, Cronin will be sure to hear that I've survived and will send more assassins until I'm finally killed. Quite frankly, I'm hopeless."

Falconer gripped Trenton's arm and forced him to his feet, "Do you hear the words escaping your own mouth? I knew that you'd make more work for me even before I knew of your injury; and as far as Cronin goes, the only power he can have over you is that which you give him," he pulled the parchment from Trenton's vest and held it before the boy's nose, "That's what this is for. Forget what you were, Trenton, and look forward to what you could be." Falconer shoved the document back into Trenton's hand and then proceeded to lead him further up the mountain, "There is great work to be done. God is not finished with you yet."

Trenton remained silent. He wasn't sure what the Arcreans' God had to do with him, but he would save that question for later. His gaze dropped to the document in his hand and Trenton saw with new clarity the crossroads that he had come to.

He had a decision to make.

Would he destroy the parchment and forget everything—Mizgalia, Arcrea, Kleyton, and Eric? Could he create a new life for himself somewhere wholly unconnected with any and all of them? Or was he willing to accept this story as his own and use Cronin's document to prove to the people of Arcrea that he was Eric's long-lost son?

The thought nearly caused Trenton to miss a step. Falconer glanced his way, but Trenton kept his eyes forward and probed deeper into his thoughts.

Was he willing to be Eric's long-lost son?

Would Eric claim a maimed Mizgalian-raised youth as his only son? Trenton frowned. Would he even have a chance to meet Eric? Would he meet Adelaide and Caroline, still held captive in Mizgalia?

Trenton suddenly turned to study his silent companion. He calculated how long it would have taken the man to reach Mockmor from the Heartland and then travel to Dragon Coast. If his guess was correct, then there was a space of time that had elapsed that could not be accounted for by this route of travel. Which meant Falconer had gone somewhere else…

"Falconer."

"Yes?"

"Where are Adelaide and Caroline now?"

Falconer turned to look at Trenton, and then allowed the smallest of smiles over the younger informant's perception, "They should be in the Heartland by now."

ꙮ

Alice was ushered into the large tent that served as Druet's headquarters in the camp west of Dormay. Renny was standing beside her husband, reading from a parchment in his hand, but the king and queen both looked up when Alice entered, observing her with similar expressions of astonishment.

Alice dropped in a curtsy, "You sent for me, Sire?"

Druet looked at Renny and then nodded for her to explain.

"Alice, word has just come from the Heartland. You must return to Olden…"

"Is it my uncle? Has his condition grown worse?"

"No," Renny shook her head, "It says nothing of Osgood. It's your…"

The queen paused and Alice looked from one face to the other, "My what?"

The king and queen exchanged another glance and Druet finally answered, "It's your mother."

Chapter 27
* Reunion *

Falconer retrieved his horse and purchased another to replace the one that Trenton had been forced to leave behind at Dragon Coast. When Trenton revealed that he had also stolen and lost Queen Aurenia's bow, the informant cleared his throat and kept his trained features from breaking into a knowing grin, saying only that the queen would not be pleased.

Trenton said no more about his identity for three days, but Falconer could see that the boy's thoughts never wandered far from the truth behind his Arcrean heritage. The informant fell into the familiar pattern of silence and observation, allowing realization and acceptance to run their course in Trenton's mind. As a result, the journey east was a relatively quiet one.

When they did begin to speak to each other, Falconer was surprised to find that Trenton was more curious to hear about God than anything else. What had King Druet meant when he spoke of God working through him? What had Falconer meant when he said that God wasn't finished with Trenton? Why would the God of the universe care for Trenton enough to spare his life, not just once, but several times? Who was Jesus? One question led to another until Falconer had shared everything he knew on the subject, but still Trenton was not satisfied.

"Why did God let so many terrible things happen to my family?"

Falconer paused to mull over Trenton's use of the word "family."

Trenton shifted in his saddle, "Well…?"

Falconer studied the road ahead with a contemplative look, "Trenton, I won't pretend to understand why God has allowed so many of the things that He has, but I do have faith that He has a purpose for everything that He does or does not do."

Trenton quirked a brow in confusion and Falconer went on, "I did not know your father when he lived in Arcrea, but I heard that he was a good man. Perhaps, if he had stayed in Arcrea, he would have become king instead of Druet."

"Wouldn't that have been a good thing?"

Falconer studied his young companion, "Not when God intended the crown to be worn by another."

Trenton shifted his gaze forward and remained silent.

"It is possible that, had he become lord of his father's region, the six other noblemen would have come to hate his integrity and plot to kill him. Such an act would not have been beyond the former Lord Frederick's capabilities—in fact, it's very likely that I would have been the man sent to kill Eric," Falconer paused a moment, "Or perhaps, as lord, the power would have turned Eric's heart away from God, whereas the life that he has led instead has drawn him closer to his Savior—or so your mother told me."

Trenton started at the unfamiliar term. Mother. It sounded so strange when he knew that the word implied *his* mother.

Falconer continued, "Maybe God used your father to reach the lost souls of Mizgalia. Truly, I don't know, and we may never know, but you can rest assured that God does know, and that is what matters most."

Travel progressed swiftly on horseback. Falconer knew the land well and so made the trip shorter by his knowledge of the numerous shortcuts. Trenton was pleased when his sword was at last returned to his possession, but felt mortified when he realized he couldn't strap it on without assistance. His left hand was healing quickly, aided by the rose tonic, and the bandage was soon a thing of the past; however, with the ability to use his hand once again, there came the need to learn how to manage with only four fingers. Falconer helped as much as he could, but both men soon realized that the best way for Trenton to relearn how to use his hand was to force him to do things on his own, determining by trial and error what would be the easiest way to accomplish any task, from mounting a horse or wielding a sword, to pulling on his boots or tying a belt.

Many mistakes were made and frustration began to ferment in the younger man, but Falconer forced Trenton to shrug off the negative attempts and try again. On several occasions, when they had stopped for the night, the two travelers held mock duels to build up the strength that Trenton would need in fighting with most of his dependence resting on one arm. By the time they reached the western border of the Heartland, Trenton felt that he had gained some familiarity with his thumbless limb.

The month of March arrived with a warm breeze in tow and eager to shed the icy cloak of winter from the realm. As he studied the surrounding landscape, Trenton determined to let his thoughts settle along with the new season. He had thought through his life and come to realize that so many curious happenings, sayings, and behaviors that he had witnessed at Mockmor were easily explained by the story he had learned from Falconer.

At last, on the day they rode passed the building site of King Druet's castle, Eubank, Trenton knew for certain that God had reconciled him to the fact that he was no longer Trenton of Mockmor, nor had he ever been. He was, in truth, Eric of Brentwood II…called Trenton. He smiled to himself; he doubted that he could ever become accustomed to using his birth name.

They left Eubank behind and traveled in continued silence for some time before Trenton turned to Falconer with a serious expression, "I accept my Arcrean heritage and will return to live with my real family as Eric's son."

"I am pleased to hear you say so."

"I've also thought much about what you told me…about Jesus—His death, burial, and resurrection…"

"Yes?"

Trenton reined his horse to a stop and Falconer did the same.

"I believe it now—that Jesus died to redeem me from the penalty of death, dealt as a reward for my sins, and that His resurrection conquered death and provides a way for me to dwell with God for eternity. I want to become a Christian, Falconer…now—before we reach Olden Weld. Will you pray with me?"

Falconer could only stare in response until he cleared his throat in a rare show of emotion and finally found his voice, "I would be honored, young sir."

ꙮ

Adelaide and Caroline were being housed at Druet and Renny's cottage in Olden Weld until a more permanent place could be made available for them. The Heartland's chief elder, Leland, had mentioned that the council believed that as Castle Brentwood was still in Lady Alice's possession, Eric's wife would doubtless be allowed to return to live in her former home; however, it was decided that she should wait at Olden Weld until word had been received from the king.

One afternoon, two weeks after their arrival in the Heartland, Adelaide and Caroline had just finished eating the midday meal when the front door flew open and a breathless young woman appeared on the threshold. Honey-colored curls spilled over her shoulders, which rose and fell with the effort to breathe. The young woman's jaw dropped and her wide eyes of a singular blue stared at Adelaide and quickly filled with tears. She shook with a sob that refused to voice itself.

Adelaide recovered from her shock and placed a

trembling hand over her mouth, "Oh my," rising from the table she made her way to the front door, nearly stumbling across the room, and put her arms around the visitor whose feet would carry her no further.

"Oh, Alice," Adelaide sobbed. Mother and daughter sank to the floor in the tearful embrace that had been twenty years in coming, and Adelaide wiped tears from her daughter's face even as she cried her own, "How I have waited and prayed for this day to come!"

"Mother!"

"Mama!" A small voice called uncertainly from beyond Adelaide's shoulder, and Alice pulled away from her mother just enough to see a little girl staring at them with uncertainty. Alice's eyes grew wide when she saw that the child's appearance was a close replica of her own.

She turned to her mother, "I have a sister?"

Adelaide nodded and blinked tears from her eyes, "And a brother…"

Alice caught her breath when she remembered Renny's reaction to the painting, "Trenton?"

Adelaide shook her head, "No, his name is Eric—your father's namesake. He was taken away as a baby, and we never heard of him again."

Adelaide's eyes filled with fresh tears and Alice held her mother close, unable to fathom all that this woman had endured during her captivity. They moved to sit in the front room and included Caroline in their joyful reunion. The little girl quickly warmed to her older sister and illuminated the room with her smiles and laughter.

Alice told them of her life at Brentwood and of

joining Druet's quest the year before. Caroline responded by telling of the cottage in the Mizgalian shepherds' village and of the night when a stranger had burst through the front door to take them away. Adelaide smiled at the little girl's animated interpretation and explained the tale in further detail to a surprised Alice.

"Falconer went to Mizgalia?"

Adelaide nodded, pulling Caroline onto her lap and wrapping her fingers around Alice's hand, "Do you know him, Alice?"

Alice nodded, but could not answer further. What had called Druet's spy to Mizgalia on such short notice? And right after a visit to Balgo. Alice shook her head, pushing the jumbled thoughts away for later and determining to ask Falconer about Trenton as soon as the informant returned to the Heartland.

ꟃ

It was dark when the two travelers reached the outskirts of Olden Weld. Windows, opened to admit the early spring breeze, revealed candlelit cottages where mothers were tucking their children into bed or, in some cases, trying in vain to herd their brood to the loft. When they passed by old Marie's cottage Trenton searched for any sign of the granddaughter's presence, but the shutters had been drawn, the candles had been snuffed, and there was no sign of his provoking young friend.

He glanced at his companion.

Falconer had ridden the last few miles in silence. A sentry had informed them that King Druet was still in Dormay overseeing preparations for the navy, and

Falconer was now anxious to report news of the Dragon Coast fleet's advance. Knowing now that the king would not be at home, they rode a short distance beyond the royal cottage to the meetinghouse. A young boy emerged from the stables next door and took their horses.

"Wait here," Falconer stepped to the door and knocked, "I'll only be a moment. I need to report to Leland and, among other things, discover where your—"

The door opened and a councilman ushered the informant inside with an exclamation that sounded strongly of relief. The door was pushed closed again and Trenton leaned against the frame with his arms crossed, preparing to wait as Falconer had asked.

The road through the village was a picture of peaceful stillness. The stars were beginning to appear, like pinpricks in a giant velvet sky. A lone bird twittered its pleasure over the warmth of the night. The soft strains of a lullaby floated by on the gentle breeze.

Trenton froze.

He listened.

The first three notes of the melody echoed across the walls of his mind.

Every fiber of his being reacted to the tune—the voice—and before he could remind himself to wait for Falconer, his shoulder had pushed away from the door of its own accord and he found himself following the familiar song down the road. When he stopped, Trenton recognized the structure before him as the home of Arcrea's king and queen. An upper window had been left open, and it was from there that the woman's voice was drifting outside.

Trenton closed his eyes and listened.

It was the same voice he had heard in his dream after the dragon's attack, when he'd slept on Miji's boat. The voice he had been so sure was his mother's. He could still picture the shadow of her head bending over him to say goodnight, but the face was vague—blurred by the loss or lack of memory.

A servant answered the door and Trenton realized he'd knocked.

He heard his own voice asking for Lady Adelaide.

The servant studied him with an odd expression, blinked once, and then motioned him into the front room. He stepped through the door and the servant quickly disappeared up the stairs.

Still listening to the lullaby, Trenton let his eyes roam absently about. His gaze landed on a table at the other side of the room, where a canvas lay partially unrolled across the rough surface to reveal half of a painting. Driven by curiosity, Trenton approached the table and, lifting the canvas at arms' length, unrolled it the rest of the way.

Upstairs, the lullaby came to an abrupt halt.

Trenton's breath caught in his throat and he stared at the canvas in disbelief.

A copy of his own face stared back at him!

Trenton blinked and looked again. It wasn't his imagination—the image in the painting was a replica of his likeness. It was like staring into a mirror.

Behind him, a woman gasped and Trenton turned to see two ladies, one middle-aged and the other much younger, standing at the bottom of the stairs. The younger woman studied Trenton with eyes that matched his own in color and likeness, and

Trenton knew instinctively that this was Lady Alice, his elder sister.

Taking a shaky breath, Trenton shifted his startled gaze to the other woman.

The painted canvas dropped to the floor.

Trenton's jaw began to tremble and he quickly blinked to clear his suddenly blurry vision—he didn't want to lose sight of her for an instant. This was the woman who had sung him to sleep, who had bent over his cradle to say goodnight. This was the woman whose image and voice had remained fixed upon the farthest reaches of his memory.

This was his mother.

Adelaide's eyelids began to blink rapidly, in time to her breathing. Her hands trembled uncontrollably as she brought them to her face. Finally, a deep sob shook her entire frame and she sank to the floor in a wash of tears. Behind her, Alice too began to cry.

Trenton's feet carried him across the room and his knees bent so that he knelt before his mother. He wasn't sure what one was supposed to do for a crying woman. He glanced at Alice and watched as she lowered herself, sobbing, to sit on the bottom step. His gaze returned to his mother and, placing a hand on either side of her auburn and gray head, he gently tilted her face up and kissed her forehead.

Adelaide tried to smile through her tears. Lifting her own hands, she placed them over Trenton's larger ones and stuttered between sobs, "You're alive! My son, my son…I was so afraid they would kill you, but God answered a mother's prayers and spared you," reaching out, she wiped a tear from Trenton's face, "Oh, my sweet little Eric…" she swallowed, "you look just like your father."

"Trenton."

The two turned, equally surprised, when they heard Alice's correction. She managed a smile through her tears as she came to kneel beside them, and placing a hand on her brother's shoulder, repeated, "His name is Trenton."

Chapter 28
* The Fate's Discovery *

Captain Black lowered his spyglass and frowned into the sunset, "They must have spotted us by now," he growled, "the sun is at their backs and not a cloud mars the sky," he lifted the glass again and ran the small circle of magnified vision over the fleet lying immobile in the distance, "Why, then, do they sit there and do nothing?"

Black snapped the spyglass shut and turned to glare at the slave behind him, as if he had expected an answer to his question, "Well?"

Nathaniel swallowed the exasperated sigh that he wished to deliver and turned his attention to pronouncing the words in Mizgalian, "I wouldn't know, sir."

Captain Black frowned. Nathaniel studied the planks at his feet and prayed that he would make it through this day. The previous lackey had served Captain Black for two years, which, Nathaniel had been told, was an impressive amount of time for one of Black's attendants to survive. The day before, the unfortunate two-year-runner had spilled the captain's ale and tried to blame the slip on the rolling of the vessel. The young man had neither been seen nor heard of since and in the morning Nathaniel had been pulled from the slave ranks to wait on Black.

Nathaniel twitched his fingers behind his back, afraid to make any obvious movement.

Captain Black was not a man easily pleased. If Nathaniel spoke, Black thundered for him to remember his place, but if Nathaniel remained silent, the captain shouted for the slave to speak up. When Nathaniel brought him a mug of hot ale, Black fumed that it was too warm; when Nathaniel served it again, it was too cold.

Nathaniel lifted his eyes and studied the view over Black's shoulder. They were a day's sail southwest of the Arcrean region of Geoffrey. The mysterious fleet on the western horizon had remained motionless for as long as the *Fate* had been close enough to make out the seven ships, each set at some distance from the others.

"Perhaps…" Nathaniel paused when Black turned to glare at him.

"Speak up, slave, 'fore I take the lash to your back!"

Nathaniel swallowed. His back had seen more of the lash in two months than Eric's had in twenty years; it was a miracle he had any flesh left, "Perhaps they have heard of the *Fate*, captain, and know her to be a vessel of fierce renown. They may not wish to become entangled with you and are hoping you'll move on without engaging them in combat."

Black stared at Nathaniel for a moment and his

expression puckered, "Don't trifle with me, slave. They've seven ships to our one—they would be daft not to advance on us."

Nathaniel shrugged.

Black eyed him and leaned closer, speaking in a voice stained by old ale, "Your wheels are turning, boy, I can see your brain spinning thoughts like they were threads of gold," he tapped Nathaniel's head with a thick finger, "What's your gold, then?"

Nathaniel's gaze flickered momentarily to the seven ships, knowing that his words could bring their destruction, while his silence would surely bring his own. He decided to be vague, "It may be that the fleet is in some sort of trouble, sir."

Black swiveled his gaze to the west, "It stands to reason…" he brought the glass to his eye and leaned forward, as if being an inch closer would reveal in detail what lay ahead. A moment passed and he suddenly stood at attention and turned to the man at the helm as if he had just come across a stunning discovery, "This fleet looks to be in some sort of trouble, Master Gloom. Run our course full west and drop sail before the wind turns. We're running in for the attack!"

Black shouted to the slaves in the rigging and the sails immediately unfurled to swallow the breeze. Nathaniel glanced at Gloom; the helmsman, looking every bit the implication of his name, rolled his eyes as he threw his weight into turning the giant wheel. Captain Black swaggered to the other side of the deck and bellowed in a seaman's ear. When he turned to face Nathaniel again a blackened grin split his beard in two, and when he leaned close Nathaniel resisted the urge to take a step away from the man's foul smell.

"Keep your wheels spinning to my liking and I won't toss you to the fish."

Nathaniel's head lifted and a daring grin pulled at his mouth, "Ho, there, if you toss me to the fish, then my wheels will spin to their liking," he tilted his head to the right, "You'd be missing out on the gold then. What have I got to lose?"

Black's eyes twitched at the corners and he stared in surprise at the bold young seaman. His shoulders suddenly jerked in a humorous lift and he threw his head back in raucous laughter. When he had finished, Black stretched his arm and pointed at Nathaniel.

"You've a head on your shoulders, boy."

Nathaniel lifted his brows in consent, "That's where the wheels are spinning, sir."

Black laughed again, "You humor me, slave. Tell me, where did I pick you up?"

Nathaniel shifted at the painful memory, "Off the coast of Stephen, sir."

"Arcrean?"

Nathaniel nodded.

Black squinted to the west to check the *Fate's* progress, "How long ago?"

"Two months, sir."

The captain's gaze darted back to his slave, "Only two? Your knowledge of our language would suggest it had been longer."

"I spent my energy on learning the language to divert my thoughts from home, sir."

Black grunted and applied his spyglass to his eyes again, "You speak openly—more than is good for a slave, I'd wager. You mind what I told you, about keeping your thoughts to my liking and good use," the glass was snapped shut as the captain turned to Nathaniel, "Now run and fetch me a pint of ale from the galley. I'd favor a drop before we strike."

The strange fleet made no move to run or advance as the *Fate* crossed the waves in its direction. No movement was detected on any of the seven ships' decks. Black kept his spyglass employed until he finally made out a faded emblem on the sail of the foremost vessel.

"You, Arcrean," he growled for Nathaniel to take the glass, "tell me what you see there."

Nathaniel studied the fleet through Black's tool, "Ho, there, the bow and sails are decorated with the likenesses of…"

"Dragons."

Nathaniel nodded and returned the spyglass, "The Dragon Coast fleet."

It was the captain's turn to nod, "Strange. They are not a people fond of the boats. In all my years on the *Fate* I've only once come across one of their vessels, and that must have been some fifteen years ago."

The sun had set, but the sky had not yet grown dark when the *Fate* approached the first Dragon Coast vessel. No sign of life was evident. Suddenly, a cry was sent down from the lookout and a Mizgalian seaman scrambled from the rigging to approach Black, "Captain, the crew of the vessel has been spotted!"

"What are their positions?" Black turned to face the starboard rail, studying the foreign vessel as they came alongside.

The seaman shook his head, "They are scattered about the decks, sir…unconscious," Black turned to him with an incredulous glare, "or dead."

"It would explain their lack of movement all day."

"Ho, there, it may be the plague," Nathaniel offered.

"Silence, Arcrean!" Black stepped away to bellow at his crew, "Make ready the grappling irons! We board the vessel's starboard rail," he glanced at Nathaniel and then added, "only take care not to handle the foreigners—there may be sickness aboard!"

Everyone froze when Black's shouts were answered by a number of eerie shrieks from the Dragon Coast vessel. The sound resonated across the calm waters and was immediately echoed by the six other Dragon Coast ships. Nathaniel's breath caught sharply at the noise and he muttered under his breath.

Black spun on his heel and leaned closer, "What's that you say?"

Nathaniel's eyes were wide. He had heard similar shrieks before and there was no mistaking the source, "Dragons!"

Captain Black turned to stare in shock at the other vessel.

The Mizgalian who had descended from the lookout shot a nervous look in the same direction, "Captain…?"

Black turned an intense glare to Nathaniel, "You've battled these creatures before?"

"Once, sir."

"How many?"

"Three, sir."

Black's brow shot upward, "Were you alone?"

Nathaniel shook his head, sending his long-unkempt hair into further disarray, "There were six of us engaged against them, sir."

"Two to one," Black muttered, shifting his gaze as another shriek shattered the still evening air, "What was the outcome, Arcrean?"

Nathaniel cast a swift glance at the lookout; both men were fairly certain of what lay ahead for them this night, "The three dragons fell dead, sir, and none of my comrades were killed."

"Cast the irons!"

A tentative silence gripped the crew—Mizgalians and slaves alike—as the grappling irons were thrown across and the two vessels became lashed together. Each man glanced at his neighbor as he hesitantly performed his part. The same thought was evident in each wide-eyed expression: It was one thing to attack a shipload of sailors and then take their fill of slaves and looted cargo, but it was quite another matter to attack a vessel carrying an unknown number of angry dragons.

From the safety of the *Fate's* quarter-deck Black's dark gaze roamed the opposite vessel, settling momentarily on the bodies of the Dragon Coast sailors where they lay prone, having collapsed haphazardly in the midst of performing various tasks. Four crates of enormous size dominated the main deck, and it was from within these that the sound of shrieking was coming.

Nathaniel stood several paces behind the captain, also eyeing the rebel clan's ship. The dragons were obviously secured within the crates, and if they hadn't escaped before now, it was very probable the creatures would provide no trouble at all for Black's men. What alarmed Nathaniel was the deathly stillness of the humans. There were no signs that the

Dragon Coast fleet had been attacked before the *Fate's* arrival—the decks were unmarred by the scars of combat, there was no blood—the clansmen looked as if they'd simply dropped in place. If they carried the plague, then Black's entire ship was in danger of contamination and death. If the sickness had not been the cause of their condition, then what had been?

"Captain Black?" a Mizgalian sailor in Black's favor climbed the steps to the quarter-deck, "What are your orders, sir?"

Black turned and brought a thoughtful expression to rest on Nathaniel, "Send the Arcrean across to scout the territory," another shriek interrupted him and he paused to let the dragon's rage die down, "If all is well, we board and loot the vessel. If there's trouble or sickness aboard, we cut the irons and be on our way."

The Mizgalian gave a sharp salute and passed word of the captain's decision along the ranks. Nathaniel glanced up into the rigging and saw Eric's face turn ashen when the news reached him. The two exchanged a solemn look before Nathaniel's attention was grabbed by Captain Black's sudden grip on his right arm.

"There's something afoot, Arcrean," his voice was low and Nathaniel was once again accosted by the stench of ale on the man's breath, "Dragon Coast clansmen do not simply sail from the safety of their encampment on a pleasure-cruise, with four dragons to a deck," his eyes darted to survey the positions of the other six vessels, "It may be a trap, but I have strong feelings against the idea. Use those brains of yours and bring me word of what's happened over there."

As he spoke, Black led Nathaniel to the railing and prepared to send him across, his fingers digging into the number branded below the slave's shoulder. When they reached the railing, a number of sailors stood in a semicircle around them, waiting to watch the event unfold. Black paused and grabbed Nathaniel's chin, gruffly jerking the slave's face around.

"No tricks, Arcrean," he growled, "The archers will know my signal to kill the moment you act against orders, and you know by now that they never miss their target."

Nathaniel had barely enough time to nod his understanding before he was all but shoved across to the Dragon Coast vessel's forecastle deck.

"One thing more," Black called and Nathaniel turned to face him, "If they carry the sickness…don't come back across."

Nathaniel nodded again as he turned away. The fear that he would die of the plague, alone on a Dragon Coast ship, set his heart to pounding.

"God, help me," he breathed, and took a step away from the railing. A moment of elation quickly filled him when he thought that this was the first time in two months that he'd left the Mizgalian *Fate*. The temptation to call out that sickness was indeed aboard, sending the *Fate* away and providing him an opportunity to strike out for land on his own, was strong; but the thought of leaving Eric behind on the pirate ship was enough to squelch the idea before it had fully formed. Nathaniel smiled to himself. Even if he had cared nothing about Eric's outcome, he doubted he could bring his honest soul to declare such an outright lie…if it was a lie.

Cautiously, Nathaniel approached a clansman who had collapsed beside the foremast. Glancing about, he caught sight of a spear that had obviously rolled out of the fallen man's grasp. Retrieving the spear, Nathaniel glanced to ensure that the *Fate's* archers didn't consider his movements treasonous. Deciding he was safe, he returned to stand several feet away from the motionless clansman and then used the spear shaft to roll the man onto his back.

The man's skin was covered in the painted signs and pictures that Nathaniel remembered seeing when he, Druet, Talon, and Bracy, had gone to rescue Renny from becoming the clan's next sacrifice. The paint was fairly new, meaning it had been refreshed within the past few days. The man's body looked gaunt, suggesting a lack of food. He had been lying here for some time.

Nathaniel jumped when the man's chest suddenly rose and fell in a shallow breath.

He was alive!

"Ho, there," Nathaniel poked the man with the spear shaft, but there was no reply. He studied the man's face and then bent for a closer look. His eyes squinted in the growing darkness, and a moment later he retreated to the railing,

"Captain Black, I need a light."

Black eyed him warily, nevertheless, he called to one of the Mizgalian crewmembers, "Raven, take a torch and accompany the Arcrean."

Raven's face blanched at the prospect, but he quickly leapt to obey and was soon standing beside Nathaniel on the Dragon Coast vessel's deck, torch in hand. Nathaniel returned to stand over the fallen clansman and Raven followed.

"He's alive," Nathaniel spoke the Mizgalian words in a hushed tone, "but there's something on his face."

Raven gave him an odd look and then lifted the torch to cast the sphere of light over the clansman. Nathaniel squatted and stared wide-eyed at the man's face. Quickly jumping to his feet again, he made his way across the forecastle deck, down the steps, across the main deck, and onto the quarter-deck. Raven followed close behind as Nathaniel examined one clansman after another, and soon the two men stood side-by-side on the quarter-deck, looking down on a particularly tall clansman.

"The clan's chief," Nathaniel muttered.

He bent to look at the chief's face. As with all the others, the man's face was coated in a powdery white substance.

"What is it?" Raven asked anxiously, obviously fearful that he was witnessing results of the plague.

"Wait here, mate," Nathaniel found a bucket by the portside railing and quickly tied a length of rope around the handle. Tossing the bucket overboard, he allowed the rope to slacken in the water a moment before hauling the full bucket up again. Crossing back to the chief, Nathaniel swung the bucket at an angle and dumped the water on the man's face. The chief shuddered at the icy impact and then took a deep breath, moaning.

"Follow me," Nathaniel motioned to Raven and then returned to the main deck. When he headed for one of the giant crates, Raven froze behind him.

"What are you doing?"

A loud shriek cut off any response Nathaniel might have made, so he remained silent as he studied the nearest crate, running a hand over its rough side. At last he found what he was looking for.

"Raven, I need the light over here."

The Mizgalian's eyes widened and he shook his head; "I'm not coming any closer to those monsters."

"Ho, there, Captain Black sent us over here. Either you bring the light, or you answer to him when you don't."

Raven took several steps closer and Nathaniel turned to the crate. When the torch's light reached the giant box he held his hand up for Raven to stop, "Stay there."

Nathaniel kicked the base of the crate and the dragon inside began to hiss.

"Don't do that!" Raven shouted as he jumped back.

"Stop moving away," Nathaniel called back, "I need the light."

"What are you doing?"

Using his fists, Nathaniel began to beat the side of the crate with relentless force. Inside, the dragon hissed, scratched, shrieked, and finally snorted through the small breathing-hole that Nathaniel had located. Hearing the snort, Nathaniel froze and stared at the small opening until, sure enough, a fine white powder escaped through the hole like a dusty-looking cloud. The three other dragons were exhibiting a show of wrath in protest of their fellow-creature's torture, but Nathaniel ignored the sounds as he watched the white powder fall to coat the deck at his feet.

Nathaniel turned and crossed to stand before Raven. Lifting his voice, he shouted over the noise of the crated dragons, "We need to see to the chief—he should be regaining consciousness about now—and then we'll inform Captain Black that there is no sickness aboard...just Death Chalk."

Chapter 29
* Retrieving a Friend *

Trenton stood across the road from Marie's cottage and swallowed the lump that had formed in his throat. The snatches of songs and laughter coming from within informed him that both occupants were at home. Now all he needed to do was overcome the strange, unwelcome, and utterly unfamiliar case of nerves that had first assailed him the moment elder Leland had told him who had been given charge of Link.

His ridiculous bird had refused to part from Leyla.

Leland's son, Kellen, had taken one look at Trenton's expression of dismayed disbelief and laughed outright, "You don't have to look so scared, Trenton."

Trenton blinked—scared was right! Leyla was smart. He had no doubt that she would have put two and two together by now, and realized that he had used her confidential words of Dragon Coast for his own purposes. He also had the uncanny suspicion that she would make his deception as a Mizgalian spy sound as if it had been a personal offense against her.

Trenton swallowed again. His frightfully limited experience with friendships and socializing in general left him clueless regarding how to face an angry female.

An angry female catawyld? Conquered.

An outraged female dragon? Defeated.

A young woman who might pin him to the wall with green-eyed fury? Out of the question.

Trenton ran a hand through his neatly trimmed hair and gently pulled at the neckline of the new tunic his mother had made for him, to replace the one devastated by his exploits at Dragon Coast.

The sound of a throat being cleared to the left brought Trenton's gaze around to where Kellen was walking two horses down the road.

"You have to knock on the door before they know to answer it, Trenton."

"I know that."

Kellen flashed his singular grin, "And you have to cross the street to knock on the door."

"I know, Kellen."

"You want me to go with—"

"No!"

"Hurry along then, friend, we're to follow Falconer to Dormay as soon as you've spent the morning with your family and retrieved your bird from Marie's granddaughter."

Trenton nodded, swallowed, and forced his feet to move across the road. His mother and sisters had treated him like a prince all morning, refusing to leave his side and ensuring that he lacked no comfort that was in their power to give. Little Caroline had roused him at an early hour by setting her face within an inch of his and tickling his nose with a golden curl. She had remained his steadfast companion through the following hours and the midday meal. He hadn't known what to do with someone that small, but she had seemed content to simply stare at the young man who looked like her father and prove to him that, yes, she could touch her small pink tongue to her nose, could he?

Trenton reached the door. He was going to miss his newfound family while he was away at Dormay, but it was possible that his knowledge of Kleyton's strengths, Mizgalia's armies, and the Dragon Coast plans, would assist King Druet in forming a scheme that would overturn the enemy. Falconer had said that Druet would also consider possible ways to track down and free his father, Eric, from the *Fate*. The council at Olden Weld had requested that Trenton present himself to the king at Dormay. Kellen would accompany him as the council's representative.

Trenton knocked with his gloved right hand and glanced at his left; his mother had tenderly cradled the maimed limb and quietly commented on the irony of which appendage had been lost. "Thumb" was the name given to Eric during his times of servitude on the Mizgalian vessel.

The door flew open and Trenton caught a glimpse of the most brilliant smile he'd ever seen before it suddenly vanished, quickly replaced by the blankest look he'd ever seen.

"Who is it, Leyla?" Marie's voice called from across the one-room interior.

The door slammed shut.

Trenton stood on the front stoop and shook his head. He still couldn't believe the girl had figured out that his signal for Link was the first three notes of "Clouds o'er an Arcrean Sea" when he himself hadn't even known the song!

"Leyla!"

Marie's exclamation sounded muffled through the barrier that had been rudely closed in Trenton's face, and he smiled at the absolute horror conveyed by the single word. One thing was certain: The door slamming had somehow swept away all fears he'd had over this meeting.

The door slowly opened again and Trenton tried to wipe the grin from his face as Leyla graced him with a single glance and muttered, "Come in."

Trenton stepped across the threshold, "It's a pleasure to see you, too."

Leyla gave the door a shove and turned away without waiting to see that it shut. Marie smiled at the guest from where she sat at the table.

"You'll have to forgive my rudeness in not rising to greet you, my boy," she waved him over to take the stool cattycorner to her own, "My old joints have been aching these last few weeks."

"No need to apol'gize, Gran'mother," Leyla stirred the contents of a wooden bowl, making no attempt to lower her voice, "if anyone 'as reason to speak their regrets for rude be'avior, then it's Master Impolite 'ere 'imself."

"Hush, Leyla."

Leyla cast a hateful glare at Trenton that would have frozen his heart with terror had he not wanted to laugh. The last time he had seen her, Leyla had been ready to poke fun at him and he had wanted her to leave. Clearly, the tide had turned.

He glanced at the bowl, "What are you making?"

"None o' your business, *Mizgal'yin*."

"Leyla, child!"

Trenton ignored the emphasis on his past and quirked his brow in amusement. He knew that word of his identity was spreading through the Heartland and beyond like wildfire, and everyone was becoming aware that the family of Brentwood was slowly being reunited. However, not all had heard of Trenton's being raised by Sir Kleyton under false pretenses, and therefore, most could not explain his initial appearance as a Mizgalian in their midst.

Trenton's gaze fell to the table and he noticed that it was covered with leaves, small clay jars, mortar and pestle… He looked up in surprise, "Are you a healer?"

Leyla huffed at an auburn curl that had escaped the new ribbon in her hair.

Marie rolled her eyes and offered Trenton an apologetic smile, "It would seem that she has taken lessons from Master Impolite."

Leyla's head jerked up at the reprimand. She studied Marie's stern expression and finally answered their guest, "I'm not exactly an 'ealer, but Rodney an' Sarah are teachin' me to be a midwife."

"Rodney is teaching you?" Trenton glanced at the table's scattered contents and thought the old healer must be the most patient man on the face of the earth.

Leyla could obviously read his thoughts, as she tilted her head and offered a painfully sweet smile, "When did you say you were leavin'?"

Suddenly the door burst open, slamming against

the wall and revealing Humphrey the goat with his two front hooves across the threshold and a look of victory on his bug-eyed face. His mouth dropped open in a noisy bleat that sounded like an odd laugh and the three at the table could only sit and stare at him in shock.

The moment quickly passed.

Humphrey darted forward into the small cottage and bedlam reigned as Trenton and Leyla jumped to catch him.

"Why'd you leave the door open?"

"Humphrey, out!"

"I didn't leave it open! You didn't close it!"

"Humphrey, *out!*"

"Close it now so 'e don't escape!"

"No, let him go or he'll tear the cottage to pieces!"

"Humphrey, behave yourself!"

"Quick, Gran'mother, put the jars in the bag before 'e knocks 'em off the table!"

Humphrey ran in circles around the one room. Trenton grabbed for the goat's legs and would have caught the animal if he'd not been without one thumb. Leyla herded the ornery critter from behind the table and tried to grab it, but failed. Humphrey scampered across the room, toppling two stools and sending a cauldron rolling. The goat bleated again, nearly tripping Leyla before turning suddenly and sending Trenton toppling onto the bed in the corner.

"Trenton, the blanket!"

Trenton scrambled to his feet and grabbed the quilt from the bed. He turned just as Humphrey rounded the table again and before he could think twice, dove to the floor with the coverlet stretched over the goat like a net. Leyla immediately dropped to her knees and reached beneath the blanket to secure a loop of rope around Humphrey's neck. When the rope was secure, Trenton removed his weight from the animal's back and lifted the blanket. Humphrey sat with his legs curled beneath him, staring at the floor as if nothing had happened.

Trenton swallowed against his heavy breathing and turned to look at Leyla. Her hair was in complete disarray and her green dress had turned a dusty shade of brown thanks to the dirt floor, but her smile had returned. The two looked from the goat to each other; a slow smile spread across Trenton's face and they suddenly began to laugh.

Marie sat at the table with her arms thrown in helpless protection about Leyla's herbs and clay jars. She looked at the two laughing young people and shook her head, "Well, I'm glad to know someone besides Humphrey enjoyed this outrage."

Leyla fell back in another fit of giggles and wiped tears of mirth from her eyes, keeping a tight hold on Humphrey's lead rope. Trenton stood and offered Leyla a hand up; she accepted the help and then handed Trenton the rope so she could dust herself off.

Marie shook out a sack and began placing the jars inside it, "Leyla, take Humphrey out to his pen and give Trenton back his bird."

Leyla paused and looked up at Trenton, "Is that why you're 'ere? To get th' 'awk?"

Trenton nodded, "Kellen and I are leaving for Dormay this afternoon, and Falconer suggested that I relieve you of your care of Link before I go."

Leyla wrinkled her nose, "Link?"

"The hawk."

"Oh," she pulled the ribbon from her hair and retied the mass at the nape of her neck. Quirking one brow, she righted the two stools and then headed for the door, "An' 'ere I thought you'd come to wish me an 'appy birthday."

"Is it your birthday?" Trenton asked, but she had already disappeared outside. Thanking Marie for her hospitality, Trenton wrapped Humphrey's rope around his wrist and followed.

Behind the cottage, Leyla poured a pail of fresh water into a shallow wooden drum inside the goat's pen and then moved to stand in readiness by the open gate. When Trenton finally managed to shove the goat inside, Leyla pushed the gate shut and secured the latch.

"That'll keep 'im in."

"Uh huh," Trenton nodded sarcastically, "for five minutes."

Leyla smiled and moved to a cage that had been built for Trenton's bird. Opening the door, she held out a wrapped arm and whistled the three notes that had only recently come to make sense in Trenton's mind. Link lifted from a perch within the cage and settled on Leyla's arm, giving Trenton an alert look with one eye.

Trenton watched, "Is it your birthday, Leyla?"

She grinned, "Maybe."

"How old are you now?"

She stroked Link with two fingers and tsked her tongue at Trenton, "It's not polite to ask a girl 'ow old she is."

Link spread his wings and when Trenton whistled the signal, the hawk found a contented perch on

Trenton's arm and screeched happily.

"Thank you for taking care of him while I was gone."

Leyla crossed her arms as the frustration of earlier returned to her gaze, "You should 'ave been 'ere to care for 'im yourself."

"I wasn't expecting him to come back, that was Falconer's doing."

"Exactly!" Leyla swung her arms out in exasperation, "You sent 'im ahead of you—you were plannin' on goin' back to Mizgal'ya without tellin' anyone!"

Trenton stared at her, "Leyla, I thought I was a Mizgalian spy. I thought I had a mission to complete."

"You said you were an 'scaped slave. You lied t' me!"

"I lied to everyone!" Trenton calmed Link when the bird dipped its head nervously, "Is that why you were mad at me inside?"

"I thought you were my friend."

"I wasn't," her mouth dropped open in shock and Trenton quickly corrected his words, "I will be now, but I wasn't then. I've always been trained not to keep friends. I didn't want friends. I was sent here to ruin your life—I wasn't going to become acquainted with you first!"

Trenton sent Link into the air and the bird flew in circles overhead before setting out to hunt for food. Leyla watched the hawk with a sullen expression. Trenton studied the glove on his left hand and finally broke the silence.

"I lost my thumb to a dragon."

Leyla's gaze darted to return his, "You did?"

He nodded.

"Can I see?"

He removed the glove and held out his hand. Leyla took a step closer and studied the spot where Falconer had cauterized the wound.

"I'm sorry. I should never 'ave tol' you about Drag'n Coast."

"This wasn't your fault, Leyla. I'm the one who decided to go," Trenton slipped his hand back into the glove and glanced at her, "God has given me a change of heart. I'm sorry now that I lied to everyone. I'm sorry that I used your confidence to further my own faulty plans; it wasn't an honorable thing to do. I understand—"

"No, you don't," Leyla shook her head as tears spilled from her eyes, "You don't un'erstand."

Trenton froze in alarm—more tears! First his mother and sister, and now Leyla. Here, where the crying began, he was at a complete loss regarding what he was supposed to do. He scratched his head, praying that Marie would experience a miraculous healing in her joints and come running around the corner to help him out. He turned back to Leyla and cleared his throat, "I don't understand…what?"

Leyla stepped up to him and jabbed a defiant finger in his face, "I 'ate lying!"

Trenton's eyes went wide and he took a step back from the condemning finger, "Leyla, I told you I'm sorry."

She ignored him, "Ever' week 'e went out to earn 'is pay, an' ever' week 'e came back an' lied 'bout 'ow much 'e made an' 'ow 'e made it."

Trenton could only stare at her in confusion as her thickly accented words slowly sank into his comprehension, "Who?"

"My father," Leyla shook with a sob and continued, "'E secretly worked as a spy for the clan at Knavesmire in Ranulf, an' also for the clans of Osgood. 'E was sellin' 'em secrets of our own region of Hugh, while 'e tol' Mother and I that 'e was workin' as a fisherman. We knew somethin' was amiss, but couldn' figure what—Father lied to us 'bout most ever'thin'. Once 'e 'ad saved enough money from 'is spyin', 'e up an' left us to live at Knavesmire, only 'e never made it there. A clan from Osgood 'eard of the doublecrossin' and killed 'im before 'e reached the border of Ranulf," Leyla wiped her eyes with the back of her hand and looked up at a stunned Trenton, "I loved my father," she shook her head, "but I couldn' trust 'im."

Trenton's jaw worked back and forth as he searched for a reply.

"I'm sorry about your father. I do understand, Leyla. I've been lied to about everything my entire life by the man who I thought was my father…but even that was a lie. I was told I was the Mizgalian son of Cronin's first knight, and trained to believe that I would be honored to bring about Arcrea's downfall. I know now that I was mistaken, and I pray that the people of Arcrea will give me a second chance as God has done. I'd be honored to know, before I leave for Dormay, that at least you will," Trenton unceremoniously plunked his finger under Leyla's chin to make her look up, "Will you give me another chance to be your friend?"

Leyla's chin quivered and she took a shaky breath. Link reappeared and settled on Trenton's shoulder. Leyla watched the hawk for a moment and then shifted her tearful gaze back to Trenton's earnest one. Slowly, her head rose and fell in a nod.

The two suddenly turned when Marie rounded the corner of the cottage with an excited cry, "Leyla, wonderful news! I tried the tonic you've been mixing and my joints feel wonderful!"

Chapter 30
* Discussion *

The overseer fastened Nathaniel's chains and shoved the slave to the floor of the hold, "Sweet dreams," the man's derisive laugh trailed away through the darkness as he climbed the rickety stairs to the main deck, and a moment later the hatch was slammed into place and locked for the night. A collective groan of temporary relief echoed across the hold as each slave anticipated several hours' rest without the slave driver watching their backs.

Nathaniel leaned his head back against the bowed wall and listened as the scraping of chains against the floor beside him announced Eric's proximity.

"What happened over there?"

Nathaniel didn't need to ask what the whispered question was about. He turned away from the moaning slave to his left and whispered in reply, "The clansmen were all affected by the Death Chalk. No doubt, the chalk became airborne in the high winds. It does not kill, though, unless the victim is left unattended for too long—the dragons use it to debilitate their prey until they are prepared to kill it themselves."

"The men of Dragon Coast were not dead then?"

"They were not. The chalk disintegrates when washed under water. Black's crew revived the clansmen on all seven ships and are keeping them as prisoners in the hold of their first vessel."

"What of the dragons?"

"Four to a vessel, mate, twenty-eight in all. The chief's interpreter was forced to explain their motives and I, in turn, translated the Arcrean's words to Captain Black," Nathaniel leaned closer and lowered his voice even more, "They were planning to release the dragons off the coast of Geoffrey, at Dormay."

"No!"

Nathaniel nodded in the dark and ran a hand over his face, "It was a Mizgalian spy who suggested the plan."

"Is he with them now?"

"No…he was sacrificed."

There was a pause, and then, "You can't be serious."

"That is what the interpreter told me. Because Mizgalia supported their plans, Black will not consider the clansmen as slaves just yet, but because they murdered Mizgalia's representative, they will be held as prisoners. The dragons on one of the faster vessels were transported to another, and the relieved ship has been sent after Sir Kleyton to ask his opinion on the matter; only he's bound to have returned to Mizgalia by now, in which case they'll consult with Cronin."

Eric sighed, "I prayed for you when I heard that Black was sending you across to determine whether or not the fleet carried the plague."

"Thank you, Thumb."

"You seem to have gained Black's favor. That may work to your advantage."

Nathaniel grunted, "His favor does not come at an easy price, mate," he gingerly fingered the new bruise on his face, "Never before have I walked through a day with so much trepidation over my next step. I shouldn't be surprised if I wake tomorrow to find that my hair has grayed with all the stress."

Eric chuckled wearily, "I've often wished that I could spare the captain's attendants by serving Black myself; he may punish me in any way he likes, but he has been ordered by Cronin not to kill me as he has the others before."

The two fell silent for a moment and Nathaniel listened to the even breathing of those around them, "Thumb, do you think Cronin and Kleyton will order Black to complete the Dragon Coast Clan's mission at Dormay?"

"It is possible. Kleyton is sure to be aware that the southern regions of Arcrea are not as experienced in battle as those in the north. Such an attack on Geoffrey's largest port city would be disastrous."

There was another pause as each man fell to his own thoughts.

Nathaniel leaned his head back, "You realize, mate, if the *Fate* sails into battle at Dormay…"

"We may have a chance to make use of the chaos and escape to shore," Eric finished the younger man's thought and the two stared at each other through the thick black of the hold.

The sweet taste of freedom was so close, Nathaniel was sure he felt its flavor on his tongue.

ꙮ

Falconer stood at attention outside the Sailor's Tailor. The captains of the new Arcrean Navy had come to collect the inventory of uniforms for the sailors on each vessel. King Druet stood in the doorway, helping Peter to find the crate designated for each captain before handing it over with a satisfied smile. Queen Aurenia watched from the shop's front window; after a busy morning of service alongside her husband, Druet had finally convinced her to take a much-needed rest.

Captain Hull shouted orders along the harbor-front street as if he were on board a vessel of his own. Falconer watched the man with well-hidden amusement and thought that Hull was much like his father had been.

A crash sounded inside the shop, accompanied by several dismayed feminine voices. Falconer didn't need to look to know that Brigit had spilled the queen's tea; standing to his right, Bracy breathed an intolerant sigh and muttered something about the young woman's hopelessness.

Peter's elder daughter, Anne, approached with a pail of fresh water and a dipper, and Falconer accepted the offered drink with quiet thanks. His first impression of the young woman with sun-washed brown hair and an easy smile had been that she closely resembled her older brother, Nathaniel. The differences between the two siblings were in their eye color and their demeanors—where the seaman was

Anne

outgoing and bold, Anne was shy and quiet. Brigit, while favoring neither brother nor sister in looks, favored Nathaniel in demeanor…by far.

The sound of a horse approaching drew Falconer's attention from the busy street to search for the returning courier. Talon directed his horse through the crowd and dismounted before his superior.

"Kellen and Trenton have arrived in camp and are resting after their journey. They should be ready to present themselves by time the king has finished here and returns to the tents."

Falconer nodded, "Very good."

Bracy finished taking a swallow from Anne's ladle and then poured the rest of the water onto Talon's head.

"Bracy!"

Bracy's expression was one of innocence, "I thought you may need a little refreshment after your ride."

"I'd rather drink it," Talon took the replenished dipper and drank most of the contents before flipping the remnants into Bracy's face and offering the ladle back to Anne.

Bracy sputtered and wiped his face, "Talon!"

"I thought you may need to be refreshed after standing here in the sun all day."

Talon gave Anne an uncharacteristically bashful grin and then led his horse to fresh water. He tethered the animal nearby before returning to take his place at Falconer's left side.

The informant shook his head and continued to stare forward, "I marvel that Druet had the patience to tolerate you two for several months worth of travel…and more still that he lived through the ordeal."

Several hours later, when Druet had inspected the liveried naval ranks and praised the men for their steadfastness in preparing for their appointments at sea, the king and his party returned to the camp west of Dormay. As they drew nearer, Falconer spotted Link floating in circles above the meadow; lowering his gaze from there, he quickly located Trenton and Kellen standing together and watching the bird. They turned as the entourage rode up and Trenton signaled for Link to land. The hawk quickly dipped to perch on the boy's shoulder and Trenton secured the bird's leg to a T-shaped perch.

Druet dismounted and then moved to help Renny do the same. When he turned to approach the two younger men, they each knelt on one knee.

"You may rise," Druet smiled and clasped Kellen's hand before turning to Trenton while Renny greeted her brother, "Welcome to Dormay, Trenton."

Trenton dipped his head, "Thank you, Sire. You are gracious to give me audience after all I've done to create trouble for you."

Druet lifted a hand, "All is forgiven. God works in mysterious ways that we do not always understand. If you had not been sent as a spy into our midst, then you would never have discovered your true identity."

Trenton nodded his head again and then shifted his gaze to the queen and cleared his throat, "I ask your pardon for the theft and loss of your bow."

Renny closed her eyes and took a deep breath at the word "loss" and Druet massaged the corners ofhis mouth to keep from grinning at her attempt to remain calm. Finally, she opened her eyes and smiled graciously at the young man.

"You are forgiven, Trenton. I'm glad that you have been returned to Arcrea. I will make another bow."

Several servants approached to lead the horses away and Druet motioned for Kellen, Trenton, and Falconer to follow him into a large central tent furnished with table, chairs, scrolls, and maps.

"Come in, good sirs. We have much to discuss."

While the men seated themselves and were served hot cider, Druet talked of his budding plans to build churches in all seven regions and to appoint men of God to preach the gospel. He spoke of the need to subdue the restless clans of Ranulf, Osgood, and Quinton—highlanders who were eager to renew their mainstay habits of mischief-making. He described the events that had taken place during his weeks in Geoffrey's port city.

"My stay in Dormay has extended longer than I thought it would. Trade has all but come to a halt, what with a mysterious vessel attacking at whim and off all points of our borders. I've come to suspect that this ship and the *Fate*, which Falconer has spoken of, are one and the same."

"It would stand to reason, Sire," Falconer nodded and took a long drink from his mug.

"With the navy prepared to set sail, I would have made ready to return to the Heartland within a day or two had you not brought me word of the Dragon Coast fleet's advance. Now I feel that I should stay and see that Dormay is readied for battle."

"Druet…Sire," Kellen sat forward in his chair, "If the clan of Dragon Coast attacks Dormay, how will you bring justice on their heads without the people murmuring that you have forsaken your duty as defender of the heart of Arcrea? After all, the clansmen are Arcrean subjects—members of the heart."

Druet studied the contents of his mug for a moment and then looked up at his brother-in-law, "Kellen, when a heart turns rebellious it becomes necessary to overthrow the unrest without crushing the heart itself if possible. However, if a sinful heart will not be subdued, then it must be crushed in order for God to make it new again."

Trenton tapped his one thumb on the other wrist, "Further still, the clansmen of Dragon Coast do not consider themselves to be under King Druet's protection. They regard the sun, dragons, and other idols, as their masters. They will not think twice of injuring the true heart of Arcrea, and those who would fall victim to them must be free to defend themselves."

Druet lifted his mug, "Well spoken. This reminds me of the discussions on politics and God's divine plan that I used to hold with my father in his smith at Oak's Branch," the young king set his mug aside and reached for a fresh parchment, quill-pen, and inkwell, "Now then…Trenton. I have been informed that you went to Dragon Coast as an ambassador of Mizgalia."

"Cronin did not send me to that clan in particular, I was told to present myself to you and infiltrate your system of rule. I decided to go to Dragon Coast on my own, knowing—or rather, believing—that my actions would be supported by the Mizgalian crown."

"What he did not know," Falconer added, "was that Cronin never intended for Trenton to make it beyond the Arcrean border. Cronin planned to have Trenton killed so that he might blame the unnecessary death of a Mizgalian on the people of Arcrea, and so create war."

Druet nodded and made a note on the parchment. He turned to Trenton, "So you went to Dragon Coast not knowing that you had ruined Cronin's plans for war, but with intentions of helping him start one on your own."

Trenton nodded and Kellen glanced at Falconer with a grin, "Helpful chap, isn't he?"

Falconer turned to the king, "Sire, the Arcrean Navy would doubtless be able to overcome the fleet from Dragon Coast. Archers in the rigging would be able to down any dragons that were released from the clan's vessels. Our problems will now arise in the form of Miji the trader."

"The round fellow who delivered Trenton to the assassins?"

"The same. He was gone before I fell upon Thomas and Delaney, and I am certain he will send word to Cronin that Trenton is dead. When Cronin believes this to be true, then he will have cause to overwhelm our northern borders in concentrated war."

Druet sat back in his chair and steepled his fingers before his mouth, "Trenton, you have a great advantage over the rest of us in that you possess firsthand knowledge of Mizgalia's strengths, weaknesses, and desires. You have even been in the close company of her rulers. I ask you, as a citizen of Arcrea; please tell us anything you think we should know."

Trenton studied each face—the acclaimed king

of Arcrea, the king's chief informant, and the representative of the royal council. He was humbled that men of such power and intelligence would include him in their conference and trust him, a former enemy, to speak the truth.

"I will do as you have asked," Trenton finally broke the silence, "but first…could we begin with prayer?"

Druet smiled and set his quill-pen aside, "Of course."

Chapter 31
* A King's Rage *

A knock sounded at Cronin's study door.

"Enter," the king of Mizgalia glanced up to see his private courier enter and bow low, "Well? What news do you bring? Speak up, man!"

"The trader, Miji, sends word that he will soon complete your second order of business. He delivered Trenton into the hands of the two assassins when the boy was in no condition to offer a defense against their attack."

There was a pause.

"And…?"

"That is all, my king."

"The trader did not stay to ensure that the job was completed?"

"He did not seem to think it necessary, my king."

"*He* did not, but perhaps I did. Trenton is dead, then?"

The courier blinked at the wall beyond Cronin's head, "I can only assume, Sire, from what I have heard, that he is."

"You assume! And why have I received no word from Thomas or Delaney to verify Miji's account?"

Silence.

"Am I to understand that the garrison has still neither seen nor heard any sign of the two men who supposedly completed their mission successfully?"

"That is correct, my king."

"And yet you bring me word from Miji, who was working in the same locality as the assassins. You and they should have started for Mockmor at the same time, following Trenton's death, yet only you have returned."

"That is correct, Sire."

After a moment, Cronin waved his hand dismissively, "Go now, and send one of the guards in," the courier bowed himself out of the room and immediately a soldier appeared in the doorway. The king did not look up when he spoke, "Send Sir Kleyton to me."

The soldier gave a sharp salute and left the study, closing the door behind him. Fifteen minutes passed before Kleyton knocked and was given admittance. The knight bowed and waited for the king to speak.

Cronin rolled a quill-pen in his fingers and spoke with unnerving calm, "I have received word that Trenton was delivered into the hands of your assassins, yet nothing has been heard from Thomas and Delaney."

The corners of Kleyton's eyes twitched as he considered the king's words, "I was not aware that you had sent a courier to Dragon Coast."

"You are not entitled to know all of my secrets, Kleyton."

"Forgive me, Sire, I did not mean to imply…"

"Kleyton," Cronin turned a look of stone on his advisor, "is Trenton dead?"

"I have no way of knowing, my king, as I have not received word from the assassins."

"Why is that, Kleyton?"

The knight searched franticly for a reply. He was well aware that Thomas and Delaney should have returned by now…if all had gone according to plan.

"It may be that Thomas and Delaney, while returning, were attacked and killed by a band of rebels in the Brikbones—"

Kleyton started visibly when Cronin slammed the quill onto the table and surged to his feet.

"Then sail round to Dragon Coast and discover what those bumbling assassins have done! And when you find them, if the Brikbone rebels have not done so already, kill them! And, Kleyton," the king leaned across the table with a dark scowl, "do not show your face again in Mizgalia until you are certain that your troublesome *son* is dead too!"

Chapter 32
• Leyla •

Four horses rode into Balgo one morning shortly before noon. Distant thunder heralded the imminent arrival of an afternoon storm. One of the riders, a soldier sent to escort the others, reported to the guardhouse and then led his three companions to a modest inn on the village square. A short time later the three visitors left the inn and asked a villager for directions to Osgood's cottage.

She pointed north, "Follow that street and take the first branch to the left, Rodney. Osgood lives near the edge of the village."

Rodney the healer stared at the young woman expectantly until his wife, Sarah, repeated the directions in little less than a shout.

"Oh! Thank you, my dear. And thank you, Elaina."

Frederick's daughter turned and walked away without another word. Sarah took Rodney's arm and led him north, following Elaina's instructions. Behind them, Leyla watched with open curiosity. Never had she met a woman who could shout so lovingly, as Sarah did; and she considered Rodney the most patient of men.

Leyla studied the cottages and shops of Balgo as they made their way to Osgood's home. The former lord's illness had taken a turn for the worse and Rodney had been sent for as a last resort to save the man's life. Leyla had been brought along as the healer's apprentice.

A clap of thunder rolled impatiently across the sky.

Sarah turned with a smile to the young girl, "The innkeeper said there is a woman in Balgo whose baby should come any day now. If her labor begins while we are here, I will take you to assist with the birth."

Leyla nodded and pulled at the strap of her shoulder bag.

They were nearing the edge of the village when the air was suddenly rent by shouts and a terrified shriek. The three startled visitors turned to look back the way they had come as more and more anxious voices were added to the mayhem. Finally, a woman appeared coming up the road; she cried out when she saw them and, dropping to her knees before Rodney, began to sob.

"Healer, please! My son…injured by a cart! Please…you must come!"

Rodney had no trouble understanding the woman's words as they were shouted in motherly concern. Placing a hand on her shoulder, he turned to Sarah.

"My dear, prepare the Common Comfrey and Solomon's Seal. I will see to this boy immediately and then visit Osgood," Sarah nodded and began searching her bag as Rodney shifted his bright gaze to the young apprentice, "Leyla, my child, I must ask you to go on and see to Osgood's condition. Take this…apply several drops of Ulric's Rose to tide him over and then come and report to me what state he is in."

"A'right, sir," Leyla nodded and watched as the healer and his wife followed the distraught mother toward the pained cries rising from the village square. Walking backwards several paces, she watched until they were out of sight and then turned to continue on to the home of the former lord. After inquiring of a washerwoman which was the right house, Leyla hurried across the dirt street to the threshold of a sorry-looking hut.

The wooden latch clacked noisily as she laid her hand to it. Clutching the vial of rose tonic, Leyla pushed the door open and squinted into the dim interior. From the light spilling in behind her, she could see that Osgood lay pale and still on his bed in the corner. The stench of illness filled the air, and Leyla thought she detected a faint toxic scent as well. Her gaze shifted and she frowned. One of the soldiers at the guardhouse had told Rodney that a fire had been kept burning on the hearth for the sick man's comfort, but one look at the darkened room was enough to prove that no fire was burning. Yet there was an element of warmth that surrounded her.

Thunder shook the village.

Leaving the door open, Leyla crossed to the fireplace and bent to examine the wood that had been laid out. Wet. Leyla touched her fingers to the rim of a bucket by the hearth. Someone had doused the fire with a pail of water.

Recently.

The door clicked shut and Leyla straightened and whirled around. Instinctively, she dropped the vial of Ulric's Rose into her bag as her eyes strained against the darkness for any sign of the intruder. The shuttered windows, aided by a storm-darkened sky beyond, made it impossible to see anything.

"'O's there?"

In the silence that answered her, Leyla realized how complete the stillness really was; there was no sound of breathing coming from the corner where Osgood lay. A chill raced up her spine as another clap of thunder echoed the pounding of her heart.

A hand clasped her arm in the dark, and Leyla shrieked. A man's voice grunted for her to be quiet. Dropping like deadweight against the stranger's hold, the young girl grabbed a handful of ashes from the hearth and threw them in her captor's face. When the man cried out in surprise, Leyla jerked her arm free and scrambled to find the exit in the black shadows. With her hands stretched out in front of her she soon ran into the door and began franticly feeling for the latch, but a thick hand suddenly clamped over her mouth and Leyla was pulled against the stranger in a solid hold; she froze when she felt the edge of a knife against her collarbone.

"Do not move or speak," the man's voice insisted.

Villagers passed by outside, speaking their concern over the boy who had been injured in the square. Leyla listened helplessly as the voices gradually faded beyond her hearing.

Behind her, the stranger chuckled, "When I

overheard that a healer was coming to see after Osgood's health, I did not expect a young woman."

Leyla growled behind the man's hand and started to struggle, but her captor's grip only tightened and the dagger pressed closer. The sound of fabric ripping, followed by the thud of a small object as it dropped to the floor, told Leyla that she had torn the man's pocket.

He grunted with the effort to keep her still, "I do not jest with you when I say do not move or speak. I have already taken one life today—I will not hesitate to bring yours to a swift end too."

Leyla froze.

The man pulled out a strip of cloth and gagged Leyla's mouth. He tied her wrists together with a strap of leather. Leyla felt herself being turned around and then shoved to sit in the corner by the door; she grunted when the floor rose to meet her in the dark. The man muttered as he searched for something and finally cursed when he discovered the torn pocket.

A moment passed and Leyla sensed that the attacker had crouched before her. The familiar sound of a cork being pulled from a vial sounded in the otherwise still room, and before Leyla had time to think, the man blew something in her face. Leyla gasped when chalky powder quickly coated her features. She felt the grainy sensation on her tongue and knew in an instant what it was.

The door opened as the man quickly made his exit. Leyla winced as light sliced a path across the room, but looked up in time to see her attacker drop a small glass vial into a pouch at his waist. She decided there was only one word that could accurately describe the man.

Round.

The door shut behind him and Leyla focused on taking a deep breath around the gag. Her tongue had gone numb and her entire being felt sluggish; her body had begun to shut down as if she were falling asleep.

Outside, the rain began to fall in solid torrents, fiercely pelting the roof and windows until Leyla was sure the cottage would collapse beneath the attack. Leyla vaguely wondered if the Rose Tonic in her bag would be of any help, but she was powerless to move her arms in order to get it out. She felt herself falling to the right and an instant later she was lying in a heap on the floor, praying that God would send help.

As the cottage and the rain melted away with consciousness, Leyla's mind drifted to another stormy day, several years before, when her father had thrown a small sack over his shoulder and sauntered from their home in Hugh. In her mind's eye, she watched again from the threshold as he disappeared into the wall of falling rain, whistling carelessly the tune that he had sung to her every night since she had been a "wee little tyke." When he had vanished from sight, the song's first three notes continued to echo repetitively on the walls of her mind. Suddenly the image of a hawk appeared, circling her dream in search of a place to land. Within her dream, Leyla tried to lift her arm in answer to Link's request for a perch, but found herself unable to do so. Her arms refused to move. As the image of Link drifted away, Leyla suddenly collapsed in a wash of tears.

The Death Chalk had rendered her helpless.

Chapter 33
* A Well-kept Secret *

Bracy pointed to a map on the table in Druet's tent, "Our patrol ship spotted a light vessel from Dragon Coast here, heading east."

"Only one?"

"Only one."

Talon added his finger to the map's surface, "The patrol followed them at a distance, but couldn't overtake the faster vessel. They did see, however, that the Dragon Coast ship sailed north around the Geoffrey peninsula."

"North," Druet mused.

"Trenton believes they'll be heading to Mizgalia to seek reinforcements or an alliance that will ensure their survival in the case of Arcrea's downfall."

There was a pause, and Druet tapped a finger on the table's edge, "We can't risk sailing after them, for fear of leaving the harbor open to the rest of the Dragon Coast fleet."

Talon nodded, "And we can't risk sailing after the

fleet, for fear of leaving the harbor open to Mizgalian reinforcements."

Bracy dropped into a chair, "And the Arcrean fleet isn't yet large enough to successfully split up and sail in pursuit of both enemies at the same time."

The tent's flap was pulled aside and Druet rose to greet Renny. Talon straightened and saluted the young queen before delivering a quick, prompting slap to Bracy's shoulder; the lounging courier seemed to suddenly register the queen's presence and quickly catapulted from the chair to execute the same formalities as Talon.

Renny smiled, "Good morning, Talon, Bracy."

Talon dipped his head in greeting while Bracy waved a hand, " 'Morning, Renny."

Druet dismissed the two couriers, asking them to send Falconer and Captain Hull to the large tent. When they had gone, he relayed to Renny the news from the patrol vessel.

"Something must happen soon," he ran a hand through his hair, "I only wish we could have it over with," he turned to Renny, "Is your party ready to leave?"

Renny fingered the edge of the map, "Yes. I came to tell you that everything is ready for my departure. Grikk and my escort of soldiers are prepared to mount, and that woman who is returning to Saxby will go by way of the Heartland in order to act as my companion since Alice is not here."

"When you reach the Heartland, tell the council to offer the woman an escort to Saxby in thanks for her services," Druet took his wife's hand, "I would not be sending you away if I did not think it necessary."

The queen smiled, "I understand. And though I am anxious about the brewing trouble and your involvement in it, I admit my relief that, in my condition, I will not be asked to wield bow and arrow in the coming conflict."

Druet smiled at this confession and reminded her, "You don't have a bow."

"Very funny, Druet."

"Just promise me that while we're apart you won't do anything that would make my hair stand on end with terror."

Renny smiled and adjusted the clasp on her cloak before moving to fix Druet's collar, "Only if you promise me that you won't do anything here that would make my hair stand on end with concern."

Druet grinned and tugged on her braid, "My dear queen, your hair is far too long to stand on end."

Renny tried to frown, "Promise. Or I'll tell Grikk to remain in Dormay to make sure you behave."

Druet's brow rose as he darted a glance at the giant guardian standing some distance away from the tent's entrance, "You couldn't keep him here if you locked him in a hut guarded by a pack of catawylds."

Renny silently crossed her arms over her swelling abdomen and waited for him to comply.

Druet laughed, "Alright! I promise you I will bear in mind the significant responsibilities that I shoulder, and will therefore act prudently."

"Thank you," Renny stood on tiptoe and kissed his nose, "And I, in turn, promise to bear in mind my duty as your wife and Arcrea's queen, and will therefore behave myself with utmost decorum."

Druet heaved a dramatic sigh, "Won't that be a sight…and I'll not be there to see it!"

Renny's brow quirked, "Very funny, Druet."

ꕥ

A day's sail northeast of Geoffrey, Sir Kleyton waited impatiently as Captain Black's messenger was brought aboard the *Griffin* from the light Dragon Coast vessel.

"Quickly, fool! I am about the king's business!"

The sailor approached and was brusquely reminded to bow before the superior knight, "Sir, Captain Black has overcome a fleet from Dragon Coast. Their chief claims that they were sent by a Mizgalian spy to attack the city of Dormay, in Geoffrey."

Kleyton clenched his teeth: Trenton.

"Captain Black wishes to know your desire. Shall we continue the work of the Mizgalian and attack the Arcrean port? Or shall we take the clansmen as slaves and sink the remaining vessels?"

A sudden thought came to Kleyton, "What has become of the Mizgalian spy?"

"Dead…"

Kleyton's heart began to ease with relief.

"…The clan offered him as a sacrifice in honor of the Dormay conquest."

Kleyton's brow lifted in surprise at this news, but he quickly recovered, "Return to your vessel my good man, and sail ahead to Captain Black. My three ships will follow and the *Fate* will aid us in finishing the business left undone by that…unfortunate Mizgalian. We will rally south of Geoffrey and attack Dormay together."

The sailor nodded and turned to go, but stopped

when Kleyton continued.

"As for the clansmen from Dragon Coast: rebels or no, they are still Arcreans. Enlist their service during the attack, but inform Captain Black that after the battle he is to consider them his slaves."

"Yes, sir."

Sir Kleyton watched as the sailor returned to the Dragon Coast vessel and then informed his officers of the coming conflict. Word was passed to the two other Mizgalian battleships and the *Griffin* and party were soon under way once again. Kleyton stood at the quarter-deck railing and watched the busyness around him with unseeing eyes.

The Dragon Coast clansmen said that Trenton had been offered as a sacrifice, but King Cronin had received word that the boy had been delivered to Thomas and Delaney.

Would the Arcrean clan admit to killing a Mizgalian if they hadn't truly done it?

Would Thomas and Delaney complete their mission and not return to Mizgalia with all haste to make their report? Did they not know whose orders they were following?

Sir Kleyton pressed his palms to his temples and went below deck to his cabin. One way or another, war was imminent. Whether Trenton had died at the hands of assassins or dragons, his death had occurred on Arcrean soil—his demise could be blamed on Druet's people. Yes, war was imminent, and it would begin at Dormay.

The knight paused on a rug centered on the floor of his cabin. Glancing at the closed door, he then stepped to a large traveling-trunk and unlocked the lid. Withdrawing a canvas, about one square foot in size, he studied the two figures depicted on its textured face. Two boys, both aged five, sat with their arms around the other's shoulder and wore cheeky grins which the artist had begged them to replace with grim stares but, in the end, had relented to portray as seen. The boy on the left had thick honey-colored hair and singularly blue eyes, while the lad on the right possessed features that were much darker. The two young cousins looked nothing alike.

Kleyton dropped the canvas back into place and closed the trunk. He crossed and exited the room and had soon returned to the quarter-deck to stand by the stern rail. With a few sharply spoken words to the officers and crew, he was left alone with his thoughts.

The small number of people who had seen the small painting had marveled that the artist had captured young Trenton's image so well. Even Trenton had come upon the canvas one day and stated that he didn't remember sitting for a portrait. He had inquired after the identity of the other boy, and Kleyton had responded, "He was your cousin."

This was nearly true, but only Kleyton knew the reality behind the statement. Only Kleyton remembered the pain of sitting for hours on the hard ottoman, waiting for Master Filligry to complete the painting so that he might go outside to play. Only Kleyton remembered the strange security of sitting arm-in-arm with his cousin, and forgetting, for a time, the troubles at home.

It had been one short week later when Kleyton's father had suddenly relocated the family to Mizgalia.

Oh, yes. Kleyton remembered.

The canvas was not just a painting, it was a depiction of the last day of happiness he had ever known—a fresh reminder of the last time Kleyton had seen his cousin before the ways of Mizgalia corrupted his family and his character.

His cousin. Sir Kleyton alone knew that the blonde in the painting was not Trenton. No, the boy seated with his arm around Kleyton's shoulder was Eric.

Eric. The boy who had brought life to Kleyton's existence. The boy who had been in line to rule an Arcrean region. The boy who had been betrayed by his younger brother and cousin. The boy who was now a grown slave on board the *Fate*, awaiting a meaningless death.

Sir Kleyton gripped the railing until his arms began to shake. Pushing away, he returned to his cabin and threw open the lid of the trunk. He grabbed the canvas from where it sat on top and placed his fingers along the upper edge. For a moment he stood transfixed by the two faces; the two boys smiled at him from his past, refusing to part from one another—refusing to relinquish their hold on a favorite cousin's shoulder.

Kleyton blinked and pulled his hands apart. The canvas followed his fingers in two directions and the painting was ripped down the middle. The boys were separated, though each had lost an arm to the other side of the canvas—still wrapped around the other lad's shoulder, as if to prove that the past's influence could never be removed. The knight closed his hands around the two pieces, reducing them to wrinkled balls. Tossing them into the trunk, he closed the lid and locked the padlock.

Returning once again to the quarter-deck, Sir Kleyton stood beside the helm and watched as the

Griffin cut a path through the sea. Behind him stretched a life best forgotten; before him lay the prospects of death, blood, and war.

Kleyton set his jaw.

Death to the adversary!

Chapter 34
* Practice *

Drop. Turn. Thrust. Turn. Cut. Lunge. Turn. Swing. Cut. Spin. Thrust. Turn. Breathe.

Trenton filled his lungs with air as he paused, waiting for the invisible foe to make the next advance. The catawylds were fierce, fast, and ruthless, but they were also predictable when one was adapted to their game. Trenton whipped his head to one side, clearing the sweat from his eyes, as he prepared for another bout.

Cut. Spin. Drop. Thrust. Turn.

Trenton talked himself through the familiar fight pattern, habitually grunting the words in Mizgalian. His sword raced to keep up with his brain.

Thrust. Turn. Slice. Spin. Cut. Uppercut. Swing. Breathe.

Trenton's gaze swiveled south, across the meadow to the sea. Somewhere out there, a fleet bearing twenty-eight dragons was coming to attack the peaceful people of Arcrea…thanks to him.

Somewhere out there, a Mizgalian vessel called the *Fate* carried his father in slavery…thanks to Osgood.

Trenton turned to study the horizon to the northwest.

Osgood. Word had come that morning that the former lord was dead. A Heartland courier had brought word forwarded from Balgo at request of the presiding guardhouse and Rodney the healer.

Osgood had been killed by a foreign brew: the combination of a deadly toxin—left behind when it fell out of the assassin's pocket—and a fine residue derived from the Substance of Fate, or, Death Chalk.

Rodney and his wife, Sarah, had discovered their young apprentice lying unconscious on the floor of Osgood's cottage, also drugged by the Death Chalk.

Trenton whirled to resume his imaginary fight, his tongue muttering in Mizgalian frustration as he finished off another invisible catawyld. God be praised, the assassin hadn't administered the poison in Leyla's case; nevertheless, it drove Trenton mad to think that someone had harmed a defenseless young girl—his friend. If the assassin hadn't dropped his vial of poison, Leyla would have undoubtedly met the same fate as Osgood!

Trenton gasped for air and retrieved his flask of water, taking a long drink before pouring the rest of the cool liquid over his head. He had stood on the outskirts of a growing crowd as King Druet had read Rodney's message aloud. Leyla had been revived from the effects of the drug and was then able to tell the Balgo soldiers all that she knew of what had happened. When Druet had read that Leyla's only account of the assassin was "round," Trenton's gaze had immediately swung to collide with Falconer's.

Miji.

Druet, too, had seemed taken aback by Leyla's choice of description. The young king had glanced up first at Falconer, and then Trenton. He had quickly linked the youth's story of the Dragon Coast hermit with Osgood's assassin. His thoughts on the matter were clear: If Miji was in the service of Mizgalia's king—as he'd proved through Trenton's betrayal—then Cronin was to blame for ordering the death of an Arcrean. A former nobleman at that!

Trenton swung his sword, balancing the weapon's use between his right arm and his thumbless left hand. His mind entrusted the fight pattern to his second nature while his thoughts took up where Druet's had left off.

"Miji had to be following Cronin's orders. Osgood was privy to information about the Mizgalians' dealings concerning Eric…Father. I was deliberately kept in ignorance of this information while I lived at Mockmor."

Thrust. Swing. Cut. Lunge.

"Falconer said that Cronin wasn't pleased to learn that Osgood and I met in Balgo two months ago. No doubt, Cronin didn't want me to learn of my Arcrean heritage and Osgood was considered a threat to those plans for silence. So he had Osgood killed."

Cut. Jump. Slice. Turn. Swing.

"But for King Druet to make such an accusation against Mizgalia without solid proof of its accuracy would be giving Cronin reason to engage us in war…"

Drop. Turn. Thrust.

"…which is exactly what Cronin wants."

Jump. Swing. Cut. Cut. Slice. Breathe.

Trenton's chest heaved with each breath. Slowly, he backed away from the spot of conflict as if surveying the victory that was only visible to his mind's eye, "Done."

"You know, I think your tactics excel when your mind is otherwise engaged."

Trenton turned at the voice and found Kellen seated on a nearby stump. The young man offered his full water flask and Trenton drank deeply.

"Thank you."

Kellen nodded, "I came out to see if you'd care to play a bout with me, but now I see you've already gotten your exercise," he pointed to where Trenton had been practicing, "You were thinking out loud?" Trenton nodded and Kellen grinned, "I thought so. I'm sure it was an admirable speech too, but as I don't understand Mizgalian, I hadn't the slightest clue what you were saying."

Trenton dropped to the ground, exhausted, "It's first nature to me…I don't even realize that I'm doing it. To me, it's even stranger having to prattle on in Arcrean," he laughed and leaned on his elbow, "You should have seen the look on the peddler's face, just the other day, when I bought an apple on my way into Dormay. I'd gotten all the way through my request before I realized I'd done it in Mizgalian. He looked ready to knock me flat!"

"Had you been in one of the northern regions, he probably would have," Kellen cast a sidelong glance at Trenton, "What do you think of Rodney's message?"

Trenton grunted, "Now there's someone who should be knocked flat."

"Rodney?"

"No! Miji."

"You think he was the assassin?"

"Positive." Trenton draped his arm over his eyes to block out the sun. "I only wish I could've been there to greet him."

Kellen smirked, "In defense of whom? Your dying Uncle Osgood or Leyla?"

A smile touched Trenton's face, "I didn't know my uncle."

"Ha!" Kellen pelted the water flask at Trenton, "You're as bad off as Talon is over Anne!"

Trenton sat up and shot back a reply in Mizgalian; at the look on Kellen's face, he rolled his eyes in realization and adjusted his tongue to repeat the words in Arcrean, "I am not!"

"Hmm," Kellen put a hand to his mouth and studied his friend with a merry expression, "I believe I've spotted a pattern. Does your speech revert to Mizgalian only when you're nervous?"

Kellen ducked when the water flask was hurled back at him.

Chapter 35
* Cookery of Exasperation *

The Sailor's Tailor was quiet. Peter sat asleep in a chair by the front hearth, Martha and Anne had gone to the butcher's for their weekly order, and Brigit stood alone in the kitchen, mixing several ingredients into a large wooden bowl.

Work on the Navy's uniforms had taken up most of the last few weeks, and now that the uniforms were complete there seemed to be a lack of things to do. Not that Brigit had been of much help where the uniforms were concerned. She knew that her father and Anne had been up late on more than one occasion, repairing the work that she had bungled during the day. Brigit huffed a sigh; sewing could be so frightfully exasperating! She marveled that her father had any patience for it, and knew for certain that Anne had been gifted with both sisters' creativity combined.

Adding a bit of water to her bowl, Brigit stirred with renewed vigor, only slowing her pace when some of the contents sloshed over the side and onto the table. Swiping at the spill with her finger, Brigit tasted the sweet dough with a feeling of accomplishment. Her father's favorite spice cake was one thing she had always been able to do right. Just take a bit of this, a dash of that, mix them together, and set it on the shelf in the hearth without igniting her skirt!

She bit her lower lip…that last step would be the tricky part.

Brigit turned when the back door opened and Bracy stepped into the kitchen. She had forgotten he'd been out back chopping wood into kindling. Waving a doughy hand, she smiled and then pointed to the large box by the hearth.

"You can put the kindling in that and then, if you don't mind, we could use some more logs in the pile by the far wall."

"I figured as much," Bracy muttered and moved to deposit the armload of kindling.

Brigit ignored his ill humor, completely understanding the young man's state of exasperation, and returned to her bowl; but as long as she had a listening ear…

"It was excessively kind of King Druet to order my father to take a day of rest after concluding the overwhelming task of making uniforms for the Navy. Oh, and you and Talon have been magnanimous in your help to us!"

Bracy straightened and brushed his hands together, "It's just me today. Talon sends his greetings, though. I'll bring some firewood inside."

"Thank you," Brigit called as she added another pinch of cinnamon. An idea suddenly struck her and she turned to glance after him. Worrying her lower lip with her teeth, she tossed the last few ingredients in and stirred with energy. Perhaps, if she finished before he left… Tasting the dough one last time, Brigit hurried to find the bread pan.

Bracy reentered the kitchen to see Brigit jumping up down, trying to reach a basket that was perched on top of the cupboard. With a forbearing sigh, he set the sling of wood down and reached for the broom. Moving to the cupboard, he lifted the basket down with the broom handle and held it out to Brigit.

"Oh, thank you," she removed a small pan from the basket and glanced up at the cupboard, "Could you put the basket back, please?"

Bracy did so, and then moved back to the load of firewood while Brigit all but ran back to the table and her wooden bowl. He couldn't help but notice that she seemed to be in a hurry. Never before had he seen anyone give the distinct impression that they were running a race while baking bread. It was a nerve-racking scenario to observe.

Brigit set the bread pan on the table and waved two flies away from her bowl. Realizing that she'd forgotten to cover the dough, she glanced down to see that one fly had already gotten himself stuck.

"Ugh," she growled.

"What's that?" Bracy called over his shoulder.

"Nothing," Brigit set her tongue between her lips and reached into the bowl to remove the fly; flicking it into the fire with a dollop of sticky dough in tow, she made a face, "Disgusting…"

"What?"

"Nothing," she wiped her fingers on her apron and glanced across the kitchen at Bracy, "Have you ever been faced with the clear certainty that the

Brigit

culinary arts have a great propensity to rendering themselves unsavory?"

Bracy turned to stare at her with wide-eyed confusion, "What did you just say?"

Brigit sighed, "Baking can be nasty."

His expression told her that he was trying to comprehend how her interpretation fit the original speech. Well…at least he was trying.

"Uh…actually I haven't."

Brigit's brow creased, "Haven't what?"

"Considered the…unsavory propensities of baking."

"Oh," she bit her lip to keep from laughing, "It sounds funny when you say it."

He grunted, "It sounds foreign when you say it."

"I like to learn new words—it's something I'm good at…that and making spice cake. Oh!" Brigit's hands fluttered in distress, "I forgot the cake!"

And she was off again: racing to oil the bread pan and pour in the dough. Bracy shook his head; it really was too stressful to watch. Grabbing the large sling used for carrying wood, he stood and headed for the door.

"Are you leaving?" Brigit's voice squeaked and the look on her face was one of terror.

"I'm going out for one more load."

"Oh," she was clearly relieved. Bracy wondered if perhaps she was scared of being alone, but her father was in the front room…

Brigit covered the pan of dough and went after an apple and a knife. She quickly peeled the apple and cut it in slices to set on top of the cake. In between the slices, she arranged several cloves. Taking a deep breath, she glanced to see if Bracy was on his way. She'd never in her young life felt so rushed to get a cake done—she felt as if she were running a race! She hoped the results would be worth the effort…and the stress.

When Bracy returned with the second load of firewood Brigit was gathering all of the culinary tools she'd used and placing them in the large wooden bowl. She dropped the loaded bowl into the washtub and then grabbed a rag to wipe the table clean.

"Ouch!"

Bracy didn't look, "What happened?"

"To use plain Arcrean for the benefit of your hearing: I gave myself a splinter."

Bracy ran a hand over his face. How could someone take a simple act, such as wiping the table, and turn it into a disaster? He cleared his throat.

"Are you alright?"

"Yes," she sounded resigned, "It's no worse than pricking myself with a needle, only a needle doesn't remain hazardously stuck in my finger as does a fragment of wood. Such particles are frightfully exasperating to extricate painlessly."

Bracy let out a low sigh, "There she goes again."

"Would you like any help with the wood?"

"No!" Bracy winced at his own startled cry, and with great effort quieted his tone, "I'm almost done."

"You've been most helpful, and I thank you. I'm going to pray that God blesses you for your kindness."

Bracy stiffened with irritation, "Don't waste your breath."

Brigit frowned in confusion, "A prayer is never a waste of breath."

"Used on me, it would be. I don't care much for God."

"But God cares much for you."

"Well, I don't expect Him to. He's never been a part of my life."

"How can you say something so preposterously absurd? God is involved in even the slightest of minute details in every life because we are His creation and He loves us!" she crossed her arms, "Have you ever looked for evidence of His work in your life?"

Bracy stacked the last of the wood with force, "No."

"Because you didn't want to find Him."

It wasn't a question. She had pinpointed all his excuses at once and left him with nothing more to say. Bracy gripped the wood sling and stood up.

"I have to go."

"Oh," Brigit stood by the table, wringing her hands. She glanced at the fireplace and then at Bracy; he'd made it to the door before she finally brought herself to stop him, "Bracy!"

He turned with one hand on the door and waited for her to speak. Only then did he realize that the bread pan was still on the table. He glanced at Brigit and saw a red flush cover her face.

She swallowed a lump in her throat, "Would…you…put the cake over the fire for me?"

Bracy's gaze swiveled to the stone shelf in the hearth and then dropped knowingly to the dancing flames—ever since the bread-browning incident, Brigit had been hesitant to go nearer to the hearth than necessary. Bracy took a deep breath and tossed the sling outside; he'd be scared too, if he had her reputation for catastrophe.

Brigit stared at the bread pan as she held it out for him, hoping she'd remembered all the ingredients in her rush to finish before he left. What a relief to know that she wouldn't be required to reach across the hearth! Mother and Anne would be back in time to take the cake out.

Bracy set the cake on the warm shelf.

"Thank you, Bracy," Brigit's tone was contrite.

He nodded and turned to go.

"Bracy?"

He sighed and turned back around.

"I want you to know that I'm still going to pray for you. If there's nothing else on this vastly immense earth that I'm good at…I do know how to pray."

"Do whatever you like," Bracy moved to the door, "Quite frankly, I don't know if I believe God exists."

Brigit looked sadly shocked, "Oh, but He does!"

"How can you know that? Have you ever seen Him?"

"No, not in person; but I see His works in…"

"You talk about God's involvement in every life, and yet He can't even help you get a cake on the hearth!"

Brigit drew herself up, "That's different! And He *can* help me, only I let my fear and justifiable discretion overpower the knowledge that He would see to my safety."

Bracy shook his head, "If your God is real and He wants me to believe in Him, He can prove to me that He exists."

"He can, and I will pray that He does!"

With a huff, Bracy pulled the door shut and was

gone. Brigit watched him go and then dropped to her knees in the middle of the kitchen, desperate to bring this lost soul's request—or rather, challenge—before the throne of God.

Having been roused by the sounds of contention, Peter came to the door between the front room and the kitchen. He took one look at his dramatic daughter kneeling on the floor, and then cast an uncertain glance around the otherwise empty room, "Brigit, are you alright?"

Brigit sniffed and wiped a tear from her eye, giving an emphatic nod. She rose from her knees and went to wash the dishes, exclaiming in a tearful voice, "Father, I never thought I'd see the day when I met anyone who was more exasperating than I am…"

There was a pause, and Peter finally prompted, "But…?"

Her words quickly dissolved into sobs like soap shavings in hot water. "Today was that day!"

ജ൫

Bracy threw his bedroll to the ground with more force than necessary, wondering how he'd let Talon, Kellen, and Trenton, talk him into leaving the tent for the night to join them around the campfire.

Talon dropped his own bedroll several feet away and grinned, "Bracy? Are you cross?"

"Be quiet, Talon. I'm in no humor to endure your teasing tonight."

For once, Talon seemed to believe him, and moved to join the merry chatter of the other two. Bracy wrapped himself in his cloak and dropped wearily to the bedroll. He closed his eyes.

I'm still going to pray for you.

Bracy's eyes flew open again when Brigit's words echoed in his mind. *Fine*, he thought, *go ahead and pray*, "Just let me sleep!"

There was a stretch of silence, broken only by the crackling fire, and then Kellen finally spoke, "Bracy…you can't expect us to be silent."

"I wasn't talking to you."

Another moment of silence, and then Talon offered, "He's a little cross."

"Talon!"

"Just stating the obvious, my good fellow."

Bracy scowled and burrowed deeper into his cloak, determined to go to sleep in spite of the noise. But it was not the noise that kept him awake. His conversation with Brigit haunted his thoughts until he felt he'd rehearsed every word a thousand times over. Gradually the others fell silent and Bracy was left alone with his thoughts and the leaping flames of the campfire.

Quite frankly, I don't know if I believe God exists. Have you ever seen Him?

No, not in person, but…

If your God is real and He wants me to believe in Him, He can prove to me that He exists.

He can, and I will pray that He does! If there's nothing else on this vastly immense earth that I'm good at…I do know how to pray.

"Bracy."

Bracy tensed when the strange voice spoke from above his head. He knew he should be troubled that someone had approached the camp without the guards raising an alarm, but, oddly enough, the thought didn't worry him. He had never heard a man's voice carry such power with such gentleness. A strong hand touched his shoulder, and Bracy felt his mind put at ease.

"Bracy."

Bracy looked up to see the silhouette of a man crouched at the head of his bedroll. With the fire at his back, the stranger's face was cast in shadows. Only his eyes were alight with an unearthly radiance. Bracy glanced to see that his three companions were sound asleep.

"Who are you? What do you want?"

Though he couldn't make out the man's features, Bracy could feel the man's patient gaze and hear a smile in his voice, "The effectual fervent prayer of a righteous man availeth much."

Bracy's brow furrowed, "What does that mean?" the man spoke like Brigit. Bracy's eyes widened with a flash of realization.

"Bracy, blessed are they that have not seen, and yet have believed."

With a start, Bracy sat up and spun around to face the stranger—but the man had vanished! Instead, Talon, Trenton, and Kellen, sat on their separate bedrolls and stared at Bracy with startled expressions. Kellen looked as if he'd been stopped mid-sentence.

"Bracy…?"

Bracy blinked in confusion and rubbed his eyes, "Weren't you just asleep?"

Trenton grinned around a yawn; "Kellen's keeping us awake with stories of his not-so-long-ago childhood."

Kellen turned in mock offense, "I was not the only one talking!"

Talon smiled, "You were the one who fell asleep,

Bracy."

"I didn't fall asleep!" Bracy's head shook in denial, "You did! I saw you…I saw the man here, and felt his hand on my shoulder. I…"

Talon frowned, "What man?"

Bracy stared at his friend and knew that Talon was truly at a loss. This was no joke—they hadn't seen the visitor. Talon rose from his bedroll and came to kneel beside Bracy; concern etched his voice.

"Are you alright? Bracy, what man did you see? What happened?"

Bracy stared at the fire. His heart was pounding and he took a shaky breath. *A prayer is never a waste of breath.* His brain belatedly took hold of Talon's question and he turned a distracted gaze to the other man.

What happened, he'd asked.

"Brigit prayed."

Chapter 36
* A Lackey's Opinion *

Nathaniel knew instinctively that the month of April had arrived. Standing behind Captain Black, with the man's elaborately braided coat draped over one arm, the slave's gaze remained locked on the northern horizon, where the land curved inward in a haven of supposed safety.

Dormay.

His hometown. The place where his parents and two sisters were, at this very moment, sitting in the little tailor shop on the waterfront street, unsuspecting of the evil that lurked in the harbor. And evil it was. Captain Black had proved beyond a doubt that he was worthy of his renowned title as the deadliest man to sail the Arcrean Sea. Twelve men—crewmembers and slaves alike—had met their demise in the past four days, thanks to the captain's temper being shortened by the stress of coming conflict. Nathaniel glanced to where Eric scrubbed the main deck on his hands and knees, and was thankful that

Black had at least been forbidden to kill the Arcrean hostage. He had feared for his own life more than once.

"Arcrean!"

Nathaniel snapped to attention when Black shouted the familiar nickname, "Sir?"

The captain squinted north and held his spyglass out for the slave, "Tell me what you see there."

Nathaniel balanced the coat and spyglass to peer at the magnified version of Dormay. He squinted through the glass and then his eyes widened in surprise, "A fleet…sir!"

Black grabbed the glass for another look, "A naval fleet; those are battleships, slave! And bulwarks on the rises east and west of the harbor…they shelter catapults, I'd wager."

Nathaniel forced his expression to remain neutral, but inwardly he shouted with glee. Druet was no fool. He had raised an army, built a Navy, and prepared the normally-tranquil city of Dormay for battle! Nathaniel's thoughts came to a standstill. There was only one question…

Black growled at the view, "How did they learn of our plans to attack?"

That was the question.

"What say you, Arcrean?" Black turned a dark look on the slave, "Have I a spy aboard the *Fate*?"

"Sir, no one's left the *Fate* without your knowledge of their going. Only the light Dragon Coast vessel left your watch to alert the Mizgalian knight of the plan to attack. The men who sailed on her couldn't have taken word to Dormay in time for a fleet to be got in order."

Captain Black seemed put out that Nathaniel had

offered sound proof against his theory.

"But how could they know? It would seem impossible."

"Nothing is impossible with God, sir."

Black scoffed, "I should toss you overboard for those words. They reek of sedition! You think that God fights for Arcrea?"

Nathaniel weighed his words carefully; he knew he was treading on dangerous ground, "I have witnessed the work of God in the life of Arcrea's king."

"The blacksmith?" Black gave a rusty laugh, "I'm sure he needed all the help he could get, the insolent pup! It's a wonder the kingdom has survived this long under his rule."

Nathaniel clenched his fingers in a fist beneath the folds of Black's coat.

A shout was suddenly heard from the lookout, "Three ships, ho! To the east!"

Black whirled to point his spyglass in the specified direction and a moment later he grunted with satisfaction, "Arcrean God or no, Sir Kleyton is a man backed by the vast armies of the undefeated Mizgalians."

Nathaniel couldn't contain his next words, "Except in the Brikbones."

Black turned to glance at the slave, "What was that?"

"The Mizgalians remain defeated in their attempts to cross the Brikbones…into Arcrea…sir."

Nathaniel thought he saw a flicker of fear or panic touch the captain's eyes, but the moment quickly passed and Black turned away again.

"Help me into my coat, slave," when Nathaniel

held the garment out, Black slipped his arms into the sleeves and then turned to grip Nathaniel by the neck, "Confidence has served you well to this day, but too much daring will lead to your swift end. One more step beyond your bounds, Arcrean, and you will follow my last lackey to a watery grave. Do you hear me?"

Nathaniel's voice croaked around Black's hold, "Yes, sir."

The captain shoved the slave away, "Now run and fetch me a pint of ale; I'd favor a drop before Sir Kleyton arrives."

Nathaniel turned and started off toward the galley, breathing deeply and rubbing his sore neck. He caught the fleeting glance of concern from Eric as he passed the older man, and then returned his gaze to the planks at his feet.

Soon.

Soon they would escape this floating death and live again. Soon these months on the *Fate* would be nothing more than a distant nightmare. Soon they would be free.

Nathaniel gave the captain's liquid request to the slaves in the galley and was soon returning to the quarter-deck with Black's ale. The man's words stuck in Nathaniel's mind like a bur.

You think that God fights for Arcrea?

Nathaniel gave precedence to a Mizgalian crewmember and waited to climb the stairs after the man had passed on his way down.

Yes, he did think that God fought for Arcrea. However, it was not a matter of one kingdom being superior to another and therefore gaining the Almighty's preference, but because Arcrea's king and the majority of the Arcrean people were turning to God and crying out for His wisdom and help. Druet—"the blacksmith"—fought against evil for the good of his people and in defense of the name of Jesus Christ. Nathaniel believed that God would protect His children regardless of their native realm, and uphold the cause of the just and righteous, even against seemingly impossible odds.

Nathaniel produced the pint of ale in silence and stood by as Captain Black and his crew reveled in the knowledge that they would soon be joining forces with Mizgalia's undefeated knight…not that they cared too much for his authority, just that their numbers would be multiplied.

It was said that Sir Kleyton scoffed at the thought of someone who challenged his abilities. Nathaniel prayed that this Kleyton would be reconciled with his Maker before it became too late.

The slave's eyes lifted and sought the city of Dormay on the Arcrean coast.

If God be for us, who can be against us?

Chapter 37
* Day of Battle *

Druet's eyes shot open and immediately he sat up to strap on his sword belt. He hadn't meant to sleep when Falconer had insisted—no, ordered—him to lie down for a few moments. If sleep had managed to overpower his active mind, he must have needed it!

The Dragon Coast fleet had been spotted off the coast the afternoon before, and in the evening it had been joined by a light vessel coming from the east. When Trenton had stated that only seven vessels had set out from Dragon Coast, a closer inspection had been made. The eighth ship was Mizgalian. Everyone was convinced that this mystery vessel could be none other than the *Fate*. Not long after this discovery had been made, a lookout from the Geoffrey peninsula had arrived with news that three more Mizgalian vessels were on the way.

The eight ships present were beyond firing range of the coast; nevertheless, the assigned companies had been detached to the eastern and western earthworks in readiness to man the catapults. The naval ranks had boarded the appropriate vessels, and the Arcrean fleet was prepared to set itself in battle formation at the slightest sign that the enemy was ready. The shops and homes along the waterfront had been evacuated as a precaution toward the damage that may be done by ammunition or dragons.

Druet's gaze swept the tent in a final search for anything that he might need as he stepped to the exit. Pulling the tent flap aside, he took one step out into the camp.

And froze.

A thick fog blanketed the meadow, making it impossible to see anything beyond a distance of fifteen feet. The city of Dormay, the harbor, and the enemy fleet, had all vanished into the penetrating walls of gray.

Somewhere off to the left, Druet heard Trenton whistle for his hawk. The three notes sounded eerie and uncertain in the dense atmosphere. Druet took a deep breath and felt his lungs fill with the heavily moistened air.

"God, help us."

Laying his left hand to the pommel at his waist, Druet started off for the central meeting-tent, where his knights and captains had gathered to review their plans. When he had gone three paces, he became aware of someone walking beside him.

"Falconer," Druet nodded his recognition.

"Sire."

The sounds of a small group coming behind them told Druet that his guard of ten was following. With this close fog making it all but impossible to see,

Falconer must have alerted the soldiers to his rising. Druet grinned, shaking his head in amazement, and spoke in a low tone.

"Falconer, how do you always know?"

The informant's gaze continued to pierce the surrounding veil, "It is my profession to know, Sire."

They entered the meeting-tent together and approached the tense gathering of soldiers. Druet's ready smile helped to ease the air of foreboding.

"A lovely morning, good sirs!"

"Sire," the men bowed before the kingdom's young sovereign.

"I am grateful that you all allowed me to rest awhile. I feel refreshed. How has strategy commenced while I've slumbered?"

A tall red-headed knight placed a finger to the battle plans on the table, "Riders have been posted in units along the coast of Geoffrey, as you requested; they are prepared to pursue any dragons that may stray for a venue wider than Dormay."

"Excellent."

"It has been calculated that the three Mizgalian vessels advancing from the east should have joined the Dragon Coast fleet by now."

"But it is doubtful they will advance on Dormay in this fog, for fear of running aground or colliding with one another in the limited view."

Druet crossed his arms and nodded thoughtfully, "The ships may not be our greatest concern," he glanced around the group, "Are dragons affected by fog?"

One of the few knights from the region of Hugh stepped forward, "They are not, Sire. I recall many an evening spent in my native region when the dragons could be heard flying through a haze."

"Then we will not be able to see their advance through this accursed fog!" a knight of Ranulf dropped his fist onto the table, "If God will fight for us, why does He blind us on the day of battle?"

Druet studied the man with a sober expression, "Sir Wiltmore. What is a blindfold, if not a tool that enforces trust?" there was a pause, "God has a purpose for the fog, my friends, and I for one anticipate the realization of what that purpose is," the king studied the marked parchments before him, "Many hours we've spent on these plans. Let us now pray for the strength to carry them out in God's order."

All occupants of the tent followed Druet's direction and circled for prayer, each man clutching the right wrist of the man to his left. When the king had finished his petition for God's wisdom and strength, his gaze was drawn to the courier standing to his right. Bracy lifted his head and gave the slightest of nods, "Amen."

Druet smiled, "Your confession of faith has brought me much joy, and I'm sure Renny will be pleased to hear of our new brother in Christ."

Talon appeared at Bracy's other side and grinned, "All I can say is, it was about time!"

Bracy shook his head and pulled Talon's cap down over his eyes. Talon pulled the hat back and glanced around the tent as everyone began to move with one accord toward the exit. Clapping Bracy on the shoulder, the blonde jerked his head to indicate that his fellow-courier was to follow.

"Let's go fight some dragons, brothers."

Druet reached for his helmet, "I thought Falconer

mentioned that you would be scouting today."

Talon grinned, "I managed to drop an obvious hint that Bracy and I would like to be stationed within the city so we can take part in the battle."

Bracy rolled his eyes and spoke in a tone that annulled his words, "Thank you, Talon, I'm indebted to you for life."

"Oh, come, Bracy! My swords are longing for another fight, and what better cause to fight for than the defense of our people?"

Falconer stepped into the tent, "Talon, Bracy, your horses are outside."

The two friends left and Druet turned to his informant while an aide helped him into his armor, "I still don't understand why I have to wear all this."

A glint of humor sparked in Falconer's eye, "You are the king, Sire; your life is highly valued by your subjects."

The aide cinched a strap at Druet's waist and he cast a long-suffering look at the spy, "I've just spent an entire summer fighting ignispats, catawylds, carnaturs, rebels, and dragons, without anyone taking any notice of my 'armorless' state. I found it much easier to move."

"I cannot and will not argue with you, Sire. Only I will say that before she left, the queen instructed me to ensure that you were prudently attired for any fighting."

"She said 'prudently'?"

"She did."

"She would," Druet grinned, "Then I suppose I shall have to endure the armor."

The king's entourage soon mounted and rode with great care through the fog and into the city of

Dormay. Heavy mist and threatening danger alike had swept the streets clean of their normal bustle. As they neared the wharf, a small group of sailors approached and were given permission to address the king.

"Sire," the leader spoke quietly, but with eagerness, "my comrades and I took the liberty of taking my boat out into the bay early this morning to discover the position of the enemy. The fog kept us hidden from sight, but we were able to distinguish the eleven vessels."

"The Mizgalians have joined them," Druet spoke to no one in particular.

"Aye, sir; there were several Mizgalian-built ships. One of my mates has drawn a map of how they sit."

Druet took the parchment and studied it before handing it to Falconer. The informant scanned it with a careful eye and passed it back as the king questioned the sailor.

"Are these words the names of the vessels?"

The man nodded, "As best we could tell through the mist, Sire."

Druet turned to Falconer and caught Trenton's gaze from beyond the spy, "The *Fate* is among them. Your father."

Trenton took a slow breath and asked, "What are the names of the three Mizgalian vessels?"

Druet searched the map, "Only two could be deciphered—the *Tyburn* and the *Griffin*. Do you know them?"

Trenton's jaw was tight as he gave a slight nod, "The *Griffin* was built and kept for Sir Kleyton's particular use."

One of the knights of Quinton spoke up from behind, "A ship built for the pleasure of a landlocked warlord? Who does the man think he is?"

Trenton smirked, "Mizgalia's greatest landlocked warlord."

Any further conversation was suddenly cut short by a chilling shriek that sliced through the fog like a sharp knife through Brigit's spice cake. Every eye lifted to search the gray overhead. In another instant a second screech was heard and the surrounding fog was stirred to the sound of leathery wings.

Trenton watched as the massive shadowy form disappeared again through the fog. Twenty-eight dragons, captured by his own ingenuity, had been kept in crates for several weeks, fed only enough to keep them alive and hungry for more. Now, one journey and an entire lifetime of realizations later, Trenton sat prepared to ward off the very attack that he had set in motion—the command of which had been transferred to the man he had called Father.

Eyes glued to the unseen sky, King Druet kept his voice low, hoping to delay detection as long as possible, "To your posts, men. It has begun."

Chapter 38
* Dragons in Dormay *

"Be prepared to drive the ships in as soon as the fog lifts."

The officer saluted in response to Kleyton's order and the knight turned to face the hidden coast of Arcrea once again. The clansmen of Dragon Coast had successfully released the caged creatures of their region and somehow forced them on a course toward the city of Dormay. Now, all they could do was wait.

Wait for the dragons to inflict their damage.

Wait for the Arcreans to tire.

Wait for this wretched fog to lift.

Sir Kleyton hated waiting.

ꟷ

On the *Fate*'s main deck, Captain Black turned from the wall of fog to the north and barked at his first-mate, "Are the catapults ready?"

"Nearly, Captain."

"Is the ammunition being brought from below?"

"Aye, Captain."

"Send some slaves to bring a barrel or two of oil from the hold. The new Arcrean Navy deserves a blazing welcome to the seas!"

The first-mate grinned, "Aye, Captain," he turned, "You, fetch a barrel of oil…"

His voice faded away and Nathaniel's stomach twisted at the thought of Druet's navy being destroyed by the same flaming missiles that had been the end of the *Seabird*. He watched through the mist as Eric was pulled from the construction of the deck-mounted catapults to help with the barrels. In spite of the tension, Nathaniel felt a thrill of excitement when he thought of the attempt they would be making to escape that day.

Another shriek sounded through the all-encompassing fog and Nathaniel's gaze darted north toward Dormay.

Home. He wanted to go home…

He rubbed a hand over his scraggly beard and through his shoulder-length mane.

…And he needed a haircut.

Suddenly, a shout turned all eyes toward the stern where a scuffle was taking place between a Mizgalian and a desperate slave. Supporters of both sides of the fight quickly joined the opponents until the quarter-deck was a flurry of brawling sailors.

"What's going on?" Black's thundered query went unanswered as he stormed toward the flight of steps that led to the deck in question.

Nathaniel followed dutifully, his mouth hanging open in disbelief. The slaves had never before dared to start an uprising! Apparently, he and Eric weren't the only ones bent on escape.

The loud snapping of iron links told everyone that the anchor had been disconnected and discharged. Instinctively, Nathaniel took a wider stance as the ship suddenly lurched, breaking free of its inactivity. A roar of excitement was delivered by the rigging-slaves and the sails were suddenly unfurled, causing the *Fate* to move toward the coast.

Captain Black's face turned the color of his name as he climbed the quarter-deck steps, "Get this deck under control before I send every one of you to an early grave! Kill the slaves before they escape!"

Black paused at the top of the stairs. Slaves. The Arcrean. Needing a quick release for his building wrath, the captain drew his sword and turned to run the weapon through his lackey.

But Nathaniel had vanished.

With an enraged growl, Black spun on his heel and lashed out at the closest man—Mizgalian or slave, it mattered little to him. His opponent fell to the deck, and Black rushed to the starboard rail to bellow fiercely over the noise of sea and strife.

"Mutiny! Mutiny aboard the *Fate*! Mutiny!"

ജ൦ൽ

Talon's fingers flexed and closed to gain a better grip on each pommel. His twin swords had gathered a layer of beaded mist as his eyes maintained a constant vigil, shifting with every noise to search the impenetrable fog.

He blinked. If Druet hadn't insisted that God had a purpose for the fog, he would have been sure that their battle was a lost cause. The archers, positioned in the rigging of each Arcrean vessel and on the waterfront rooftops, were the army's greatest asset against the dragons. They could fell one of the beasts quickly and from a distance. But with this fog it would be impossible for the archers to see the dragons until it was too late to take a shot; and they couldn't shoot if they were unsure of their fellow-Arcreans' positions.

"Dragons don't like fire," Bracy spoke from where he stood some distance away, nearly lost to Talon's vision in the gray mist, "Why did we not construct massive fire pits to keep them away?"

"We don't want to keep them away, Bracy; we need to kill them before they get away."

"Where are they?"

"How should I know? Lower your voice, you harebrained rebel!"

"Who's calling who a rebel?" Bracy huffed, but his voice dropped to a whisper, "Maybe they flew beyond the fog, and are terrorizing the Geoffrey countryside."

"Oh, that's comforting."

"Well, I don't hear any—"

"They're here, Bracy. I can feel it. Just wait for…"

Both men froze when a rustling sounded overhead and then settled somewhere off to the right. A heavy rustling.

Bracy held his breath, unsure whether the dragon was aware of their location or waiting for a noise to reveal their whereabouts. He still couldn't believe that Talon had actually asked Falconer to place them along the waterfront…and Falconer had heeded the request! It was true the two former clansmen had fought dragons before, but it wasn't necessarily one of Bracy's favorite pastimes.

Talon took a slow breath and waited, straining to hear the first indication that the dragon was ready to attack. As soon as the fight began, he and Bracy would have to make noise—stay alert to each other's position in order to keep from striking out at one another in the confusion of a fog-wrapped battle.

Suddenly, a low growl—like the unnerving purr of a lion—sent a shiver up Talon's spine. In the next instant, a snort was heard from the direction where Bracy was standing, while simultaneously Talon felt a forked tongue brush the back of his neck.

He stiffened.

And then whirled with both swords poised.

"Now, Bracy! We've got two!"

ᘐᘎ

With the assistance of three other slaves, Eric threw his weight into tipping the barrel on its side. The first barrel had already been lifted to the deck.

The ship lurched and the four men froze.

"We're moving!"

"Has the fog lifted?"

"SH! Listen!"

The sounds of shouting could be heard, gaining intensity with every moment, and then…

"Mutiny! Mutiny aboard the Fate*! Mutiny!"*

"Come, lads! We're getting out of here today or dying in the attempt!"

Eric's thoughts sped to Nathaniel and he wondered if his young friend had done something to cause the uproar, but his mind made a swift return to the hold when the other three men left their positions around the barrel and rushed for the ladder.

"Wait! I can't hold it by myself!"

Eric's shout came too late. The heavy barrel surrendered to the pitching of the vessel and started to roll. In his attempt to get out of the way, Eric tripped and landed with a thud on the plank floor. The barrel charged, heedless of anything in its wake, and Eric heard himself yell when its crushing weight found his right leg. The barrel crashed into the wall and oil burst in all directions. The hold began to spin around him and Eric gritted his teeth against the pain.

He had to get out.

He had to get off the *Fate*.

Putting every ounce of strength he possessed into his desperate bellow, Eric looked toward the hatch and roared, "NATHANIEL!"

ꝏ

"Sir Kleyton, there's trouble with the *Fate*! She's abandoned her position!"

Kleyton moved to the railing. He had barely made out the shape of the drifting *Fate* before word arrived from his scouts that the seven Dragon Coast vessels, under command of Black's choicest officers, had weighed anchor to follow their leader further into the harbor.

"Idiots!" Kleyton pounded his fist on the railing, "They'll collide with one another or run aground in this fog if the Arcreans do not become aware of their advance and sink them first! What are they thinking?"

Suddenly, across the water, a single voice rose above the shouts of war.

"Mutiny! Mutiny aboard the Fate*! Mutiny!"*

Captain Black!

"Mutiny, he says. Sir, the slaves!"

Kleyton swore, "I told that fool to secure his slaves as long as he was this near the coast!"

Sir Kleyton's thoughts suddenly came to a standstill. Slaves! The Arcrean! The startling realization drove him to the main deck and to a group of eight or so waiting sailors, "Lower a boat and row me to the *Fate* with all speed!"

They glanced at one another and one sailor spoke up, "But, Sir…"

Kleyton ignored the protest and turned to address an officer, "Captain Holbrook, alert the *Tyburn* and the *Doldrum* that they are to await my signal. If the fog lifts before I return, you may advance and overwhelm the coast. Otherwise, we will leave these bumbling pirates to their demise and sail for Mizgalia on my return."

The sailor persisted, "But, Sir Kleyton, the *Fate* will be a hornet's nest…"

Kleyton shoved the man to the deck at his feet and towered over him with a menacing glare, "There is a small piece of business that must be finished, and I will conclude it today. Not one of you will rest at ease until my sword has done its work and cut down my prey. Now climb in the boat and row!"

ꙮ

Talon felt a scaly paw slap his face and he dropped to roll away before the claws had a chance to find him. In an instant, he was on his feet again. By now, the city was alive with the shouts of man and beast alike. From all around, the sounds of numerous skirmishes reached his ears. The battle for Dormay was well under way. Talon ducked and just missed a blow from the dragon's tree-trunk of a tail.

"Bracy, are you—whoa!—are you still alive?"

"I think so! How—back up, you monster!—how about you?"

"Still breathing!"

"That is a positive sign of life."

Talon spun and felt the dragon lurch closer; he quickly delivered a slice that sent the beast into momentary retreat. Turning towards Bracy's scuffle, he shouted at the blurred figure of his friend.

"Get ready to drive a thrust!"

With a run and a leap, Talon landed behind Bracy's dragon and brought his sword down in an overhead slice. The beast shrieked and turned when the weapon met its tail, and Talon quickly jumped away to meet the return of his first opponent while Bracy delivered the advised thrust to his. Bracy's adversary writhed and twisted until it finally dropped to the ground and Bracy served the deathblow.

"Is it dead?"

"Yes."

"Good! Come and help me!"

Bracy moved around the fallen dragon and through the swirling fog to meet up with Talon, "What do you need me to do?"

"Distract him."

Bracy maneuvered around the dragon and swung his sword to deliver a teasing blow. The beast growled in annoyance and twisted its neck around, backing Bracy against a shop's outer wall and bringing its face close to the young man's. Bracy stared at the giant head before him, and out of the corner of his eye, saw

Talon advancing on the dragon.

"Bracy, duck!"

Before the words had left Talon's mouth, the dragon's nostrils flared before Bracy's eyes, and the beast gave a sharp snort that was accompanied by a thick chalky powder.

ꕥ

Trenton whirled his horse where the street opened onto the docks and leveled his bow, using his left forefinger to balance the arc in place of his lost thumb. He eyed the shot and let the arrow loose when the shadow of his target turned back out to sea, and a moment later the massive beast coiled with a jerk and fell to the surf.

Though an official count would be impossible to tally amid the confusion, it was guessed along the city's main thoroughfare that, all told, nine dragons had been slain. His would make ten. That left eighteen alive in Dormay. Trenton turned his horse to glance back up the street. Though he had helped to trap the dragons in the mountains of Hugh, it was an entirely different arena in the city. In the fog.

A splash from behind him startled his horse and Trenton quickly reined the animal in before turning to see the head of dragon rising from the waves. At first, Trenton thought the "tenth dragon" had survived his arrow and swum back to shore, but as the beast continued to climb onto the docks, Trenton got a better view and his eyes widened.

This dragon had no wings!

Trenton stared in shock when Wings spotted him and gave a wrathful shriek. He hadn't known of the clan's decision to bring the wingless beast along! Wings flicked a forked tongue and snapped its jaws as it scurried closer for the kill. Trenton reached for another arrow and brought his bow up for a shot. The arrow zipped across the closing distance and found its mark with a thud.

Eleven down. Seventeen to go.

ജ്ജ

Nathaniel raced along the rail of the main deck. The fight had quickly spread to all sections of the ship, and if he and Eric were going to use chaos as cover for an escape, now would be the time to go. Leaving the railing, Nathaniel cut to the left and made his way towards the hatch, where Eric had been sent to fetch oil.

The deck was quickly becoming littered and slippery with unthinkable gore. Nathaniel found a sword in the hand of a fallen Mizgalian and grabbed the weapon for his own safety. As he neared the hatchway, three slaves ascended from below to enter the mêlée. Eric wasn't with them. Nathaniel reached the top of the ladder and looked down into the dimly lit hold.

A Mizgalian roared and swung for an attack, and Nathaniel turned to block the sword with his own. Another slave turned to help and the Mizgalian fell a moment later.

Nathaniel glanced his thanks and the slave nodded to the port railing, "We've a boat ready to sail for the shore. You'd best come and find a seat."

"But…" Nathaniel turned back to the hatch.

"It's now or never, mate!"

"Eric may be down there!"

"Who?"

Nathaniel realized his error, "Thumb!"

"I've just come up from the hold, and the four of us who went down left a barrel of oil and came running when we heard the noise up here."

The slave ran off to the portside rail and Nathaniel found his feet carrying him in the same direction.

"NATHANIEL!"

Nathaniel whirled and searched for the owner of the muffled but strong voice that had called his name. His eyes scanned the crowded deck for the familiar face of his friend, but Eric was nowhere to be seen. Perhaps he had climbed into the escape boat, knowing that Nathaniel would find his way there too. Nathaniel turned portside again.

"Wait!"

Nathaniel's steps had been too slow. The slave-laden boat dropped to the waves without him and the oars quickly propelled it towards the coast. Nathaniel rushed to the rail and his eyes darted to scrutinize the passengers. There was a man with dark-blond hair, but in the fog Nathaniel couldn't be certain…

A hand suddenly gripped his shoulder, and Nathaniel adjusted his grip on the pommel of his sword as the attacker whirled him around. He paused and searched the face before him.

Raven.

Chapter 39
* The Fate *

"What's the count, Falconer?" Trenton reined his horse to a halt beside the informant's.

"The last guess was fifteen."

"It's climbed since I saw you last. I just killed two on the docks."

"Seventeen is my guess, then," Falconer's gaze searched the fog overhead, "Eleven more. I'm riding now to check the scouts on the east—"

Falconer turned as the king and his guard rode up. Druet brought his horse to the informant's other side.

"Word from the harbor scouts has come in. The *Fate* is advancing on western Dormay with the seven vessels of Dragon Coast."

"In this fog? Are they mad?"

Druet shook his head, "I don't understand it, either, but its true. I've ordered the naval captains to row their vessels to the east and then prepare to move south and west to block the enemies' escape. The harbor scouts will help to lead them through the fog as best they can in their small boats."

Falconer nodded and turned to stare in the general direction of the harbor, "They'll have a greater chance of success with your plan; if they remain where they are, they run the risk of blind collision with the advancing enemy fleet. What of the three Mizgalian ships?"

"They remain behind. One of the scouts reported a possible mêlée on board the *Fate*, and wondered if there might be some trouble with the slaves."

"Mutiny?" Trenton lurched forward in his saddle. Falconer turned to study him as Druet nodded in reply.

Falconer spoke thoughtfully, "Then I would not be surprised if the *Fate*'s advance is by accident, Sire. If so, the Mizgalians will be sure to retreat before their association with the battle is marred by defeat. I say this from my own experience in the Brikbones."

"Then our focus must turn to western Dormay. If the enemy lands there, we must have a battalion ready to greet them."

The king nodded to Falconer and Trenton and then motioned for his guards to ride out. As they disappeared through the fog, Falconer turned to Trenton.

"You think a slave revolt is a sign of trouble for your father?"

Trenton lifted a tense look to return the informant's gaze, "My father has been kept hidden away on the *Fate* for twenty years. I can only imagine his captors will do everything in their power to prevent his escape now. Sir Kleyton will think that my father's escape would bring ruin to Mizgalia's plans for war—Father knows too much."

Falconer nodded, "Eric must be rescued."

"Thumb."

"What's that?"

"He is called Thumb on board the *Fate*."

Falconer glanced at Trenton's left hand and then met the younger man's gaze.

Suddenly, a shriek rent the fog and a dragon's massive form swept by just over their heads. The two men ducked and tried to calm their horses. Falconer swung his mount around to face the north, staring after the dragon.

"Trenton, he's going to come back around. We need to…Trenton? Trenton!"

Falconer searched the street for the youth and then heard the sound of Trenton's horse moving swiftly toward the docks. Half a smile touched the informant's face and he shook his head, reminded of his own adolescence.

"Impetuous hoodlum."

The circling dragon landed with a thud behind Falconer and stretched its neck in an angry scream. Falconer's horse skittered forward. The dragon gave another shriek, anticipating its next meal, and the cry was echoed from several points throughout the city.

A thought struck Falconer and he suddenly dismounted and pushed through the door of a nearby shop. The shopkeeper appeared in the doorway of a back room, a fearful look on his face. Falconer shouted to the man as he ran through the shop to the back stairs.

"My horse—in the street! Go stand beside it and on my signal slap its hindquarters!"

"I, sir?"

"Go, man!"

Falconer raced upstairs and threw open the shutters on a front window. In the narrow street below, the shopkeeper stood beside the informant's black mare, shaking in terror at the sight of the dragon. *God bless the man for his aid.* Falconer hopped onto the sill and eyed the dragon's posture—ready to strike.

"Now!" the shopkeeper looked up in surprise at Falconer's shout and the informant repeated his cry, "Do it now!"

The man delivered a slap to the horse's hindquarters and then darted back inside. Just up the street, the dragon hissed angrily and began flapping its leathery wings, preparing to fly after the retreating horse. Perfect. Falconer hovered in the window, waiting in tense silence for the right moment.

"What are you about, sir?" the shopkeeper appeared at the top of the stairs, but came no closer to Falconer's position.

Falconer kept his eyes on the dragon, "I'm catching a ride to the harbor, good sir. Thank you for your kind assistance."

Before the man had a chance to question further, the moment came. The dragon had gained height for its flight and as the beast passed under the spy's position, Falconer launched himself from the sill with a powerful shove and landed on the dragon's back. The beast growled in fury and rolled in an attempt to shake its rider, but Falconer dug his hands and feet into the scaly flesh and maintained his grip.

"Now then," he mused, "how does one fly a dragon?"

Falconer observed the pattern of the wings and

felt the dragon's muscles quiver beneath him with every shift in direction. The fog-wrapped city flew by at a safe distance, and Falconer marveled at the beast's sense of direction. Finally moving his grip to the front edge of each wing, Falconer located a nerve and pulled up on the left, simultaneously digging his right knee into the dragon's back.

The dragon curved to the right.

Falconer allowed himself one exclamation of victory and then removed the pressure of his knee to level the dragon's flight toward western Dormay, where the *Fate* would be approaching the coast. His thoughts shifted to Trenton, and Falconer offered up a swift prayer for the youth's safety. If Trenton was indeed anything like the informant had been at that age, there was bound to be trouble ahead.

ຣ໑ຉ

Out on the water, the fog had begun to lift. Trenton caught sight of the Arcrean fleet rowing into position to the south, barring the enemy's access to the open sea.

After leaving Falconer, he had been fortunate to come upon one of the harbor-scouts' boats, and the man had agreed to carry Trenton west with him. Trenton looked over his shoulder to the shrouded docks. He should have waited for Falconer—helped his friend kill the circling dragon and then ridden together to save Eric. Falconer was far more experienced in… With a shake of his head, Trenton faced forward again; he couldn't risk another moment when his father's life was hanging in the balance.

At last, the sounds of chaos and confusion drifted

across the waves and Trenton could make out the shapes of the Dragon Coast fleet. Some of the ships had run aground on rocky shallows and others had run into them from behind. One vessel had crashed into the docks, creating horrible damage.

"It appears enemy battalions have landed to enter into combat with our king's troops," the scout pointed to the waterfront street and his rowers craned their necks to see. Trenton sacrificed a glance to see what was happening, but his eyes quickly returned to scan the forest of masts.

"The *Fate*, where's the *Fate*?" the men turned to stare at him, and Trenton quickly realized he'd spoken in Mizgalian; he repeated his question in Arcrean and added, "Please, sir, my father is aboard and I seek to rescue him."

The scout gave him a long look, "I'll take you to her starboard side, but after that you're on your own. I must be about the king's business."

"Thank you, that is all I ask," Trenton gripped the sides of the boat as the scout gave orders to his rowers. The long poles rose and dipped into the surf with rapid precision and Trenton felt his heart beginning to pound to the steady beat.

Please, God, let me be in time.

Trenton adjusted his gloves and then lowered his four left fingers to grip the pommel at his side. Trenton glanced down at the maimed limb and suddenly a vision of Miji's face flashed across his memory; the round man's words flooded his mind with new and terrible meaning.

The dragon's final strike took your thumb.

"Here you are, lad. Quickly now, and take care. It sounds like there's a war aboard."

The scout's words propelled Trenton from the boat and sent him scrambling up the side of a vessel that he hoped was the *Fate*.

The dragon's final strike took your thumb.

My Thumb.

Trenton heaved himself over the starboard rail and into the midst of a wild brawl. Steadying himself against the pitch of the vessel and its slippery deck, he scanned the multitude of faces before him in hopes of locating one that looked like his own…but older. Dodging a swinging club, Trenton jumped to one side and drew his sword. The glint of a helmet caught his eye and he started across the deck with as much speed as circumstances would allow.

He'd found his dragon.

ጿጸ

Eric opened his eyes as consciousness returned, and then shut them again when a wave of excruciating pain and nausea washed over him. The fighting on deck had reached a deadly climax. He prayed Nathaniel had made it off of the *Fate* and reached the shore in safety.

The sound of boots descending the ladder was followed by a firm tread crossing the floor of the hold. Eric opened his eyes as a shadow fell across his face and Sir Kleyton drew his sword with a derisive laugh.

"So, we meet again…Thumb."

ጿጸ

Druet whirled to block a cut from behind and

then delivered a fatal thrust that finished the Mizgalian. The docks of western Dormay had become the stage for a desperate struggle between the royal army and the clan of Dragon Coast, led by a company of Mizgalians who had supposedly sailed on the *Fate* before commandeering the other fleet.

Druet took a deep breath and eyed a wrathful man from Dragon Coast. Growing up in a blacksmith shop had honed Druet's muscles well, but he still felt inadequate when it came to the knowledge of applying those muscles to swordplay.

The clansman offered a bitter glare and then rushed forward with a shriek as unnerving as that of the dragons. Druet gave a shout of his own before delivering a combination his father had taught him. The clansman fell to the ground beside the Mizgalian.

Druet grabbed another breath and looked up to see that he had become separated from his guard. Seeing an opening between two skirmishes, he ducked through only to find himself before a wall of three Mizgalians.

"God, help me," he breathed, and brought his sword up to block an overhead slice.

Druet felt strength seep into his arms as his sword flashed to ward off the enemy blows. He didn't know how long he'd fought before one Mizgalian met his death, fueling the wrath of the others to new intensity. One slipped out of his vision to circle behind him.

"Meet at the back!"

A voice shouted from several yards behind him, and Druet heard the scrape of metal as a blow was intercepted. Druet's eyes darted to keep up with his mind, which was racing to keep pace with the

Mizgalian's sword. Inching his way toward the sound of his aide's voice, he somehow managed to make his way to where the other man stood in combat. Back to back, the two fought until the other man's rival roared fiercely and dropped to the ground. Druet shoved his attacker backward and delivered a final lunge. A glance told him that the rest of the fight was coming to a close in Arcrea's favor.

"You did well…for a blacksmith."

Druet froze at the familiar voice. It couldn't be… Whirling to face the man behind him, Druet could only stare in disbelief. The man was filthy, ragged, unkempt, clearly malnourished, and in desperate need of a haircut. Nevertheless, he stood with a familiar poise about him, and the gray eyes that smiled back at Druet shone with a familiar spark of ease and amusement. His grin said that he was ready to take on the world…a world which he had supposedly left three months before.

Druet's head began to shake. One knee buckled, causing him to stumble forward, and he felt his lungs empty with one mighty exhale.

"Nathaniel!"

The seaman reached out a hand to steady the king, "In person, brother."

"You were dead!"

The two turned to meet the advance of several wild clansmen.

"It felt like death," swords locked at the cross-guard, Nathaniel shoved his opponent backward, "I've been kept as a slave aboard the *Fate*," he spun to deflect a blow meant for Druet's back, "I was helped to shore just moments ago by a Mizgalian who begged me to obtain his sanctuary in return,"

Nathaniel delivered a thrust that finished the fight and then turned to face Druet, "I believe he's sincere, so I promised to ask that you grant him a fair trial."

Suddenly, the commotion on the docks stilled when a deep thunderous noise sounded in the harbor and a ball of fire appeared in the sky, soaring quickly towards the coast.

Nathaniel's eyes widened, "The catapults!"

ꕥ

Sir Kleyton widened his stance in the hold when the catapult's momentum caused the vessel to dip. He rolled his eyes. That idiot, Captain Black, would land a strike against the Arcreans if he died trying, which he probably would. Eric moaned and Kleyton brought his focus back to the matter at hand.

"You and your family have given me more grief these twenty years than a man ought to endure in twenty lifetimes. I was forced to arrange for your kidnapping, find a remote spot where you could live unknown and undiscovered, see that you were taken to and from the *Fate* to serve your time, and even raise your impudent son."

Eric managed a look of surprise through his painful grimace, and Kleyton smirked with pleasure.

"Oh, yes. My dear son, sacrificed for the cause of Mizgalia, was in truth your little Eric," Kleyton leaned down with a cruel laugh, "You would have been proud, Thumb—my Trenton grew to be a fine Mizgalian youth."

"Is that so?"

Kleyton froze when the voice to his right was accompanied by a sword's tip being placed beneath his chin. The blade was slowly drawn upward, forcing the knight to straighten with the elevation.

From the floor, Eric's eyes followed the length of the sword and took in the strange sight of a young man whose face was the mirror image of his own younger appearance.

Trenton kept his sword in place as Kleyton glared at him in surprise.

"I was told you were dead! You were sacrificed!"

"Which sacrifice are you referring to, sir? Your plot to have me killed in the Brikbones, slaughtered in Hugh, or thrown off a cliff to the dragons?"

Kleyton's eyes narrowed, "How dare you speak to me in such a tone? Do not forget I am the man who taught you everything you know."

"No. You are the man who lied to me and taught me everything you *wanted* me to know. God is the one who spared me from your traps and deceit, and taught me what I *needed* to know."

"Ungrateful wretch!"

Trenton quirked a brow, "What, exactly, did you want me to be grateful for?"

In a sudden deft movement, Kleyton swung his sword arm and forced Trenton to retreat before a fierce combination. The ship lurched with another launch of the catapults and moments later a massive object struck the bow with force, but the two combatants were oblivious to everything beyond their next strike.

Eric winced as he pushed himself onto his elbows and tried to drag himself to a wall. His ears were alert to the clashing of the two swords—his longtime nemesis and his long lost son—absorbed in a deadly fight for his life as well as their own. Suddenly, Eric's nostrils flared with an undeniable scent and he turned to look toward the *Fate*'s bow.

Smoke!

"Fire in the hold!"

ꕥ

The fog was lifting from the harbor.

Falconer saw the first flaming missile rise from the *Fate*'s deck and complete an arc of destruction to the street along Dormay's waterfront. A shop was struck and the fire quickly began to spread.

Finding the correct nerves and persuading the wings just so, Falconer shifted the dragon's path of fury toward the Mizgalian vessel. The informant held the angry beast to its course and ducked low over the dragon's back when arrows zipped passed from below.

The second catapult flipped to hurl its mass of fire and Falconer readied himself for the hit. The dragon hissed and twisted, and then ran headlong into the *Fate*'s missile. As his waning ride plummeted to strike the bow of the *Fate*, Falconer jumped to his feet on the creature's back and dove for a rope that dangled from the fore mast. With the fore sail in pitiful shreds, thanks to the mutiny at a climax below, Falconer managed to swing through from starboard to port, and then circle around to the bowsprit for a landing. Sliding between jibs, Falconer quickly made his way down to the forecastle deck.

God, help me. His eyes made a quick sweep of the deck's warring occupants, detecting no sign of Trenton or Eric. An awareness of smoke pricked at the back of his mind and Falconer made a mental note that this rescue was going to have to take place quickly, before the ship burned down around their ears.

The alarm of fire was suddenly shouted, spilling across the vessel like a watchword, and the mutiny on board the *Fate* quickly turned into a dash for survival. Mizgalians and slaves, hailing from every kingdom within a radius of one hundred miles, all rushed as one for the rails. Some jumped, others hacked off planks to use as rafts, while still others clambered to find a seat in the last few leaky boats. Falconer's eyes trailed them all, still searching for the purpose behind his presence on board. When his search produced nothing, the informant pushed his way through a mob of frightened men toward the stairs that would take him to the main deck.

ഇന്ദ

Trenton blinked fiercely to cleanse his eyes of the stinging smoke. The burning sensation was making it much harder to focus on his opponent. Blood matted his right sleeve just below his shoulder, warning him that if the fight didn't come to a quick close he was sure to suffer.

Sir Kleyton had suffered his own share of wounds, but doggedly performed as if he hadn't a scratch. With every advance, he reprimanded Trenton; with every retreat, he rebuked the boy for rebelling against his king and forsaking the cause of his people. The Mizgalian words spewed forth like a poison intent to kill.

Exhausted, Trenton ignored the knight's verbal buffeting and forced his mind instead to focus on the next combination. His thoughts cried out to God for strength.

"You were always ungrateful; after all I did for you, after all I said on your behalf in the king's presence…"

With a roar, Trenton cut off Kleyton's words with an intricate combination that landed a clout on the knight's left arm. Kleyton growled and reacted swiftly, throwing Trenton off balance. The younger man tripped and fell against the curved wall of the hold just as the *Fate* shuddered and settled on a shelf of rocks in the quay. Water began pouring in through the hull.

The lurch upset Kleyton's stance and he stumbled to the floor. Trenton saw him fall, but couldn't move to finish the fight; his arm throbbed painfully and the lack of oxygen in the hold made him lightheaded. Gasping for a breath filled his lungs with smoke and sent him into a fit of coughing. By now, fire engulfed much of the hold and seawater swirled at his ankles.

Trenton felt the tip of a sword pressed against his chest and Kleyton rasped another string of admonition, "King Cronin was always right, I placed far too much confidence in you. You could have been so great, but your foolishness has brought you to the brink of death."

"Eric! Eric!" the voice sounded far away and it took a moment for Trenton to realize that he was the one being addressed by Thumb, "Eric! Er—Trenton! Son!"

Kleyton turned, "Silence you rogue!"

"His words are lies, son. Greatness is not found in a man's social status, nor in the count of deaths he causes in the king's name. Greatness is found in the hearts of men who have committed their life to God and who purpose to follow His ways!"

With his last ounce of strength and a roar of determination, Trenton delivered a kick to Kleyton's stomach and then lunged forward with a swift thrust. Before he could know if his sword had found its mark, Trenton's world turned dark and he collapsed into the knee-deep flood that surrounded him.

ꕥ

Falconer dropped into the flaming hold and immediately spotted Trenton's form as it sank beneath the water's surface. Sir Kleyton's lifeless figure had dropped nearby. Falconer quickly trudged across the space and lifted the youth out by his collar. Throwing his arm around Trenton in a supportive hold, Falconer turned to yell through the smoke.

"Eric! Thumb!"

"Here!"

The voice that answered was weak and Falconer hefted Trenton's unconscious weight to go after the boy's father. He found Eric clinging to a crate above the surface of the fast-rising water. Even through the grime and the beard, Falconer was struck by the resemblance between the two men. Though he had known Trenton and seen Eric's painting, it was still remarkable to witness the likeness firsthand.

Eric winced, "My leg is broken."

"Can you swim at all?"

"I'll certainly try."

Falconer glanced over his shoulder at the hole in the bow of the hull, where the fallen dragon had struck. The incoming water would keep the fire from wrapping all the way to the floor, but they had to get out before the water rose to make escape nearly impossible. It had already risen to chest-level.

Falconer turned and called over his shoulder, "Grab onto Trenton and I'll pull you to the hole."

As soon as Eric released his hold on the crate and gripped Trenton's tunic from behind, Falconer set off for the bow of the ship. Eric paddled with his left leg and kept his eyes glued on the massive hole ahead. At any other time he would have been elated by the news that the *Fate* had met its demise, but now, with three lives stuck in the ship's belly, the celebration would have to be delayed.

They reached the breach just as the water level covered the top of the gap. Eric reached out and gripped the rough edge of a plank. Needing the young man's cooperation, Falconer shifted to pin Trenton against the wall, and then gave a sharp slap to the youth's face.

"What?" Trenton's eyes flew open and then darted to take in the sights that surrounded him. His ears pounded with the thunderous noise of water, and his head felt hot beneath the flaming planks of the ceiling. His arm still throbbed and his lungs hurt.

"Hold your breath."

"What?"

Falconer glanced at Eric, "Grab hold as we go under. Kick if you can."

Trenton looked confused, "What's happening?"

"We're executing your brilliant escape plan."

"*My* brilliant…?"

"Hold your breath and swim!"

Trenton took a gulp of murky air and then felt his ears close with the pressure of the underwater world.

A hand found his and held tightly as Falconer planted his feet on the jagged edge of the breach, and shoved them through the opening. The force of the shove thrust them through the water like a missile and all three men paddled to the best of their individual ability.

Falconer spotted a grouping of driftwood on the surface above them and used his free arm to pull them toward the surface. When his head emerged, the informant threw his arm over a large plank and then reached to haul Eric up from behind; Trenton gripped the other end of the board and helped to place his father in the middle. The three men gasped to fill their burning lungs. Trenton coughed and turned his head to see Eric studying him.

"Thank you for coming for me."

Trenton nodded and the two stared at one another, finally comprehending the reality of their reunion.

"We must paddle to shore," Falconer pulled their attention back to the danger at hand, "before the *Fate* slips from the rock shelf and pulls us down with it."

Chests heaving with every breath, father and son nodded and prepared for the next leg of their journey.

Chapter 40
* Battle's End *

The fog had lifted. The last dragon had been slain. The eight advancing ships had all been run aground, sunk, burned, or trapped. Sir Kleyton's three vessels were sailing away in retreat. The battle had come to an end, and the city of Dormay sighed with relief.

King Druet strolled along the docks, eying the damage done by ships, dragons, and missiles. The fire was being extinguished by a crowd of diligent citizens and the docks would be repaired as soon as possible. The Mizgalian pirates and Dragon Coast clansmen who had survived were being rounded up as prisoners. Druet watched as the rebels from Hugh were led away, and he clenched his jaw when tears threatened. Beside him, Nathaniel gave him a curious look.

"I wonder," Druet's eyes moved over the death-strewn docks, "if this is how our heavenly Father feels when His children stray from His protection,"

Nathaniel's gaze shifted to the clansmen as Druet continued, "I should have fought *for* them, as their king. It pains me to know that, out of necessity, I fought against them today."

They were silent for a moment and Nathaniel turned to stare at the wreckage in the harbor, "You say Falconer knew of Eric's presence on board the *Fate*?"

"He did."

Nathaniel nodded and savored a breath of freedom; "I pray he made it off the ship in time."

The sound of horses drew their attention eastward to see two scouts approaching.

"Sire!" Bracy pulled his horse to a stop and dismounted, giving a brief nod of greeting to the filthy slave who stood beside the king, "Druet, Talon and I discovered God's purpose for the fog!"

Nathaniel's brow lifted in surprise at Bracy's open acknowledgment of God. Talon dismounted behind his comrade, staring at the seaman with a look of vague recognition…and disbelief.

Bracy went on, oblivious to his friend's distraction, "The Death Chalk! The moist air created by the fog disabled the effects of the Death Chalk so that no one would be left lying in the streets at its mercy! I know—I was hit!"

Druet smiled at his enthusiasm, "Praise the Lord that you're alright."

The two turned as Talon stepped up to Nathaniel, peering intently into the seaman's face.

"Who is this?" Bracy asked, studying the slave for the first time.

Nathaniel grinned and Talon's jaw dropped in shock. Throwing his arms around the seaman in a fierce embrace, he lifted the seaman from the ground with a shout.

"You're alive!"

Bracy stared in disbelief at his comrade's behavior, "Talon?"

"Ho there, mate," Nathaniel's feet touched the ground again and he reached out to clasp Bracy's shoulder, "I gather you deserve a warm welcome to the faith."

Bracy's jaw dropped lower, "Nathaniel?"

Druet threw his head back and laughed, "I think it's his hair," he clapped Nathaniel on the back and ruffed the brown mane, "My friend, you're in dire need of a trim."

Nathaniel's grin broadened, "Advice accepted," his eyes shifted to look beyond Druet and his face suddenly lit up with relief, "Eric!"

The group turned to see Falconer and Trenton approaching, carrying a man stretched out on a litter between them; his right leg wrapped in a temporary bandage. The three men were soaked to the skin, battered, weary, and bleeding, but they were alive.

Druet ordered two soldiers to take charge of the litter and its burden, and immediately Trenton collapsed.

"Bring another litter," Druet motioned, "and carry them to the camp. Word has been sent to the surrounding healers, and they have agreed to come and care for the wounded. I also sent a summons to Rodney on his return from Balgo; he should arrive some time today or tomorrow."

Falconer greeted Nathaniel before the seaman excused himself to walk further down the street. The informant then turned to the king and described what had happened aboard the *Fate*. Druet listened in silence until Falconer had finished.

"You are certain that Kleyton was dead?"

"Yes, Sire; as was Captain Black on the quarter-deck."

Druet nodded soberly, "I can't say I'm sorry for an end to their evil, only that they never turned from it."

ℵ

The shop's front door opened and a shadow fell across the room. Peter glanced up from the mess of splintered shutters on the floor and promptly dropped every piece he had already picked up.

"Father," Nathaniel's voice shook over the single word.

Trembling and speechless, Peter rose to his feet and stumbled into his son's arms. The two men embraced with sobs until the father found his voice.

"Martha! Martha, come quickly!"

"What is it, Peter?" Nathaniel's mother called from the kitchen as she dried her hands on her apron and rushed into the front room, followed closely by his two sisters.

Martha took one look at the scene and then screamed as she rushed forward to hold her son. Behind her, Anne began to cry as she too found an opening and added herself to the family embrace. Brigit remained standing in the doorway, and Nathaniel could tell by the look on her face that she couldn't decide whether crying or fainting would be the occasion's appropriate response.

"Brigit…?"

Her face suddenly crumpled and she sobbed, "You're ali-i-ive!" before taking a single deep breath and falling forward in a faint.

ꕥ

"Ouch!" Trenton winced at the tightened bandage and jerked his sleeve back into place, "You did that on purpose."

"Stop fussin' afore I call Rodney an' tell 'im you're misbe'avin'."

"That hurt!"

Leyla's green eyes snapped, "If you'd stopped movin' around when I tol' ya, I wouldn'a had to pull it so tight!"

Trenton threw his back against the tree trunk behind him and glared, "Where's Rodney?"

"Seein' t' the hun'reds of other wounded," Leyla huffed as she tossed the extra length of bandage into her bag and shoved auburn curls from her face, "I woulda joined 'im ages ago if not for some ill-tempered boy 'o won' stop sulkin'!"

"Trenton?"

Trenton looked up to see Druet approaching and he quickly stood to salute, "Sire."

Druet glanced at Leyla, "Have I come at a bad time?"

"No, Sire," Leyla took Trenton's offered hand and rose from her knees, "I'm expected t' join Rodney an' Sarah when I've finished 'ere," she offered a curtsy before the king and then shot another scowl at Trenton, " 'E's all yours, Sire, only tread with care on account 'e's got an ill temper."

Leyla marched away and Druet cast a glance at

Trenton, "Renny tells me she's quite amiable."

Trenton shot a glance at Druet and saw the king's barely suppressed smile, "Was there something you needed to discuss, Sire?"

Druet sobered instantly, "Yes. I wanted you to know that a plan is under discussion in the war council, and word of the scheme has been sent to the royal council at Olden Weld. A party will soon be sent to Mockmor to inform Cronin that we are aware of his dealings within our borders. It was suggested that the journey take place after you've had time to heal from your wounds so that you might accompany them. Falconer tells me that you have a document in your possession that might be of influence in the conference."

"I have. Falconer gave me the parchment that reveals the truth of my past. It's marked by Cronin's seal and proves that Mizgalia was responsible for my abduction."

"Excellent. Then I can count on you to make the journey?"

Trenton nodded, "Of course, Sire."

The two turned when Sarah drew near. She nodded her respect to Druet and then looked to Trenton and laid a hand on his arm, "Eric has asked to see you."

When Trenton entered the tent, his eyes immediately flew to where his father lay stretched out on a cot. The coverlet draped over him dipped just below the knee, accentuating the lack of a limb. Eric looked up and motioned Trenton forward, and the youth went to kneel beside the cot.

"I'm sorry I wasn't there in time to save your…"

Eric waved a hand for silence, "You were there in

time to save my life, and for that I am most grateful. The fact that you were there at all—that you are alive and well—still causes my heart to sing praises to our God," he placed his hand alongside Trenton's face as a tear crept down his own cheek, "I've dreamed of this day, when you and I would be reunited, but I never dared to hope that it would ever truly come to pass."

They were silent for a moment, Eric holding Trenton's face while Trenton gripped Eric's wrist, until Trenton gave a slight laugh.

"We're quite the pair, you and I. I'm without my left thumb and you've lost everything below your right knee!"

Eric chuckled, "We'll strike a bargain then. You'll have to do some of my walking for me, and I'll be more than happy to help carry your burdens."

Trenton smiled and the two clasped hands in a pact, "Fair enough."

ഇ൦൩

The army's eventual departure from Dormay was marked with great celebration among the citizens. The king's entourage journeyed northwest to the Heartland in high spirits. A clean-shaven Nathaniel rode with the company and laughed as Talon and Bracy bantered good-naturedly over who would fill him in on the details of the past three months. Trenton utilized the journey to become better acquainted with his father, and often found he had a second riding companion in Leyla.

The group's arrival in Olden Weld was a time of sweet rejoicing and tears as everyone was welcomed home.

Trenton and Eric—whose lower leg had been replaced by a wooden peg—were delivered to Adelaide, Alice, and Caroline, and the family of Brentwood was at last restored as a whole. Alice embraced her father for the first time in twenty years and praised God for the safekeeping of her family. Some time later, her beloved Nathaniel joined them and another tearful reunion took place.

When King Druet led a large company across the border of Quinton and into Mizgalia two weeks later, Falconer, Trenton, Leland, and Kellen, were among the entourage. Bracy and Talon acted as the party's scouts and prevented an ambush in the Brikbones. At Mockmor, Cronin was effectually reprimanded and brought to acknowledge a position of acquiescence before the Arcrean king. A peace-treaty was drawn up and Cronin vowed to observe the written boundaries…for a time.

Osgood's death was investigated and a search made for Miji the trader, but the round man had disappeared, leaving those who had known him in Arcrea with a sense that he might return.

The building of Castle Eubank progressed at a steady pace and the king and queen anticipated life in their new home, but anticipated even more was the event that would take place before Eubank's completion: The birth of their first child.

And so, a measure of peace settled over the seven united regions of Arcrea, though the clans of Ranulf, Frederick, and Quinton, once again began to pester one another with vague threats of unrest. But then, as Druet observed to his father one day,

"Unrest will come; it must, for we live in a world

of imperfect men. But as long as we expect the unrest and depend on God to see us safely through it, we can be sure to find that we have grown somehow through the ordeal. You'll remember it was unrest that first started me on my journey to seek out the heart of Arcrea," he paused and grinned, "You know, unpleasant as trouble can be, I truly believe that if we lived in a world that had no obstacles to overcome, no growth to be gained, no fight to be finished for the cause of Christ…life here on earth might prove to be rather dull."

Epilogue
* Falconer's Trade *

T*wo-and-a-half months later…*

Falconer reined in and dismounted before his horse had come to a complete stop. A woman's agonized cries filled the air. Falconer gave a quick rap at the front door of Druet and Renny's cottage and then let himself in. The king came pounding down the stairs from the loft and rushed toward the kitchen.

"Sire?" Falconer followed him.

Druet grabbed a shallow pan and filled it with water, "Yes?"

"You sent for me, Sire? You sent an urgent summons…"

Druet straightened as another cry was heard from above and he looked at Falconer for a long moment before the distracted look cleared from his eyes, "I did."

He started for the stairs again, balancing the pan.

Falconer followed again, "Sire, the summons! The

courier made it clear that your message was very urgent. Was there something you needed?"

"Yes."

Falconer waited as the king climbed the first three stairs.

Finally, Druet paused, "I need you here."

Falconer's mask of composure slipped for an instant and he quirked a brow, "I beg your pardon, Sire?"

Druet glanced over his shoulder and Falconer read the panic in his gaze, "My father and mother are still on their way from the Eubank site, and I simply needed to know that someone was here. Now."

Falconer stared at the king and tried to recall the last time someone had needed him. Not his skills, his stealth, or his services—just his presence as a friend.

"I'll be outside, out of the way, if you need me…Druet."

Druet gave a tight smile and nodded, and then disappeared up the rugged stairs.

Falconer walked outside and slipped around the corner to the side of the cottage. Leaning his back and head against the wall, he let his eyes roam one half of the village while his thoughts strayed to the events leading from the previous months until now.

Old Marie had passed away in May. Rodney and Sarah had taken Leyla in as their own, along with Humphrey the goat, and the young girl was thriving in the active lifestyle led by the healer and his wife.

Nathaniel and Alice had been married in June and were currently living with her family at Castle Brentwood, where Nathaniel was steadily recovering from his time aboard the *Fate*. Upon Eubank's completion, the couple would make their home in the royal palace, where Alice would return to her service as the queen's companion while her husband served as Druet's ambassador.

Eric had been restored to his former home and was named the first governor of southern Osgood. As each of the seven regions were charted to contain a number of districts, a man was placed in authority over each quarter; the people would report to this governor and he, in turn, would bring the cries of the people before their king.

Trenton was a frequent visitor at Olden Weld, coming both to spend time with Kellen and to court Leyla. As if the latter action were a contagious disease, Talon somehow managed to claim responsibility for every message requiring delivery in southern Geoffrey so that he might call on Nathaniel's sister, Anne. Bracy didn't seem to mind the repetitive route.

It was now nearing the end of a sultry July, and the queen was about to deliver her baby. From the windows above, the voices of Druet, Renny's mother, Rodney, Sarah, and Leyla, drifted down to Falconer in a soothing cadence as they coaxed Renny, as well as one another, through the age-old event.

The front door suddenly opened and Druet's voice called, "Falconer?"

"Here, Sire."

Druet appeared with a flushed face and rambled for several minutes about the stress of childbirth as he paced back and forth before the silent informant. When he had finished ranting, he turned to face the other man, "Do you think I'm right?"

"Undoubtedly, Sire."

"Yes…well," with a short exhale and a stiff nod of his head, Druet turned to reenter the cottage,

"Thank you, Falconer."

"Sire?"

"Yes?"

"The kingdom's prayers are with you, as are my own."

As he lifted up another silent petition for the king, Falconer shifted to study the other half of the village. It was relatively still today, though an air of excitement hung in the air as thick and obvious as the heat itself. Natives passed by with glances to the upper windows and whispered comments to their companions; many paused across from the cottage, long enough to say a prayer on the queen's behalf.

Falconer kept his position and watched as the shadows in the village moved from one slant to the opposite.

As the afternoon waned, Gregory the blacksmith and his wife, Ruth, arrived from the building-site in the west to be present at the birth of their grandchild. A crowd began to gather; bearing torches and expectant faces, they looked to the royal cottage and waited. Falconer's gaze studied the masses, fully aware that one or more of these curious onlookers were foreigners—spies, such as himself—ready to dispatch news of Arcrea's royal child to their homeland. A man with yellow hair falling to his shoulders caught Falconer's eye, and he recognized Blunt the minstrel, another member of Druet's heart-seeking band of the year before.

At last, with the sun burnishing the western fields to a warm gold, Renny's cries reached a climax and then came to a relieved halt as the bawling of a newborn took their place. The crowd cheered and soon began chanting for a sight of the child. Falconer looked up when Leyla appeared beside him several minutes later.

"The king sent me t' fetch you."

Falconer pulled away from the wall and followed Leyla back inside. She led the way to the top of the stairs, where Grikk stood on guard, and knocked on a door; it was quickly opened and they entered. Every eye in the room was focused on the tiny bundle in Druet's arms. When the door opened the king turned and with glowing countenance motioned for Falconer to approach.

"You devoted your time today in order to give me peace of mind and the presence of a friend. In thanks I would like you to be the first person, outside of the few already present, to be introduced to my son and heir, Prince Samuel."

A fold of the blanket was pulled aside and Falconer beheld the tiniest human being he had ever seen. A thin layer of dark fuzz topped a pink face, the features of which were squished in contented rest. Fingers that had to be the length of his own thumbnail were curled beside the babe's cheek, and a mouth the size of a pebble was propped open in a miniscule O.

Falconer glanced up to see Druet watching him; he cleared his throat, "I am honored, Sire, and humbled," he turned and nodded to the queen, "Congratulations, your majesty. He is a beautiful child."

Renny nodded her thanks and Falconer bowed before leaving the room. Once outside again, he took a post beside the door and waited. It was not long before Druet appeared in the doorway, bearing the prince, to appease the expectant throng. The people hushed momentarily, eager to hear whether the child was a boy or a girl, an heir or a princess.

Druet smiled on his subjects, "Arcreans, your prince!"

A cheer was raised and the villagers began to sing and dance in honor of the birth that had provided them with a future king. Eventually Druet moved inside again and, as the celebration continued, Falconer slipped from his post and walked east; he needed to check on his mare and hear the reports brought in from his scouts and couriers. Movement snagged his peripheral vision and Falconer turned as a woman addressed him.

"Excuse me, sir, is this the village of Olden Weld?"

Her lilting accent instantly alerted Falconer to a nationality beyond both Arcrea and Mizgalia, "It is," he replied, "Are you seeking someone?"

Her expressive brown eyes closed briefly in a look of relief, "I seek an audience before your king."

Falconer glanced at the festivities down the road and the woman followed his gaze.

"The king has just been given a son, and is…"

"Busy," the woman nodded and turned to Falconer with a somber but determined expression, "I'll wait."

Falconer studied her for a moment and then spoke again, "Perhaps one or more members of the royal council would be available to hear you."

She nodded eagerly, "Please, will you take me to them?"

Falconer nodded and motioned toward the eastern end of the street, where the meetinghouse glowed in the evening light. As the two set off,

Falconer's mind considered the woman's eager pace and the way she kept twisting her fingers in an agitated manner.

She turned to look back at the celebrating crowd; "You are kind to help me at such a busy time. Thank you."

He acknowledged her words with a nod and mentally prepared himself for whatever lay ahead. For an entire day he had been nothing more than the king's friend, a presence of strength in a time of uncertainty, and he had relished the time of inactivity. But now, as he walked beside another person in distress, he knew that he thrived on the prospect of going back to work. Behind him, the kingdom of Arcrea rejoiced, unconcerned—if only for one night—with the problems of the world beyond their borders; before him lay the task that he did best.

Falconer paused to knock at the meetinghouse door, realizing for the first time that the council had not been alerted to the prince's birth. He turned and noticed a solitary tear in the woman's eye.

"What is your name?"

She looked up at him, "Meredith, sir."

A servant opened the door and gave them entrance upon seeing Falconer. The informant made a small sweep with his arm, motioning her inside before the waiting council.

"Come then, Mistress Meredith, let us find a solution to your troubles."

ꙮ

LOOK FOR BOOK 3 OF
THE ARCREAN CONQUEST!

The Isle of Arcrea

Subject to the designing rule of evil men,
one island's future rests in the hands of an Arcrean.

Lady Meredith of Gilbrenor seeks help from the land of Arcrea in a desperate attempt to rescue her son from the clutches of Lord Brock and to claim his rightful legacy. When Falconer undertakes the seemingly simple mission and travels to the isle with Meredith and her two young daughters, he is unprepared for the painful memories from his own past that wait to confront him on the distant shores.

Seth is an Arcrean shepherd whose cares are simple and few…until the discovery of a costly heirloom compels him to set off on a mission of justice. His humble life quickly becomes a tangled web of betrayal that will test the strength of his faith and unlock the truth of his life's purpose.

A lost parchment, a devastating secret, and an evil lord who seeks their ruin. Will the puzzle of Gilbrenor be solved and the isle's future secured before it is too late?

ABOUT THE AUTHOR

Nicole Sager is an avid reader and coffee drinker who lives in the Midwest. Besides reading and writing, Nicole also enjoys a quirky array of interests that include tap dancing, ziplining, musical theatre, hedgehogs, buying stacks of books at a time, and all things Roger & Anita Radcliffe.

"In writing each book, I pray that it will bring honor and glory to God, and that He will use it as a tool to bring at least one person to the saving knowledge of Jesus Christ. I pray that my books would be a blessing to readers (individuals & families alike) as they search for wholesome yet exciting reading material for all ages."

~ *N.S.*

Author Fun Fact!
Nicole's favorite character from
The Fate of Arcrea is Brigit!

Connect with Nicole online!
Instagram: @arcrea_author
Facebook: @arcreabooks
Pinterest: @heartofarcrea
www.arcreabooks.wix.com/nicole-sager